ELLIS PETERS

SAINT PETER'S FAIR

THE CADFAEL CHRONICLES IV

Brother
CADFAEL

WARNER FUTURA

A *Warner Futura* Book

First published in Great Britain in 1981
by Macmillan London Limited
Published in 1984
Reprinted 1984, 1985 (twice), 1986 (twice), 1989, 1990, 1991
This edition published in 1992 by Warner Futura
Reprinted 1994

ISBN 0 7515 1104 8

Photoset in North Wales by
Derek Doyle & Associates, Mold, Clwyd
Printed in England by Clays Ltd, St Ives plc

Warner Futura
A Division of
Little, Brown and Company (UK) Limited
Brettenham House
Lancaster Place
London WC2E 7EN

SHREWSBURY ABBEY
and
TOWN
(not to scale)

The Eve of the Fair

Chapter One

I t began at the normal daily chapter in the Benedictine monastery of Saint Peter and Saint Paul, of Shrewsbury, on the thirtieth day of July, in the year of Our Lord 1139. That day being the eve of Saint Peter ad Vincula, a festival of solemn and profitable importance to the house that bore his name, the routine business of the morning meeting had been devoted wholly to the measures necessary to its proper celebration, and lesser matters had to wait.

The house, given its full dedication, had two saints, but Saint Paul tended to be neglected, sometimes even omitted from official documents, or so abbreviated that he almost vanished. Time is money, and clerks find it tedious to inscribe the entire title, perhaps as many as twenty times in one charter. They had had to amend their ways, however, since Abbot Radulfus had taken over the rudder of this cloistral vessel, for he was a man who brooked no slipshod dealings, and would have all his crew as meticulous as himself.

Brother Cadfael had been out before Prime in his enclosed herb-garden, observing with approval the blooming of his oriental poppies, and assessing the time when the seed would be due for gathering. The summer season was at its height, and promising rich harvest, for the spring had been mild and moist after plenteous early snows, and June and July hot and

sunny, with a few compensatory showers to keep the leafage fresh and the buds fruitful. The hay harvest was in, and lavish, the corn looked ripe for the sickle. As soon as the annual fair was over, the reaping would begin. Cadfael's fragrant domain, dewy from the dawn and already warming into drunken sweetness in the rising sun, filled his senses with the kind of pleasure on which an ascetic church sometimes frowns, finding something uneasily sinful in pure delight. There were times when young Brother Mark, who worked with him this delectable field, felt that he ought to confess his joy among his sins, and meekly accept some appropriate penance. He was still very young, there were excuses to be found for him. Brother Cadfael had more sense, and no such scruples. The manifold gifts of God are there to be delighted in, to fall short of joy would be ingratitude.

Having put in two hours of work before Prime, and having no office in connection with the abbey fair, which was engaging all attention, Cadfael was nodding, as was his habit, behind his protective pillar in the dimmest corner of the chapter-house, perfectly ready to snap into wakefulness if some unexpected query should be aimed in his direction, and perfectly capable of answering coherently what he had only partially heard. He had been sixteen years a monk, by his own considered choice, which he had never regretted, after a very adventurous life which he had never regretted, either, and he was virtually out of reach of surprise. He was fifty-nine years old, with a world of experience stored away within him, and still as tough as a badger – according to Brother Mark almost as bandy-legged, into the bargain, but Brother Mark was a privileged being. Cadfael dozed as silently as a closed flower at night, and hardly ever snored; within the Benedictine rule, and in genial companionship with it, he had perfected a daily discipline

10

of his own, that suited his needs admirably.

It is probable that he was fast asleep when the steward of the grange court, with an appropriate apology, ventured into the chapter-house and stood waiting the abbot's permission to speak. He was certainly awake when the steward reported: 'My lord, here in the great court is the provost of the town, with a delegation from the Guild Merchant, asking leave to speak with you. They say the matter is important.'

Abbot Radulfus allowed his steely, level brows to rise a little, and indicated graciously that the fathers of the borough should be admitted at once. Relations between the town of Shrewsbury on one side of the river and the abbey on the other, if never exactly cordial – that was too much to expect, where their interests so often collided – were always correct, and their skirmishes conducted with wary courtesy. If the abbot scented battle, he gave no sign. But for all that, thought Cadfael, watching the shrewd, lean hatchet-face, he has a pretty accurate idea of what they're here for.

The worthies of the guild entered the chapter-house in a solid phalanx, no less than ten of them, from half the crafts in the town, and led by the provost. Master Geoffrey Corviser, named for his trade, was a big, portly, vigorous man not yet fifty, clean-shaven, brisk and dignified. He made some of the finest shoes and riding-boots in England, and was well aware of their excellence and his own worth. For this occasion he had put on his best, and even without the long gown that would have been purgatory in this summer weather, he made an impressive figure, as clearly he meant to do. Several of those grouped at his back were well known to Cadfael: Edric Flesher, chief of the butchers of Shrewsbury, Martin Bellecote, master-carpenter, Reginald of Aston, the silversmith – men of substance every one. Abbot Radulfus did not know them, not yet.

He had been only half a year in office, sent from London to trim an easy-going provincial house into more zealous shape, and he had much to learn about the men of the borders, as he himself, being no man's fool, was well aware.

'You are welcome, gentlemen,' said the abbot mildly. 'Speak freely, you shall have attentive hearing.'

The ten made their reverences gravely, spread sturdy feet, and stood planted like a battle-square, all eyes alert, all judgments held in reserve. The abbot was concentrating courteous attention upon them with much the same effect. In his interludes of duty as shepherd, Cadfael had once watched two rams level just such looks before they clashed foreheads.

'My lord abbot,' said the provost, 'as you know, Saint Peter's Fair opens on the day after tomorrow, and lasts for three days. It's of the fair we come to speak. You know the conditions. For all that time all shops in the towns must be shut, and nothing sold but ale and wine. And ale and wine are sold freely here at the fairground and the Foregate, too, so that no man can make his living in the town from that merchandise. For three days, the three busiest of the year, when we might do well out of tolls on carts and pack-horses and man-loads passing through the town to reach the fair, we must levy no charges, neither murage nor pavage. All tolls belong only to the abbey. Goods coming up the Severn by boat tie up at your jetty, and pay their dues to you. We get nothing. And for this privilege you pay no more than thirty-eight shillings, and even that we must go to the trouble to distrain from the rents of your tenants in the town.'

'*No more* than thirty-eight shillings!' repeated Abbot Radulfus, and elevated the iron-grey brows a shade higher, but still with an urbane countenace and a gentle voice. 'The sum was appointed as fair. And not by us. The terms of the charter have been known to

12

you many years, I believe.'

'They have, and often before now have been found burdensome enough, but bargains must be kept, and we have never complained. But bad years or good, the sum has never been raised. And it falls very hard on a town so pressed as we are now, to lose three days of trade, and the best tolls of the year. Last summer, as you must know, though you were not then among us, Shrewsbury was under siege above a month, and stormed at last with great damage to the town walls, and great neglect of the streets, and for all our efforts there's still great need of work on them, and it's costly labour, after all last summer's losses. Not the half of the dilapidations are yet put right, and in these troublous times, who knows when we may again be under attack? The very traffic of your fair will be passing through our streets and adding to the wear, while we get nothing to help make good the damage.'

'Come to the point, Master Provost,' said the abbot in the same tranquil tone. 'You are come to make some demand of us. Speak it out plainly.'

'Father Abbot, so I will! We think – and I speak for the whole guild merchant and borough gathering of Shrewsbury – that in such a year we have the best possible case for asking that the abbey should either pay a higher fee for the fair, or, better by far, set aside a proportion of the fair tolls on goods, whether by horse-load or cart or boat, to be handed over to the town, and spent on restoring the walls. You benefit by the protection the town affords you; you ought, we think, to bear a part with us in maintaining its defences. A tenth share of the profits would be welcomed, and we should thank you heartily for it. It is not a demand, with respect, it is an appeal. But we believe the grant of a tenth would be nothing more than justice.'

Abbot Radulfus sat, very erect and lean and lofty,

13

gravely considering the phalanx of stout burgesses before him. 'That is the view of you all?'

Edric Flesher spoke up bluntly: 'It is. And of all our townsmen, too. There are many who would voice the matter more forcibly than Master Corviser has done. But we trust in your fellow-feeling, and wait your answer.'

The faint stir that went round the chapter-house was like a great, cautious sigh. Most of the brothers looked on wide-eyed and anxious; the younger ones shifted and whispered, but very warily. Prior Robert Pennant, who had looked to be abbot by this time, and been sorely disappointed at having a stranger promoted over his head, maintained a silvery, ascetic calm, appeared to move his lips in prayer, and shot sidelong looks at his superior between narrowed ivory lids, wishing him irredeemable error while appearing to compassionate and bless. Old Brother Heribert, recently abbot of this house and now degraded to its ranks, dozed in a quiet corner, smiling gently, thankful to be at rest.

'We are considering, are we not,' said Radulfus at length, gently and without haste, 'what you pose as a dispute between the rights of the town and the rights of this house. In such a balance, should the judgment rest with you, or with me? Surely not! Some disinterested judge is needed. But, gentlemen, I would remind you, there has been such a decision, now, within the past half-year, since the siege of which you complain. At the beginning of this year his Grace King Stephen confirmed to us our ancient charter, with all its grants in lands, rights and privileges, just as we held them aforetime. He confirmed also our right to this three-day fair on the feast of our patron Saint Peter, at the same fee we have paid before, and on the same conditions. Do you suppose he would have countenanced such a grant, if he had not held it to be just?'

14

'To say outright what I suppose,' said the provost warmly, 'I never supposed for a moment that the thought of justice entered into it. I make no murmur against what his Grace chose to do, but it's plain he held Shrewsbury to be a hostile town, and most like still does hold it so, because FitzAlan, who is fled to France now, garrisoned the castle and kept it over a month against him. But small say we of the town ever had in the matter, and little we could have done about it! The castle declared for the Empress Maud, and we must put up with the consequences, while FitzAlan's away, safe out of reach. My lord abbot, is that justice?'

'Are you making the claim that his Grace, by confirming the abbey in its rights, is taking revenge on the town?' asked the abbot with soft and perilous gentleness.

'I am saying that he never so much as gave the town a thought, or its injuries a look, or he might have made some concession.'

'Ah! Then should not this appeal of yours be addressed rather to the Lord Gilbert Prestcote, who is the king's sheriff, and no doubt has his ear, rather than to us?'

'It has been so addressed, though not with regard to the fair. It is not for the sheriff to give away any part of what has been bestowed on the abbey. Only you, Father, can do that,' said Geoffrey Corviser briskly. It began to be apparent that the provost knew his way about among the pitfalls of words every bit as well as did the abbot.

'And what answer did you get from the sheriff?'

'He will do nothing for us until his own walls at the castle are made good. He promises us the loan of labour when work there is finished, but labour we could supply, it's money and materials we need, and it will be a year or more before he's ready to turn over even a handful of his men to our needs. In such a case,

Father, do you wonder that we find the fair a burden?'

'Yet we have our needs, too, as urgent to us as yours to you,' said the abbot after a thoughtful moment of silence. 'And I would remind you, our lands and possessions here lie outside the town walls, even outside the loop of the river, two protections you enjoy that we do not share. Should we, then, be asked to pay tolls for what cannot apply to us?'

'Not all your possessions,' said the provost promptly. 'There are within the town some thirty or more messuages in your hold, and your tenants within them, and their children have to wade in the kennels of broken streets as ours do, and their horses break legs where the paving is shattered, as ours do.'

'Our tenants enjoy fair treatment from us, and considerate rents, and for such matters we are responsible. But we cannot be held responsible for the town's dilapidations, as we can for those here on our own lands. No,' said the abbot, raising his voice peremptorily when the provost would have resumed his arguments, 'say no more! We have heard and understood your case, and we are not without sympathy. But Saint Peter's Fair is a sacred right granted to this house, on terms we did not draw up; it is a right that inheres not to me as a man, but to this house, and I in my passing tenure have no authority to change or mitigate those terms in the smallest degree. It would be an offence against the king's Grace, who has confirmed the charter, and an offence against those my successors, for it could be taken and cited as a precedent for future years. No, I will not set aside any part of the profits of the fair to your use, I will not increase the fee we pay you for it, I will not share in any proportion the tolls on goods and stalls. All belong here, and all must be gathered here, according to the charter.' He saw half a dozen mouths open to protest against so summary a dismissal, and rose in his place,

very tall and straight, and chill of voice and eye. 'This chapter is concluded,' he said.

There were one or two among the delegation who would still have tried to insist, but Geoffrey Corviser had a better notion of his own and the town's dignity, and a shrewder idea of what might or might not impress that self-assured and austere man. He made the abbot a deep, abrupt reverence, turned on his heel, and strode out of the chapter-house, and his defeated company recovered their wits and marched as haughtily after him.

There were booths already going up in the great triangle of the horse-fair, and all along the Foregate from the bridge to the corner of the enclosure, where the road veered right towards Saint Giles, and the king's highway to London. There was a newly-erected wooden jetty downstream from the bridge, where the long riverside stretch of the main abbey gardens and orchards began, the rich lowland known as the Gaye. By river, by road, afoot through the forests and over the border from Wales, traders of all kinds began to make their way to Shrewsbury. And into the great court of the abbey flocked all the gentry of the shire, and of neighbouring shires, too, lordlings, knights, yeomen, with their wives and daughters, to take up residence in the overflowing guest-halls for the three days of the annual fair. Subsistence goods they grew, or bred, or brewed, or wove, or span for themselves, the year round, but once a year they came to buy the luxury cloths, the fine wines, the rare preserved fruits, the gold and silver work, all the treasures that appeared on the feast of Saint Peter ad Vincula, and vanished three days later. To these great fairs came merchants even from Flanders and Germany, shippers with French wines, shearers with the wool-clip from Wales, and clothiers with the finished goods, gowns,

17

jerkins, hose, town fashions come to the country. Not many of the vendors had yet arrived, most would appear next day, on the eve of the feast, and set up their booths during the long summer evening, ready to begin selling early on the morrow. But the buyers were arriving in purposeful numbers already, bent on securing good beds for their stay.

When Brother Cadfael came up from the Meole brook and his vegetable-fields for Vespers, after a hard and happy afternoon's work, the great court was seething with visitors, servants and grooms, and the traffic in and out of the stables flowed without cease. He stood for a few minutes to watch the pageant, and Brother Mark at his elbow glowed as he gazed, dazzled by the play of colours and shimmer of movement in the sunlight.

'Yes,' said Cadfael, viewing with philosophical detachment what Brother Mark contemplated with excitement and wonder, 'the world and his wife will be here, either to buy or sell.' And he eyed his young friend attentively, for the boy had seen little enough of the world before entering the order, being thrust through the gates willy-nilly at sixteen by a stingy uncle who grudged him his keep even in exchange for hard work, and he had only recently taken his final vows. 'Do you see anything there to tempt you back into the secular world?'

'No,' said Brother Mark, promptly and serenely. 'But I may look and enjoy, just as I do in the garden when the poppies are in flower. It's no blame to men if they try to put into their own artifacts all the colours and shapes God put into his.'

There were certainly a few of God's more charming artifacts among the throng of visitors moving about the great court and the stable-yard, young women as bright and blooming as the poppies, and all the prettier for being in a high state of expectation,

looking forward eagerly to their one great outing of the year. Some came riding their own ponies, some pillion behind husbands or grooms, there was even one horse-litter bringing an important dowager from the south of the shire.

'I never saw it so lively before,' said Mark, gazing with pleasure.

'You've not lived through a fair as yet. Last year the town was under siege all through July and into August, small hope of getting either buyers or sellers into Shrewsbury for any such business. I had my doubts even about this year, but it seems trade's well on the move again, and our gentlefolk are hungrier than ever for what they missed a year ago. It will be a profitable fair, I fancy!'

'Then could we not have spared a tithe to help put the town in order?' demanded Mark.

'You have a way, child, of asking the most awkward questions. I can read very well what was in the provost's mind, since he spoke it out in full. But I'm by no means so sure I know what was in the abbot's, nor that he uttered the half of it. A hard man to read!'

Mark had stopped listening. His eyes were on a rider who had just entered at the gatehouse, and was walking his horse delicately through the moving throng towards the stables. Three retainers on rough-coated ponies followed at his heels, one of them with a cross-bow slung at his saddle. In these perilous times, even here in regions summarily pacified so short a time ago, no gentleman would undertake a longer journey without provision for his own defence, and an arbalest reaches further than a sword. This young man both wore a sword and looked as if he could use it, but he had also brought an archer with him for security.

It was the master who held Mark's eyes. He was perhaps a year or two short of thirty, past the uncertainties of first youth – if, indeed, he had ever

19

suffered them – and at his resplendent best. Handsomely appointed, elegantly mounted on a glistening dark bay, he rode with the negligent ease of one accustomed to horses almost from birth. In the summer heat he had shed his short riding-cotte, and had it slung over his lap, and rode with his shirt open over a spare, muscular chest, hung with a cross on a golden chain. The body thus displayed to view in simple linen shirt and dark hose was long and lissome and proud of its comeliness, and the head that crowned it was bared to the light, a smiling, animated face nicely fashioned about large, commanding dark eyes, and haloed in a cropped cap of dark gold hair, that would have curled had it been allowed to grow a little longer. He came and passed, and Mark's eyes followed him, at once tranquil and wistful, quite without any shade of envy.

'It must be a pleasant thing,' he said thoughtfully, 'to be so made as to give pleasure to those who behold you. Do you suppose he realises his blessings?'

Mark was rather small himself, from undernourishment from childhood, and plain of face, with spiky, straw-coloured hair round his tonsure. Not that he ever viewed himself much in the glass, or realised that he had a pair of great grey eyes of such immaculate clarity that common beauty faltered before them. Nor was Cadfael going to remind him of any such assets.

'As the world usually goes,' he said cheerfully, 'he probably has a mind that looks no further ahead or behind than the length of his own fine eyelashes. But I grant you he's a pleasure to look at. Yet the mind lasts longer. Be glad you have one that will wear well. Come on, now, all this will keep till after supper.'

The word diverted Brother Mark's thoughts very agreeably. He had been hungry all his life until he entered this house, and still he preserved the habit of hunger, so that food, no less than beauty, was

20

unflawed pleasure. He went willingly at Cadfael's side towards Vespers, and the supper that would follow. It was Cadfael who suddenly halted, hailed by name in a high, delighted voice that plucked his head about towards the summons gladly.

A lady, a slender, young, graceful lady with a heavy sheaf of gold hair and a bright oval face, and eyes like irises in twilight, purple and clear. Her body, as Brother Mark saw in his first startled glance, though scarcely swollen as yet, and proudly carried, was girdled high, and rounded below the girdle. There was a life there within. He was not so innocent that he did not know the signs. He should have lowered his eyes, and willed to do so, and could not; she shone so that it was like all the pictures of the Visiting Virgin that he had ever seen. And this vision held out both hands to Brother Cadfael, and called him by his name. Brother Mark, though unwillingly, bent his head and went on his way alone.

'Girl,' said Brother Cadfael heartily, clasping the proffered hands with delight, 'you bloom like a rose! And he never told me!'

'He has not seen you since the winter,' she said, dimpling and flushing, 'and we did not know then. It was no more than a dream, then. And *I* have not seen you since we were wed.'

'And you are happy? And he?'

'Oh, Cadfael, can you ask it!' There had been no need, the radiance Brother Mark had recognised was dazzling Cadfael no less. 'Hugh is here, but he must go to the sheriff first. He'll certainly be asking for you before Compline. I have come to buy a cradle, a beautiful carved cradle for our son. And a Welsh coverlet, in beautiful warm wool, or perhaps a sheepskin. And fine spun wools, to weave his gowns.'

'And you keep well? The child gives you no distress?'

'Distress?' she said, wide-eyed and smiling. 'I have

21

not had a moment's sickness, only joy. Oh, Brother Cadfael,' she said, breaking into laughter, 'how does it come that a brother of this house can ask such wise questions? Have you not somewhere a son of your own? I could believe it! You know far too much about us women!'

'As I suppose,' said Cadfael cautiously, 'I was born of one, like the rest of us. Even abbots and archbishops come into the world the same away.'

'But I'm keeping you,' she said, remorseful. 'It's time for Vespers, and I'm coming, too. I have so many thanks to pour out, there's never enough time. Say a prayer for our child!' She pressed him by both hands, and floated away through the press towards the guest-hall. Born Aline Siward, now Aline Beringar, wife to the deputy sheriff of Shropshire, Hugh Beringar of Maesbury, near Oswestry. A year married, and Cadfael had been close friend to that marriage, and felt himself enlarged and fulfilled by its happiness. He went on towards the church in high content with the evening, his own mood, and the prospects for the coming days.

When he emerged from the refectory after supper, into an evening still all rose and amber light, the court was as animated as at noon, and new arrivals still entering at the gatehouse. In the cloister Hugh Beringar sat sprawled at ease, waiting for him; a lightweight, limber, dark young man, lean of feature and quizzical of eyebrow. A formidable face, impossible to read unless a man knew the language. Happily, Cadfael did, and read with confidence.

'If you have not lost your cunning,' said the young man, lazily rising, 'or met your overmatch in this new abbot of yours, you can surely find a sound excuse for missing Collations – and a drop of good wine to share with a friend.'

'Better than an excuse,' said Cadfael readily, 'I have

an acknowledged reason. They're having trouble in the grange court with scour among the calves, and want a brewing of my cure in a hurry. And I daresay I can find you a draught of something better than small ale. We can sit outside the workshop, such a warm evening. But are you not a neglectful husband,' he reproved, as they fell companionably into step on their way into the gardens, 'to abandon your lady for an old drinking crony?'

'My lady,' said Hugh ruefully, 'has altogether abandoned me! A breeding girl has only to show her nose in the guest-hall, and she's instantly swept away by a swarm of older dames, all cooing like doves, and loading her with advice on everything from diet to midwives' magic. Aline is holding conference with all of them, hearing details of all their confinements, and taking note of all their recommendations. And since I can neither spin, nor weave, nor sew, I'm banished.' He sounded remarkably complacent about it, and being well aware of it himself, laughed aloud. 'But she told me she had seen you, and you needed no telling. How do you think she is looking?'

'Radiant!' said Cadfael. 'In full bloom, and prettier than ever.'

In the herb-garden, shaded along one side by its high hedge from the declining sun, the heavy fragrances of the day hung like a spell. They settled on a bench under the eaves of Cadfael's workshop, with a jug of wine between them.

'But I must start my draught brewing,' said Cadfael. 'You may talk to me while I do it. I shall hear you within, and I'll be with you as soon as I have it stirring. What's the news from the great world? Is King Stephen secure on his throne now, do you think?'

Beringar considered that in silence for a few moments, listening contentedly to the soft sounds of Cadfael's movements within the hut. 'With all the west

still holding out for the empress, however warily, I doubt it. Nothing is moving now, but it's an ominous stillness. You know that Earl Robert of Gloucester is in Normandy with the empress?'

'So we'd heard. It's not to be wondered at, he is her half-brother, and fond of her, so they say, and not an envious man.'

'A good man,' agreed Hugh, doing an opponent generous justice, 'one of the few on either side not grasping for what he himself can get. The west, however quiet now, will do what Robert says. I can't believe he'll hold off for ever. And even out of the west, he has kinsmen and influence. The word runs that he and Maud, from their refuge in France, are working away quietly to enlist powerful allies, wherever they see a hope. If that's true, this civil war is by no means over. Promised enough support, there'll be a bid for the lady's cause, soon or late.'

'Robert has daughters married about the land,' said Cadfael thoughtfully, 'and all of them to men of might. One of them to the earl of Chester, I recall. If a few of that measure declared for the empress, you might well have a war on your hands to some purpose.'

Beringar drew a long face, and then shrugged off the thought. Earl Ranulf of Chester was certainly one of the most powerful men in the kingdom, virtually king himself of an immense palatine where his writ ran, and no other. But for that very reason he was less likely to feel the need to declare for either side in the contention for the throne. Himself supreme, and unlikely ever to be threatened in his own possessions by either Maud or Stephen, he could afford to sit back and watch his own borders, not merely with a view to preserving them intact, rather to extending them. A land at odds with itself offers opportunities, as well as threats.

'Ranulf will need a lot of persuading, kinsman or no.

He's very well as he is, and if he does move it will be because he sees profit and power in it for himself, and the empress will come a poor second. He's not the man to risk anything for any cause but his own.'

Cadfael came out from the hut to sit beside him, drawing grateful breath in the evening coolness, for he had his small brazier burning within, beneath his simmering brew. 'That's better! Now fill me a cup, Hugh, I'm more than ready for it.' And after a long and satisfying draught he said thoughtfully: 'There were some fears this disturbed state of things could ruin the fair even this year, but it seems trade keeps on the move while barons skulk in their castles. The prospects are excellent, after all.'

'For the abbey, perhaps,' agreed Hugh. 'The town is less happy about the outlook, from all we heard as we passed through. This new abbot of yours has set the burgesses properly by the ears.'

'Ah, you've heard about that?' Cadfael recounted the course of the argument, in case his friend had caught but one side of it. 'They have a case for seeking relief, no question. But so has he for refusing it, and he's standing firm on his rights. No way round it in law, he's taking no more than is granted to him. And no less!' he added, and sighed.

'Feelings are running high in the town,' warned Beringar seriously. 'I would not be sure you may not have trouble yet. I doubt if the provost made any too much of their needs. The word in the town is that this may be law, but it is not justice. But what's the word with you? How are you faring in the new dispensation?'

'You'll hear murmurs even within our walls,' admitted Cadfael, 'if you keep your ears open. But for my part, I have no complaint. He's a hard man, but fair, and at least as hard on himself as on others. We've been spoiled and easy with Heribert, and the new curb

pulled us up pretty sharply, but that's the sum of it. I have much confidence in the man. He'll chasten where he sees fault, but he'll stand by his own against any power where they are threatened blameless. He's a man I'd be glad to have beside me in any battle.'

'But his loyalty's limited to his own?' said Beringar slyly, and cocked a slender black brow.

'We live in a contentious world,' said Brother Cadfael, who had lived more than half his life in the thick of the battles. 'Who says peace would be good for us? I don't know the man well enough yet to know what's in his mind. I have not found him limited, but his vows are to his vocation and this house. Give him room and time, Hugh, and we shall see what follows. Time was when I was in two minds, or more, about *you*!' His voice marvelled and smiled at the thought. 'Not very long, however! I shall soon get the measure of Radulfus, too. Hand me the jug, lad, and then I must go and stir this brew for the calves. How long have we yet to Compline?'

Chapter Two

On the thirty-first of July the vendors came flooding in, by road and by river. From noon onward the horse-fair was marked out in lots for stalls and booths, and the abbey stewards were standing by to guide pedlars and merchants to their places, and levy the tolls due on the amount of merchandise they brought. A halfpenny for a modest man-load, a penny for a horse-load, from twopence to fourpence for a cart-load, depending on the size and capacity, and higher fees in proportion for the goods unloaded from the river barges that tied up at the temporary landing-stage along the Gaye. The entire length of the Foregate hummed and sparkled with movement and colour and chatter, the abbey barn and stable outside the wall was full, children and dogs ran among the booths and between the wheels of the carts, excited and shrill.

The discipline of the day's devotions within the walls was not relaxed, but between offices a certain air of holiday gaiety had entered with the guests, and novices and pupils were allowed to wander and gaze without penalty. Abbot Radulfus held himself aloof, as was due to his dignity, and left the superintendence of the occasion and the collection of tolls to his lay stewards, but for all that he knew everything that was going on, and had measures in mind to deal with any emergency. As soon as the arrival of the first Flemish merchant was

reported to him, together with the news that the man had little French, he dispatched Brother Matthew, who had lived for some years in Flanders in his earlier days, and could speak fluent Flemish, to deal with any problems that might arise. If the fine-cloth merchants were coming, there was good reason to afford them every facility, for they were profitable visitors. It was a mark of the significance of the Shrewsbury fair that they should undertake so long a journey from the East Anglian ports where they put in, and find it worth their while to hire carts or horses for the overland pilgrimage.

The Welsh, of course, would certainly be present in some numbers, but for the most part they would be the local people who had a foot on either side the border, and knew enough English to need no interpreters. It came as a surprise to Brother Cadfael to be intercepted once again as he left the refectory after supper, this time by the steward of the grange court, preoccupied and breathless with business, and told that he was needed at the jetty, to take care of one who spoke nothing but Welsh, and a man of consequence, indeed of self-importance, who would not be fobbed off with the suspect aid of a local Welshman who might well be in competition with him on the morrow.

'Prior Robert gives you leave, for as long as you're needed. It's a fellow by the name of Rhodri ap Huw, from Mold. He's brought a great load up the Dee, and ported it over to Vrnwy and Severn, which must have cost him plenty.'

'What manner of goods?' asked Cadfael, as they made for the gatehouse together. His interest was immediate and hearty. Nothing could have suited him better than a sound excuse to be out among the noise and bustle along the Foregate.

'What looks like a very fine wool-clip, mainly. And also honey and mead. And I thought I saw some

28

bundles of hides – maybe from Ireland, if he trades out of the Dee. And there's the man himself.'

Rhodri ap Huw stood solid as a rock on the wooden planking of the jetty beside his moored barge, and let the tides of human activity flow round him. The river ran green and still, at a good level for high summer; even boats of deeper draught than usual had made the passage without mishap, and were unloading and unbaling on all sides. The Welshman watched, measuring other men's bales with shrewd, narrowed dark eyes, and pricing what he saw. He looked about fifty years old, and so assured and experienced that it seemed strange he had never picked up English. Not a tall man, but square-built and powerful, fierce Welsh bones islanded in a thick growth of thorny black hair and beard. His dress, though plain and workmanlike, was of excellent material and well-fitted. He saw the steward hurrying towards him, evidently having carried out his wishes to the letter, and large, white teeth gleamed contentedly from the thicket of the black beard.

'Here am I, Master Rhodri,' said Cadfael cheerfully, 'to keep you company in your own tongue. And my name is Cadfael, at your service for all your present needs.'

'And very welcome, Brother Cadfael,' said Rhodri ap Huw heartily. 'I hope you'll pardon my fetching you away from your devotions …'

'I'll do better. I'll thank you! A pity to have to miss all this bustle, I can do with a glimpse of the world now and again.'

Sharp, twinkling eyes surveyed him from head to toe in one swift glance. 'You'll be from the north yourself, I fancy. Mold is where I come from.'

'Close by Trefriw I was born.'

'A Gwynedd man. But one who's been a sight further through the world than Trefriw, by the look of

29

you, brother. As I have. Well, here are my two fellows, ready to unload and porter for me before I send on part of my cargo downriver to Bridgnorth, where I have a sale for mead. Shall we have the goods ashore first?'

The steward bade them choose a stand at whatever point Master Rhodri thought fit when he had viewed the ground, and left them to supervise the unloading. Rhodri's two nimble little Welsh boatmen went to work briskly, hefting the heavy bales of hides and the wool-sacks with expert ease, and piling them on the jetty, and Rhodri and Cadfael addressed themselves pleasurably to watching the lively scene around them; as many of the townsfolk and the abbey guests were also doing. On a fine summer evening it was the best of entertainments to lean over the parapet of the bridge, or stroll along the green path to the Gaye, and stare at an annual commotion which was one of the year's highlights. If some of the townspeople looked on with dour faces, and muttered to one another in sullen undertones, that was no great wonder, either. Yesterday's confrontation had been reported throughout the town, they knew they had been turned away empty-handed.

'A thing worth noting,' said Rhodri, spreading his thick legs on the springy boards, 'how both halves of England can meet in commerce, while they fall out in every other field. Show a man where there's money to be made, and he'll be there. If barons and kings had the same good sense, a country could be at peace, and handsomely the gainer by it.'

'Yet I fancy,' said Cadfael dryly, 'that there'll be some hot contention here even between traders, before the three days are up. More ways than one of cutting throats.'

'Well, every wise man keeps a weapon about him, whatever suits his skill, that's only good sense, too. But

we live together, we live together, better than princes manage it. Though I grant you,' he said weightily, 'princes make good use of these occasions, for that matter. No place like one of your greater fairs for exchanging news and views without being noticed, or laying plots and stratagems, or meeting someone you'd liefer not be seen meeting. Nowhere so solitary as in the middle of a market-place!'

'In a divided land,' said Cadfael thoughtfully, 'you may very well be right.'

'For instance – look to your left a ways, but don't turn. You see the meagre fellow in the fine clothes, the smooth-shaven one with the mincing walk? Come to watch who's arriving by water! You may be sure if *he's* here at all, he's come early, and has his stall already up and stocked, to be free to view the rest of us. That's Euan of Shotwick, the glover, and an important man about Earl Ranulf's court at Chester, I can tell you.'

'For his skill at his trade?' asked Cadfael dryly, observing the lean, fastidious, high-nosed figure with interest.

'That and other fields, brother. Euan of Shotwick is one of the sharpest of all of Earl Ranulf's intelligencers, and much relied on, and if he's setting up a booth here as far as Shrewsbury, it may well be for more purposes than trade. And then on the other side, look, that great barge standing off ready to come alongside – downstream of us. See the cut of her? Bristol-built, for a thousand marks! Straight out of the west country, and the city the king failed to take last year, and has let well alone ever since.'

Above the softly-flowing surface of Severn, its green silvered now with slanting evening sunlight, the barge sidled along the grassy shore towards the end of the jetty. She loomed impressively opulent and graceful, cunningly built to draw hardly more water than boats half her capacity, and yet steer well and ride steadily.

She had a single mast, and what seemed to be a neat, closed cabin aft, and three crewmen were poling her inshore with easy, light touches, and waiting to moor her alongside as soon as there was room. Twenty pence, as like as not, thought Cadfael, before *she* gets her load ashore and cleared!

'Made to carry wine, and carry it steady,' said Rhodri ap Huw, narrowing his sharply-calculating eyes on the boat. 'Some of the best wines of France come into Bristol, they should have a ready sale as far north as this. I should know that rig!'

A considerable number of onlookers, whether they recognised her port and rig or not, were curious enough to come down from the bridge and the highroad to see the Bristol boat come in. She was remarkable enough among her fellow-craft to draw all eyes. Cadfael caught sight of a number of known faces craning among the crowd: Edric Flesher's wife Petronilla, Aline Beringar's maid Constance leaning over the bridge, one of the abbey stewards forgetting his duties to stare; and suddenly sunlight on a head of dark gold hair, cropped short, and a young man came running lightly down from the highway, to halt on the grass slope above the jetty, and watched admiringly as the Bristol boat slid alongside, ready to be made fast. The lordling whose assured beauty had aroused Mark's wistful admiration was evidently just as inquisitive as the raggedest barefoot urchin from the Foregate.

The two Welshmen had completed their unloading by this time, and were waiting for orders, and Rhodri ap Huw was not the man to let his interest in other men's business interfere with his own.

'They'll be a fair while unloading,' he said briskly. 'Shall we go and choose a good place for my stall, while the field's open?'

Cadfael led the way along the Foregate, where

several booths had already been set up. 'You'll prefer a site on the horse-fair itself, I fancy, where all the roads meet.'

'Ah, my customers will find me, wherever I am,' said Rhodri smugly; but for all that, he kept a shrewd eye on all the possibilities, and took his time about selecting his place, even when they had walked the length of the Foregate and come to the great open triangle of the horse-fair. The abbey servants had set up a number of more elaborate booths, that could be closed and locked, and supply living shelter for their holders, and these were let out for rents. Other traders brought their own serviceable trestles and light roofs, while the small country vendors would come in early each morning and display their wares on the dry ground, or on a woven brychan, filling all the spaces between. For Rhodri nothing was good enough but the best. He fixed upon a stout booth near the abbey barn and stable, where all customers coming in for the day could stable their beasts, and in the act could not fail to notice the goods on the neighbouring stalls.

'This will serve very well. One of my lads will sleep the nights here.' The elder of the two had followed them, balancing the first load easily in a sling over his shoulders, while the other remained to guard the merchandise stacked on the jetty. Now he began to stow what he had brought, while Rhodri and Cadfael set off back to the river to dispatch his fellow after him. On the way they intercepted one of the stewards, notified him of the site chosen, and came to terms for the rental. Brother Cadfael's immediate duty was done, but he was as interested in the growing bustle along the road and by the Severn as any other man who saw the like but once a year, and there was time to spare yet before Compline. It was good, too, to be speaking Welsh, there was seldom need within the walls.

They reached the point where the track turned aside from the highway to go down to the waterside, and looked down upon a lively scene. The Bristol boat was moored, and her three crewmen beginning to hoist casks of wine on to the jetty, while a big, portly, red-faced elderly gentleman in a long gown of fashionable cut, his capuchon twisted up into an elaborate hat, swung wide sleeves as he pointed and beckoned, giving orders at large. A fleshy but powerful face, round and choleric, with bristly brows like furze, and bluish jowls. He moved with surprising agility and speed, and plainly he considered himself a man of importance, and expected others to recognise him as such on sight.

'I thought it might well be!' said Rhodri ap Huw, pleased with his own acuteness and knowledge of widespread affairs. 'Thomas of Bristol, they call him, one of the biggest importers of wine into the port there, and deals in a small way in fancy wares from the east, sweetmeats and spices and candies. The Venetians bring them in from Cyprus and Syria. Costly and profitable! The ladies will pay high for something their neighbours have not! What did I say? Money will bring men together. Whether they hold for Stephen or the empress, they'll come and rub shoulders at your fair, brother.'

'By the look of him,' said Cadfael, 'a man of consequence in the city of Bristol.'

'So he is, and I'd have said in very good odour with Robert of Gloucester, but business is business, and it would take more than the simple fear of venturing into enemy territory to keep him at home, when there's good money to be made.'

They had turned to begin the descent to the riverside when they were aware of a growing murmur of excitement among the people watching from the bridge, and of heads turning to look towards the town

34

gates on the other side of the river. The evening light, slanting from the west, cast deep shadows under one parapet and half across the bridge, but above floated a faint, moving cloud of fine dust, glittering in the sunset rays, and advancing towards the abbey shore. A tight knot of young men came into sight, shearing through the strolling onlookers at a smart pace, like a determined little army on the march. All the rest were idling the time pleasurably away on a fine evening, these were bound somewhere, in resolution and haste, the haste, perhaps, all the more aggressive lest the resolution be lost. There might have been as many as five and twenty of them, all male and all young. Some of them Cadfael knew. Martin Bellecote's boy Edwy was there, and Edric Flesher's journeyman, and scions of half a dozen respected trades within the town; and at their head strode the provost's own son, young Philip Corviser, jutting a belligerent chin and swinging clenched hands to the rhythm of his long-striding walk. They looked very grave and very dour, and people gazed at them in wonder and speculation, and drew in at a more cautious pace after their passing, to watch what would happen.

'If this is not the face of battle,' said Rhodri ap Huw alertly, viewing the grim young faces while they were still safely distant, 'I have never seen it. I did hear that your house has a difference of opinion with the town. I'll away and see all those goods of mine safely stacked away under lock and key, before the trumpets blow.' And he tucked up his sleeves and was off down the path to the jetty as nimbly as a squirrel, and hoisting his precious jars of honey out of harm's way, leaving Cadfael still thoughtfully gazing by the roadside. The merchant's instincts, he thought, were sound enough. The elders of the town had made their plea and been sent away empty-handed. To judge by their faces, the younger and hotter-headed worthies of the town of

Shrewsbury had resolved upon stronger measures. A rapid survey reassured him that they were unarmed, as far as he could see not even a staff among them. But the face, no question, was the face of battle, and the trumpets were about to blow.

Chapter Three

The advancing phalanx reached the end of the bridge, and checked for no more than a moment, while their leader cast calculating glances forward along the Foregate, now populous with smaller stalls, and down at the jetty, and gave some brisk order. Then he, with perhaps ten of his stalwarts on his heels, turned and plunged down the path to the river, while the rest marched vehemently ahead. The interested townspeople, equally mutely and promptly, split into partisan groups, and pursued both contingents. Not one of them would willingly miss what was to come. Cadfael, more soberly, eyed the passing ranks, and was confirmed in believing that they came with the most austere intentions; there was not a bludgeon among them, and he doubted if any of them ever carried knives. Nothing about them was warlike, except their faces. Besides, he knew most of them, there was no wilful harm in any. All the same, he turned down the path after them, not quite easy in his mind. The Corviser sprig was known for a wild one, clever, bursting with hot and suspect ideas, locked in combat with his elders half his time, and occasionally liable to drink rather more than at this stage he could carry. Though this evening he had certainly not been drinking; he had far more urgent matters on his mind.

Brother Cadfael sighed, descending the path to the waterside half-reluctantly. The earnest young are so

dangerously given to venturing beyond the point where experience turns back. And the sharper they are, the more likely to come by wounds.

He was not at all surprised to find that Rhodri ap Huw, that most experienced of travellers, had vanished from the jetty, together with his second porter and all his goods. Rhodri himself would not be far, once he had seen all his merchandise well on its way to being locked in the booth on the horse-fair. He would want to watch all that passed, and make his own dispositions accordingly, but he would be out of sight, and somewhere where he could make his departure freely whenever he deemed it wise. But there were half a dozen boats of various sizes busy unloading, dominated by Thomas of Bristol's noble barge. Its owner heard the sudden surge of urgent feet on the downhill track, and turned to level an imperious glance that way, before returning to his business of supervising the landing of his goods. The array of casks and bales on the boards was impressive. The young men surging down to the river could not fail to make an accurate estimate of the powers they faced.

'Gentlemen ...!' Philip Corviser hailed them all loudly, coming to a halt with feet spread, confronting Thomas of Bristol. He had a good, ringing voice; it carried, and lesser dealers dropped what they were doing to listen. 'Gentlemen, I beg a hearing, as you are citizens all, of whatever town, as I am of Shrewsbury, and as you care for your own town as I do for mine! You are here paying rents and tolls to the abbey, while the abbey denies any aid to the town. And we have greater need than ever the abbey has, of some part of what you bring.'

He drew breath hard, having spent his first wind. He was a gangling lad, not yet quite in command of his long limbs, being barely twenty and only just at the end of his growing. Spruce in his dress, but down at the

heel, Cadfael noticed – proof of the old saying that the shoemaker's son is always the one who goes barefoot! He had a thick thatch of reddish dark hair, and a decent, homely face now pale, with passion under his summer tan. A good, deft workman, they said, when he could be stopped from flying off after some angry cause or other. Certainly he had a cause now, bless the lad, he was pouring out to these hard-headed business men all the arguments his father had used to the abbot at chapter, in dead earnest, and – heaven teach him better sense! – even with hopes of convincing them!

'If the abbey turns a cold eye on the town's troubles, should you side with them? We are here to tell you our side of the story, and appeal to you as men who also have to bear the burdens of your own boroughs, and may well have seen at home what war and siege can do to your own walls and pavings. Is it unreasonable that we should ask for a share in the profits of the fair? The abbey came by no damage last year, as the town did. If they will not bear their part for the common good, we address ourselves to you, who have no such protection from the hardships of the world, and will have fellow-feeling with those who share the like burdens.'

They were beginning to lose interest in him, to shrug, and turn back to their unloading. He raised his voice sharply in appeal.

'All we ask is that you will hold back a tithe of the dues you pay to the abbey, and pay them instead to the town for murage and pavage. If all hold together, what can the abbey stewards do against you? There need be no cost to you above what you would be paying in any event, and we should have something nearer to justice. What do you say? Will you help us?'

They would not! The growl of indifference and derision hardly needed words. What, set up a challenge to what was laid down by charter, when they had nothing to gain by it? Why should they take the

risk? They turned to their work, shrugging him off. The young men grouped at his back set up among themselves a counter murmur, still controlled but growing angry. And Thomas of Bristol, massive and contemptuous, waved a fist in their spokesman's face, and said impatiently: 'Stand out of the way, boy, you are hindering your betters! Pay a tithe to the town indeed! Are not the abbey rights set down according to law? And can you, dare you tell me they do not pay the fee demanded of them by charter? If you have a complaint that they are failing to keep the law, take it to the sheriff, where it belongs, but don't come here with your nonsense. Now be off, and let honest men get on with their work.'

The young man took fire. 'The men of Shrewsbury are as honest as you, sir, though something less boastful about it. We take honesty for granted here! And it is not nonsense that our town goes with broken walls and broken streets, while abbey and Foregate have escaped all such damage. No, but listen ...'

The merchant turned a broad, hunched back, with disdainful effect, and stalked away to pick up the staff he had laid against his piled barrels, and motion his men to continue their labours. Philips started indignantly after him, for the act was stingingly deliberate, as though a gnat, a mere persistent nuisance, had been brushed aside.

'Master merchant,' he called hotly, 'one word more!' And he laid an arresting hand to Thomas's fine, draped sleeve.

They were two choleric people, and it might have come to it even at the best, sooner or later, but Cadfael's impression was that Thomas had been genuinely startled by the grasp at his arm, and believed he was about to be attacked. Whatever the cause, he swung round and struck out blindly with the staff he held. The boy flung up his arm, but too late

40

thoroughly to protect his head. The blow fell heavily on his forearms and temple, and laid him flat on the planking of the jetty, with blood oozing from a cut above his ear.

That was the end of all peaceful and dignified protest, and the declaration of war. Many things happened on the instant. Philip had fallen without a cry, and lay half-stunned, but someone had certainly cried out, a small, protesting shriek, instantly swallowed up in the roar of anger from the young men of the town. Two of them rushed to their fallen leader, but the rest, bellowing for vengeance, lunged to confront the equally roused traders, and closed with them merrily. In a moment the goods newly disembarked were being hoisted and flung into the river, and one of the raiders soon followed them, with a bigger splash. Fortunately those who lived all their lives by Severn usually learned to swim even before they learned to walk, and the youngster was in no danger of drowning. By the time he had hauled himself out and returned to the fray, there was a fully-fledged riot in progress all along the riverside.

Several of the cooler-headed citizens had moved in, though cautiously, to try to separate the combatants, and talk a little sense into the furious young; and one or two, not cautious enough, had come in for blows meant for the foe, the common fate of those who try to make peace where no one is inclined for it.

Cadfael among the rest had rushed down to the jetty, intent on preventing what might well be a second and fatal blow, to judge by the merchant's congested countenance and brandished staff. But someone else was before him. A girl had clambered frantically up out of the tiny cabin of the barge, kilted her skirts and leaped ashore, in time to cling with all her weight to the quivering arm, and plead in agitated tones:

'Uncle, don't, please don't! He did no violence!

41

You've hurt him badly!'

Philip Corviser's brown eyes, all this time open but unseeing, blinked furiously at the sound of so unexpected a voice. He heaved himself shakily to his knees, remembered his injury and his grievance, and gathered sprawled limbs and faculties to surge to his feet and do battle. Not that his efforts would have been very effective; his legs gave under him as he tried to rise, and he gripped his head between steadying hands as though it might fall off if he shook it. But it was the sight of the girl that stopped him short. There she stood, clinging to the merchant's arm and pleading angelically into his ear, in tones that could have cooled a dragon, her eyes all the time dilated and anxious and pitying on Philip. And calling the old demon 'uncle'! Philip's revenge was put clean out of his reach in an instant, but he scarcely felt a pang at the deprivation, to judge by the transformation that came over his bruised and furious face. Swaying on one knee, still dazed, he stared at the girl as pilgrims might stare at miraculous visions, or lost wanderers at the Pole star.

She was well worth looking at, a young thing of about eighteen or nineteen years, bare-armed and bare-headed, with two great braids of blue-black hair swinging to her waist, and framed between them a round, childish face all roses and snow, lit by two long-lashed dark blue eyes, at this moment huge with alarm and concern. No wonder the mere sound of her voice could tame her formidable uncle, as surely as the sight of her had checked and held at gaze the two young men who had rushed to salvage and avenge their leader, and who now stood abashed, gaping and harmless.

It was at that moment that the fight on the jetty, which had become a melee hopelessly tangled, reeled their way, thudding along the planks, knocked over the stack of small barrels, and sent them rolling

thunderously in all directions. Cadfael grasped young Corviser under the arms, hoisted him to his feet and hauled him out of harm's way, thrusting him bodily into the arms of his friends for safe-keeping, since he was still in a daze. A rolling cask swept Thomas's feet from under him, and the girl, flung aside in his fall, swayed perilously on the edge of the jetty.

An agile figure darted past Cadfael with a flash of gold hair, leaped another rolling cask as nimbly as a deer, and plucked her back to safety in a long arm. The almost insolent grace and assurance was as familiar as the yellow hair. Cadfael contented himself with helping Thomas to his feet, and drawing him aside out of danger, and was not particularly surprised, when that was done, to see that the long arm was still gallantly clasped round the girl's waist. Nor was she in any hurry to extricate herself. Indeed, she was gazing at the smiling, comely, reassuring face of her rescuer wide-eyed, much as Philip Corviser had gazed at her.

'There, you're quite safe! But let me help you back aboard, you'd do best to stay there a while, your uncle, too. I advise it, sir,' he said earnestly. 'No one will offer you further offence. With this lady beside you, no one could be so ungallant,' he said, his eyes wide in candid admiration. The cream of the girl's fair skin turned all to rose.

Thomas of Bristol dusted himself down with slightly shaky hands, for he was a big man, and had fallen heavily. 'I thank you, sir, warmly, for your help. You, too, brother. But my wines – my goods –'

'Leave them to us, sir. What can be salvaged, shall be. You stay safe aboard, and wait. This cannot continue, the law will be out after these turbulent young fools any moment. Half of them are off along the Foregate, overturning stalls and hounding the abbey stewards. Before long they'll be in the town gaol with sore heads,

wishing they'd had better sense than pick a fight with the abbot of a Benedictine house.'

His eye was on Cadfael, who was busy righting and retrieving the fugitive casks, and still within earshot. He felt himself being drawn companionably into this masterful young man's planning, perhaps as reassurance and guarantee of respectability. The eyes were slightly mischievous, though the face retained its decent gravity. The nearest Benedictine was being gently teased as representative of his order.

'My name,' said the rescuer blithely, 'is Ivo Corbière, of the manor of Stanton Cobbold in this shire, though the main part of my honour lies in Cheshire. If you'll allow me, I'm happy to offer my help ...' He had taken his arm from about the girl's waist by then, decorously if reluctantly, but his gaze continued to embrace and flatter her; she was well aware of it, and it did not displease her. 'There!' cried Corbière triumphantly, as a shrill whistle resounded from a youth hanging over the parapet of the bridge above them. 'Now watch them dive to cover! Their look-out sees the sheriff's men turning out to quell the riot.'

His judgment was accurate enough. Half a dozen heads snapped up sharply at the sound, noted the urgently waving arm, and half a dozen dishevelled youths extricated themselves hastily from the fight, dropped whatever they were holding, and made off at speed in several directions, some along the Gaye, towards the coverts by the riverside, some up the slope into the tangle of narrow lanes behind the Foregate, one under the arch of the bridge, to emerge on the upstream side with no worse harm than wet feet. In a few moments the sharp clatter of hooves drummed over the bridge, and half a dozen of the sheriff's men came trotting down to the jetty, while the rest of the company swept on towards the horse-fair.

'As good as over!' said Ivo Corbière gaily. 'Brother,

will you lend an oar? I fancy you know this river better than I, and there's many a man's hard-won living afloat out there, and much of it may yet be saved.'

He asked no leave; he had selected already the smallest and most manageable boat that swung beside the jetty, and he was across the boards and down into it almost before the sheriff's men had driven their mounts in among the still-locked combatants, and begun to pluck the known natives out by the hair. Brother Cadfael followed. With Compline but ten minutes away, by his mental clock, he should have made his escape and left the salvage to this confident and commanding young man, but he had been sent out here to aid a client of the abbey fair, and could he not argue that he was still about the very same business? He was in the borrowed boat, an oar in his hand and his eye upon the nearest cask bobbing on the bright sunset waters, before he had found an answer; which was answer enough.

The noise receded soon. Everyone left here was busily hooking bales and bundles out of the river, pursuing some downstream to coves where they had lodged, abandoning one or two small items too sodden and too vulnerable to be saved, writing off minor losses, thankfully calculating profits still to be made after fees and rentals and tolls were paid. The damage was not so great, after all, it could be carried. Along the Foregate stalls were being righted, goods laid out afresh. Doubtful if the pandemonium had ever reached the horse-fair, where the great merchants unrolled their bales. In the stony confines of the castle and the town gaol, no doubt, some dozen or so youngsters of the town were nursing their bruises and grudges, and wondering how their noble and dignified protest had disintegrated into such a shambles. As for Philip Corviser, nobody knew where he had fetched up, once

he shook off the devotees who had helped him away from the jetty in a daze. The brief venture was over, the cost not too great. Not even the sheriff, Gilbert Prescote, was going to bear down too hard on those well-meaning but ill-advised young men of Shrewsbury.

'Gentlemen,' said Thomas of Bristol, eased and expansive, 'I cannot thank you enough for such generous help. No, the casks will have taken no hurt. Those who buy my wines should and do store them properly a good while before tapping, their condition will not be impaired. The sugar confections, thanks be, were not yet unloaded. No, I have suffered no real hurt. And my child here is much in your debt. Come, my dear, don't hide there within, make your respects to such good friends! Let me present my niece Emma, my sister's daughter, Emma Vernold, heiress to her father, who was a master-mason in our city, and also to me, for I have no other kin. Emma, my dear, you may pour the wine!'

The girl had made good use of the interval. She came forth now with her braids of hair coiled in a gilded net on her neck, and a fine tunic of embroidered linen over her plain gown. Not, thought Cadfael, for my benefit! It was high time for him to take his leave and return to his proper duties. He had missed Compline in favour of retrieving goods from the waters, and he would have to put in an hour or so in his workshop yet before he could seek his bed. No one would be early to bed on this night, however. Thomas of Bristol was not the man to leave the supervision of his booth and the disposition of his goods to others, however trustworthy his three servants might be; he would soon be off to the horse-fair to see everything safely stowed to his own satisfaction, ready for the morrow. And if he thought fit to leave those two handsome young people together

46

here until his return, that was his affair. Mention of the manor of Stanton Cobbold, and as the least part of Corbière's honour, at that, had made its impression. There had been no real need for that careful mention of Mistress Emma's prospective wealth; but dutiful uncles and guardians must be ever on the alert for good matches for their girls, and this young man was already taken with her face before ever he heard of her fortune. Small wonder, she was a beautiful child by any standards.

Brother Cadfael excused himself from lingering, wished the company goodnight, and walked back at leisure to the gatehouse. The Foregate stretched busy and populous, but at peace. Order had been restored, and Saint Peter's Fair could open on the morrow without further disruption.

Chapter Four

hugh Beringar came back from a final patrol along the Foregate well past ten o'clock, an hour when all dutiful brothers should have been fast asleep in the dortoir. He was by no means surprised to find that Cadfael was not. They met in the great court, as Cadfael came back from closing his workshop in the herb-garden. It was still a clear twilight, and the west had a brilliant afterglow.

'I hear you've been in the thick of it,' said Hugh, stretching and yawning. 'Did ever I know you when you were not? Mad young fools, what did they hope to do, that their elders could not! And then to run wild as they did, and ruin their case even with those who had sympathy for them! Now their sires will have fines to pay, and the town lose more for the night's work than ever it stood to gain. Cadfael, I take no joy in heaving decent, silly lads into prison, I have a foul taste in my mouth from it. Come into the gatehouse for a while, and share a cup with me. You may as well stay awake until Matins now.'

'Aline will be waiting for you,' objected Cadfael.

'Aline, bless her good sense, will be fast asleep, for I'm bound to the castle yet to report on this disturbance. I doubt I shall be there over the night. Come and tell me how all this went wrong, for they tell me it began down at the jetty, where you were.'

Cadfael went with him willingly. They sat together in

48

the anteroom of the gatehouse, and the porter, used to such nocturnal activities when the deputy sheriff of the shire was lodged within, brought them wine, made tolerant enquiry of progress, and left them to their colloquy.

'How many have you taken up?' asked Cadfael, when he had given an account of what had happened by the river.

'Seventeen. And it should have been eighteen,' owned Hugh grimly, 'if I had not hauled Bellecote's boy Edwy aside without witnesses, put the fear of God into him, and sent him home with a flea in his ear. Not sixteen yet! But sharp enough to know very well what he was about, the imp! I should not have done it.'

'His father was one of yesterday's delegates,' said Cadfael, 'and he's a loyal child, as well as a bold one. I'm glad you let him away home. And young Corviser?'

'No, we've not laid hand on him, though a dozen witnesses say he was the ringleader, and captained the whole enterprise. But he has to go home some time, and he'll not get in at the gate a free man. Not a hope of it!'

'He came lecturing like a doctor,' said Cadfael seriously, 'and never a threatening move. It was when he was struck down that the wild lads took the bit between their teeth and laid about them. I saw it! The man who struck him lashed out in alarm, I grant you, but without cause.'

'I take your word for that, and I'll stand by it. But he led the attack, and he'll end with the rest, as he should, seeing he loosed this on us all. They'll be bailed by their fathers, the lot of them,' said Hugh wearily, and passed long fingers over tired eyelids. 'Do I seem to you, Cadfael, to be turning horribly into a crown official? That I should not like!'

'No,' said Cadfael judicially, 'you're not too far gone. Still a glint in the eye and a quirk in the mind. You'll do

yet!'

'Gracious in you! And you say this Bristol merchant struck the silly wretch down without provocation?'

'He imagined provocation. The boy laid a detaining hand on his arm from behind, meaning no ill, but the man took fright. He had a staff in his hand, he turned on him and hit out. Felled him like an ox! I doubt if he had the strength to knock the trestle from under a stall, after that. For all I know, he may be fallen out of his senses, somewhere, unless his friends have kept their hands on him.'

Hugh looked at him across the trestle on which their own elbows were spread, and smiled. 'If ever I want for an advocate, I'll come running to you. Well, I do know the lad, he has a well-hung tongue, and lets it wag far too freely, and he has a hot temper and a warm heart, and lets the pair of them run away with his own sense – if you claim he has any!'

The lay porter put his bald brown crown and round red face into the room. 'My lord, there's a lady here at the gate has a trouble on her mind, and asks a word. One Mistress Emma Vernold, niece to the merchant Thomas of Bristol. Will you have her come in?'

They looked at each other across the board with raised brows and startled eyes. 'The same man?' said Beringer, marvelling.

'The same man, surely! And the same girl! But the uproar was all over. What can she be wanting here at this hour, and what's her uncle about, letting her venture loose into the night?'

'We'd best be finding out,' said Hugh, resigned. 'Let the lady come in, if I'm the man she wants.'

'She asked first for a guest here, Ivo Corbière, but I know he's still out viewing the preparations along the Foregate. And when I mentioned that you were here, she begged a word with you. Glad to find the law here and awake, seemingly.'

'Ask her to step in, then. And Cadfael, stay, if you'll be so good, she's had speech with you already, she may be glad of a known face.'

Emma Vernold came in hurriedly yet hesitantly, unsure of herself in this unfamiliar place, and made a hasty reverence. 'My lord, I pray your pardon for troubling you so late ...' She saw Brother Cadfael, and half-smiled, relieved but distracted. 'I am Emma Vernold, I came with my uncle, Thomas of Bristol, we have our own living-space on his barge by the bridge. And this is my uncle's man Gregory.' It was the youngest of the three who attended her, a gawky, lean but powerful fellow of about twenty.

Beringar took her by the hand and put her into a seat by the table. 'I'm here to serve you, as best I can. What's your trouble?'

'Sir, my uncle went to see to the stocking of his booth at the horse-fair, it was not long after the good brother here left us. You'll have heard all that happened, below there? My uncle went to join his other two men, who were busy there before him, and left only Gregory with me. But that's nearly two hours ago, and he has not come back.'

'He will have brought a great deal of merchandise with him,' suggested Hugh reasonably. 'It takes time to arrange things to the best vantage, and I imagine your uncle will have things done well.'

'Oh, yes, indeed he will. But it isn't just that he is so long. The two men with him were his journeyman, Roger Dod, and the porter Warin, and Warin sleeps in the booth to mind the goods. Roger came back to the barge an hour ago, and was surprised not to find my uncle back, for he said he left the booth well before him. We thought perhaps he had met some acquaintance on the way, and stopped to exchange the news with him, so we waited some while, but still he did not come. And now I have been back to the booth with

51

Gregory, to see if by some chance he had turned back there for something, something forgotten, perhaps. But he has not, and Warin says, as Roger does, that my uncle left first, intending to come straight home to me, it being so late. He never liked – he does not like,' she amended, paling, 'for me to be alone with the men, without his company.' Her eyes were steady and clear, but her lip quivered, and there was the faint suggestion of disquiet even in the unflinching firmness of her regard.

She knows she is fair, Cadfael thought, and she's right to take account of it. It may even be that one of them – Roger Dod, the most privileged of the three, perhaps? – has a fancy for her, and she knows that, too, and has no fancy for him, and whether justly or not, is uneasy about being close to him without her guardian by.

'And you are sure he has not made his way home by some other way,' asked Hugh, 'while you've been seeking him at his booth?'

'We went back. Roger waited there, for that very case, but no, he has not come. I asked those still working in the Foregate if they had seen such a man, but I could get no news. And then I thought that perhaps –' She turned in appeal to Cadfael. 'The young gentleman who was so kind, this evening – he is staying here in the guest-hall, so he told us. I wondered if perhaps my uncle had met him again on his way home, and lingered … And he, at least, knows his looks, and could tell me if he has seen him. But he is not yet back, they tell me.'

'He left the jetty earlier than your uncle, then?' asked Cadfael. The young man had looked very well settled to spend a pleasant hour or two in the lady's company, but perhaps her formidable uncle had ways of conveying, even to lords of respectable honours, that his niece was to be approached only when he was

52

present to watch over her.

Emma flushed, but without averting her eyes; eyes which were seen to be thoughtful, resolute and intelligent, for all her milk-and-roses baby-face. 'Very soon after you, brother. He was at all points correct and kind. I thought to come and ask for him, as someone on whom I could rely.'

'I'll ask the porter to keep a watch for him,' offered Cadfael, 'and have him step in here when he returns. Even the horse-fair should be on its way to bed by now, and he'll be needing his own sleep if he's to hunt the best bargains tomorrow, which is what I take it he's here for. What do you say, Hugh?'

'A good thought,' said Hugh. 'Do it, and we'll make provision to look for Master Thomas, though I trust all's well with him, for all this delay. The eve of a fair,' he said, smiling reassurance at the girl, 'and there are contacts to be made, customers already looking over the ground … A man can forget about his sleep with his mind on business.'

Brother Cadfael heard her sigh: 'Oh, yes!' with genuine hope and gratitude, as he went to bid the porter intercept Ivo Corbière when he came in. His errand could hardly have been better timed, for the man himself appeared in the gateway. The main gate was already closed, only the wicket stood open, and the dip of the gold head stepping through caught the light from the torch overhead, and burned like a minor sun. Bare-headed, with his cotte slung on one shoulder in the warm last night of July, Ivo Corbière strolled towards his bed almost rebelliously, with a reserve of energy still unspent. The snowy linen shirt glowed in the lambent dark with a ghostly whiteness. He was whistling a street tune, more likely Parisian than out of London, by the cadence of it. He had certainly drunk reasonably deep, but not beyond his measure, nor even up to it. He was alert at a word.

53

'What, you, brother? Out of bed before Matins?' Amiable though his soft laughter was, he checked it quickly, sensing something demanding gravity of him. 'You were looking for me? Something worse fell out? Good God, the old man never killed the fool boy, did he?'

'Nothing so dire,' said Cadfael. 'But there's one within here at the gatehouse came looking for you, with a question. You've been about the Foregate and the fairground all this time?'

'The whole round,' said Ivo, his attention sharpening. 'I have a new and draughty manor to furnish in Cheshire. I'm looking for woollens and Flemish tapestries. Why?'

'Have you seen, in your wanderings, Master Thomas of Bristol? At any time since you left his barge earlier this evening?'

'I have not,' said Ivo, wondering, and peered closely in the strange, soft light of midsummer, an hour short of midnight.

'What is this? The man made it clear – he has practice, which is no marvel! – that his girl is to be seen only in his presence and with his sanction, and small blame to him, for she's gold, with or without his gold. I respected him for it, and I left. Why? What follows?'

'Come and see,' said Cadfael simply, and led the way within.

The young man blinked in the sudden light, and opened his eyes wide upon Emma. It was a question which of them showed the more distracted. The girl rose, reaching eager hands and then half-withdrawing them. The man sprang forward solicitously to welcome the clasp.

'Mistress Vernold! At this hour? Should you ...' He had a grasp of the company and the urgency by then. 'What has happened?' he asked, and looked at Beringar.

Briskly, Beringar told him. Cadfael was not greatly surprised to see that Corbière was relieved rather than dismayed. Here was a young, inexperienced girl, growing nervous all too easily when she was left alone an hour or so too long, while no doubt her uncle, very travelled and experienced indeed, and well able to take care of himself, was in no sort of trouble at all, but merely engaged in a little social indulgence with a colleague, or busy assessing the goods and worldly state of some of his rivals.

'Nothing ill will have happened to him,' said Corbière cheerfully, smiling reassurance at Emma, who remained, for all that, grave and anxious of eye. And she was no fool, Cadfael reflected, watching, and knew her uncle better than anyone else here could claim to know him. 'You'll see, he'll come home in his own good time, and be astonished to find you so troubled for him.'

She wanted to believe it, but her eyes said she could not be sure. 'I hoped he might have met you again,' she said, 'or that at least you might have seen him.'

'I wish it were so,' he said. 'It would have been my pleasure to set your mind at rest. But I have not seen him.'

'I think,' said Beringar, 'this lies now with me. I have still half a dozen men here within the walls, we'll make a search for Master Thomas. In the meantime, the hour is late, and you should not be wandering in the night. It will be best if your man here returns to the barge, while you, madam, if you consent, can very well join my wife, here in the guest-hall. Her maid Constance will make room for you, and find you whatever you need over the night.' There was no knowing whether he had noted her uneasiness about returning to the barge, just as acutely as Cadfael had, or was simply placing her in the nearest safe charge, and the best; but she brightened so eagerly, and thanked

him so fervently, that there was no mistaking the relief she felt.

'Come, then,' he said gently, 'I'll see you safely into Constance's care, and then you may leave the searching to us.'

'And I,' said Corbière, shrugging enthusiastically into the sleeves of his cotte, 'will bear a hand with you in the hunt, if you'll have me.'

They combed the whole length of the Foregate, Beringar, with his six men-at-arms, Ivo Corbière, as energetic and wide-awake as at noon, and Brother Cadfael, who had no legitimate reason to go with them at all, beyond the pricking of his thumbs, and the manifest absurdity of going to his bed at such an hour, when he would in any case have to rise again at midnight for Matins. If that was excuse enough for sharing a drink with Beringar, it was excuse enough for taking part in the hunt for Thomas of Bristol. For truly, thought Cadfael, shaking his head over the drastic events of the evening, I shall not be easy until I see that meaty blue-jowled face again, and hear that loud, self-confident voice. Corbière might shrug off the merchant's non-return as a mere trivial departure from custom, such as every man makes now and again, and on any other day Cadfael would have agreed with him; but too much had happened since noon today, too many people had been trapped into outrageous and uncharacteristic actions, too many passions had been let loose, for this to be an ordinary day. It was even possible that someone had stepped so far aside from his usual self as to commit deliberate violence by stealth in the night, to avenge what had been done openly and impulsively in the day. Though God forbid!

They had begun by making certain that there was still no word or sign at the jetty. No, Thomas had

neither appeared nor sent word, and Roger Dod's forays among the other traders along the riverside, as far as he dared go from the property he guarded, had elicited no news of his master.

He was a burly, well-set-up young man of about thirty, this Roger Dod, and very personable, if he had not been so curt and withdrawn in manner. No doubt he was anxious, too. He answered Hugh's questions in the fewest possible words, and gnawed an uncertain lip at hearing that his master's niece was now lodged in the abbey guest-hall. He would have come with them to help in their search, but he was responsible for his master's belongings, and would have to be answerable for their safety when his master returned. He stayed with the barge, and sent the mute and sleepily resentful Gregory to lead them straight to the booth Master Thomas had rented. Beringar's sergeant, with three men, was left behind to work his way gradually along the Foregate after them, questioning every waking stallholder as he went, while the rest followed the porter to the fairground. The great open space was by this time half-asleep, but still winking with occasional torches and braziers, and murmuring with subdued voices. For these three days in the year it was transformed into a tight little town, busy and populous, to vanish again on the fourth day.

Thomas had chosen a large booth almost in the centre of the triangular ground. His goods were neatly stacked within, and his watchman was awake and prowling the ground uneasily, to welcome the arrival of authority with relief. Warin was a leathery, middle-aged man, who had clearly been in his present service many years, and was probably completely trusted within his limits, but had not the ability ever to rise to the position Roger Dod now held.

'No, my lord,' he said anxiously, 'never a word since, and I've been on watch every moment. He set off for

his barge a good quarter of an hour before Roger left. We had everything stowed to his liking, he was well content. And he'd had a fall not so long before – you'd know of that? – and was glad enough, I'd say, to be off home to his bed. For after all, he's none so young, no more than I am, and he carried more weight.'

'And he set off from here, which way?'

'Why, straight to the highroad, close by here. I suppose he'd keep along the Foregate.'

Behind Cadfael's shoulder a familiar voice, rich and full and merrily knowing, said in Welsh: 'Well, well, brother, out so late? And keeping the law company! What would the deputy sheriff of the shire want with Thomas of Bristol's watchman at this hour? Are they on the scent of all Gloucester's familiars, after all? And I claimed commerce was above the anarchy!' Narrowed eyes twinkled at Cadfael in the light of the dispersed torches and the far-distant stars in a perfect midsummer sky. Rhodri ap Huw was chuckling softly and fatly at his own teasing wit and menacing sharpness of apprehension.

'You keep a friendly eye out for your neighbours?' said Cadfael, innocently approving. 'I see you brought off all your own goods without scathe.'

'I have a nose for trouble, and the good sense to step out of its way,' said Rhodri ap Huw smugly. 'What's come to Thomas of Bristol? He was not so quick on the scent, it seems. He could have loosed his mooring and poled out into the river till the flurry was over, and been as safe as in the west country.'

'Did you see him struck down?' asked Cadfael deceitfully; but Rhodri was not to be caught.

'I saw him strike down the other young fool,' he said, and grinned. 'Why, did he come to grief after I left? And which of them is it you're looking for, Thomas or the lad?' And he stared with marked interest to see the sheriff's men probing at the backs of stalls, and under

58

the trestles, and followed inquisitively on their heels as they worked their way back along the highroad. Evidently nothing of moment was to be allowed to happen at this fair without Rhodri ap Huw being present at it, or very quickly and minutely informed of it. And why not make use of his perspicacity?

'Thomas's niece is in a taking because he has not come back to his barge. That might mean anything or nothing, but now it's gone on so long, his men are getting uneasy, too. Did you see him leave his booth?'

'I did. It might be as much as two hours ago. And his journeyman some little while after him. A fair size of a man, to be lost between here and the river. And no word of him anywhere since then?'

'Not that we've found, or likely to find, without questioning every trader and every idler in all this array. And the wiser half of them getting their sleep in ready for the morning.'

They had reached the Foregate and turned towards the town, and still Rhodri strode companionably beside Cadfael, and had taken to peering into the dark spaces between stalls just as the sheriff's men were doing. Lights and braziers were fewer here, and the stalls more modest, and the quiet of the night closed in drowsily. On their left, under the abbey wall, a few compact but secure booths were arrayed. The first of them, though completly closed in and barred for the night, showed through a chink the light of a candle within. Rhodri dug a weighty elbow into Cadfael's ribs.

'Euan of Shotwick! No one is ever going to get at *him* from the rear, he likes a corner backed into two walls if he can get it. Travels alone with a pack-pony, and wears a weapon, and can use it, too. A solitary soul because he trusts nobody. His own porter – luckily his wares weigh light for their value – and his own watchman.'

Ivo Corbière had loitered to go aside between the

stalls, some of which in this stretch were still unoccupied, waiting for the local traders who would come with the dawn. The consequent darkness slowed their search, and the young man, not at all averse to spending the night without sleep, and probably encouraged by the memory of Emma's bright eyes, was tireless and thorough. Even Cadfael and Rhodri ap Huw were some yards ahead of him when they heard him cry after them, high and urgently:

'Good God, what's here? Beringar, come back here!'

The tone was enough to bring them running. Corbière had left the highway, probing between stacked trestles and leaning canvas awnings into darkness, but when they peered close there was lambent light enough from the stars for accustomed eyes to see what he had seen. From beneath a light wooden frame and stretched canvas jutted two booted feet, motionless, toes pointed skywards. For a moment they all stared in silence, dumbstruck, for truth to tell, not one of them had believed that the merchant could have come to any harm, as they all agreed afterwards. Then Beringar took hold of the frame and hoisted it away from the trestles against which it leaned, and dim and large in the darkness they saw a man's long shape, from the knees up rolled in a cloak that hid the face. There was no movement, and no noticeable sound.

The sergeant leaned in with the one torch they had brought with them, and Beringar reached a hand to the folds of the cloak, and began to draw them back from the shrouded head and shoulders. The movement of the cloth released a powerful wave of an odour that made him halt and draw suspicious breath. It also disturbed the body, which emitted an enormous snore, and a further gust of spirituous breath.

'Dead drunk and helpless,' said Beringar, relieved. 'And not, I fancy, the man we're looking for. The state he's in, this fellow must have been here some hours

already, and if he comes round in time to crawl away before dawn it will be a miracle. Let's have a look at him.' He was less gingerly now in dragging the cloak away, but the drunken man let himself be hauled about and dragged forth by the feet with only a few disturbed grunts, and subsided into stertorous sleep again as soon as he was released. The torch shone its yellow, resinous light upon a shock-head of coarse auburn hair, a pair of wide shoulders in a leather jerkin, and a face that might have been sharp, lively and even comely when he was awake and sober, but now looked bloated and idiotic, with open, slobbering mouth and reddened eyes.

Corbière took one close look at him, and let out a gasp and an oath. '*Fowler!* Devil take the sot! Is this how he obeys me? By God, I'll make him sweat for it!' And he filled a fist with the thick brown hair and shook the fellow furiously, but got no more out of him than a louder snort, the partial opening of one glazed eye, and a wordless mumble that subsided again as soon as he was dropped, disgustedly and ungently, back into the turf.

'This drunken rogue is mine … my falconer and archer, Turstan Fowler,' said Ivo bitterly, and kicked the sleeper in the ribs but not savagely. What was the use? The man would not be conscious for hours yet, and what he suffered afterwards would pay him all his dues. 'I've a mind to put him to cool in the river! I never gave him leave to quit the abbey precinct, and by the look of him he's been out and drinking – Good God, the reek of it, what raw spirit can it be? – since ever I turned my back.'

'One thing's certain,' said Hugh, amused, 'he's in no case to walk back to his bed. Since he's yours, what will you have done with him? I would not advise leaving him here. If he has anything of value on him, even his hose, he might be without it by morning. There'll be

scavengers abroad in the dark hours – no fair escapes them.'

Ivo stood back and stared down disgustedly at the oblivious culprit. 'If you'll lend me two of your men, and let us borrow a board here, we'll haul him back and toss him into one of the abbey's punishment cells, to sleep off his swinishness on the stones, and serve him right. If we leave him there unfed all the morrow, it may frighten him into better sense. Next time, I'll have his hide!'

They hoisted the sleeper on to a board, where he sprawled aggravatingly into ease again, and snored his way along the Foregate so blissfully that his bearers were tempted to tip him off at intervals, by way of recompensing themselves for their own labour. Cadfael, Beringar and the remainder of the party were left looking after them somewhat ruefully, their own errand still unfulfilled.

'Well, well!' said Rhodri ap Huw softly into Cadfael's ear, 'Euan of Shotwick is taking a modest interest in the evening's happenings, after all!'

Cadfael turned to look, and in the shuttered booth tucked under the wall a hatch had certainly opened, and against the pale light of a candle a head leaned out in sharp outline, staring towards where they stood. He recognised the high-bridged, haughty nose, the deceptively meagre slant of the lean shoulders, before the hatch was drawn silently to again, and the glover vanished.

They worked their way doggedly, yard by yard, all the way back to the riverside, where Roger Dod was waiting in a fume of anxiety, but they found no trace of Thomas of Bristol.

A late boat coming up the Severn from Buildwas next day, and tying up at the bridge about nine in the

morning, delayed its unloading of a cargo of pottery to ask first that a message be sent to the sheriff, for they had other cargo aboard, taken up out of a cove near Atcham, which would be very much the sheriff's business. Gilbert Prestcote, busy with other matters, sent from the castle his own sergeant, with orders to report first to Hugh Beringar at the abbey.

The particular cargo the potter had to deliver lay rolled in a length of coarse sail-cloth in the bottom of the boat, and oozed water in a dark stain over the boards. The boatman unfolded the covering, and displayed to Beringar's view the body of a heavily-built man of some fifty to fifty-five years, fleshy, with thinning, grizzled hair and bristly, bluish jowls, his pouchy features sagging doughily in death. Master Thomas of Bristol, stripped of his elaborate capuchon, his handsome gown, his rings and his dignity, as naked as the day he was born.

'We saw his whiteness bobbing under the bank,' said the potter, looking down upon his salvaged man, 'and poled in to pick him up, the poor soul. I can show you the place, this side of the shallows and the island at Atcham. We thought best to bring him here, as we would a drowned man. But this one,' he said very soberly, 'did not drown.'

No, Thomas of Bristol had now drowned. That was already evident from the very fact that he had been stripped of everything he had on, and hardly by his own hands or will. But also, even more certainly, from the incredibly narrow wound under his left shoulder-blade, washed white and closed by the river, where a very fine, slender dagger had transfixed him and penetrated to his heart.

The First Day of the Fair

Chapter One

The first day of Saint Peter's Fair was in full swing, and the merry, purposeful hum of voices bargaining, gossiping and crying wares came over the wall into the great court, and in at the gatehouse, like the summer music of a huge hive of bees on a sunny day. The sound pursued Hugh Beringar back to the apartment in the guest-hall, where his wife and Emma Vernold were very pleasurably comparing the virtues of various wools, and the maid Constance, who was an expert spinstress, was fingering the samples critically and giving her advice.

On this domestic scene, which had brought back the fresh colour to Emma's cheeks and the animation to her voice, Hugh's sombre face cast an instant cloud. There was no time for breaking news circuitously, nor did he think that this girl would thank him for going roundabout.

'Mistress Vernold, my news is ill, and I grieve for it. God knows I had not expected this. Your uncle is found. A boat coming up early this morning from Buildwas picked up his body from the river.'

The colour ebbed from her face. She stood with frightened, helpless eyes gazing blindly before her. The prop of her life had suddenly been plucked away, and for a moment it seemed that all balance was lost to her, and she might indeed fall for want of him. But by

the time she had drawn breath deep, and shaped soundlessly: 'Dead!' It was clear that she was firm on her own feet again, and in no danger of falling. Her eyes, once the momentary panic and dizziness passed, looked straight at Hugh and made no appeal.

'Drowned?' she said. 'But he swam well, he was raised by the river. And if he drank at all, it was sparingly. I do not believe he could fall into Severn and drown. Not of himself!' she said, and her large eyes dilated.

'Sit down,' said Hugh gently, 'for we must talk a little, and then I shall leave you with Aline, for of course you must remain here in our care for this while. No, he did not drown. Nor did he come by his death of himself. Master Thomas was stabbed from behind, stripped, and put into the river after death.'

'You mean,' she said, in a voice low and laboured, but quite steady, 'he was waylaid and killed by mere sneak-thieves, for what he had on him? For his rings and his gown and his shoes?'

'It is what leaps to the mind. There are no roads in England now that can be called safe, and no great fair that has not its probable underworld of hangers-on, who will kill for a few pence.'

'My uncle was not a timid man. He has fought off more than one attack in his time, and he never avoided a journey for fear in his life. After all these years,' she said, her voice aching with protest, 'why should he fall victim now to such scum? And yet what else can it be?'

'There are some people recalling,' said Hugh, 'that there was an ugly incident on the jetty last evening, and violence was done to a number of the merchants who were unloading goods and setting up stalls for the fair. It's common knowledge there was bad blood between town and traders, of whom Master Thomas was perhaps the most influential. He was involved bitterly with the young man who led the raid. An attack made

in revenge, by night, perhaps in a drunken rage, might end mortally, whether it was meant or no.'

'Then he would have been left where he lay,' said Emma sharply. 'His attacker would think only of getting clean away unseen. Those angry people were not thieves, only townsmen with a grievance. A grievance might turn them into murderers, but I do not think it would turn them into thieves.'

Hugh was beginning to feel considerable respect for this girl, as Aline, by her detached silence and her attentive face, had already learned to do. 'I won't say but I agree with you there,' he admitted. 'But it might well occur to a young man turned murderer almost by mishap, to dress his crime as the common sneak killing for robbery. It opens so wide a field. Twenty young men bitterly aggrieved and hot against your uncle for his scorn of them could be lost among a thousand unknown, and the most unlikely suspects among them, at that, if this passes as chance murder for gain.'

Even in the bleak newness of her bereavement, this thought troubled her. She bit a hesitant lip. 'You think it may have been one of those young men? Or more of them together? That they burned with their grudge until they followed him in the dark, and took this way?'

'It's being both thought and said,' owned Hugh, 'by many people who witnessed what happened by the river.'

'But the sheriff's men,' she pointed out, frowning, 'surely took up many of those young men long before my uncle went to the fairground. If they were already in prison, they could not have harmed him.'

'True of most of them. But the one who led them was not taken until the small hours of the morning, when he came reeling back to the town gate, where he was awaited. He is in a cell in the castle now, like his fellows, but he was still at liberty long after Master Thomas failed to come back to you, and he is under

strong suspicion of this death. The whole pack of them will come before the sheriff this afternoon. The rest, I fancy, will be let out on their fathers' bail, to answer the charges later. But for Philip Corviser, I greatly doubt it. He will need to have better answers than he was able to give when they took him.'

'This afternoon!' echoed Emma. 'Then I should also attend. I was a witness when this turmoil began. The sheriff should hear my testimony, too, especially if my uncle's death is in question. There were others – Master Corbière, and the brother of the abbey, the one you know well …'

'They will be attending, and others besides. Certainly your witness would be valuable, but to ask it of you at such a time …'

'I would rather!' she said firmly. 'I want my uncle's murderer caught, if indeed he was murdered, but I pray no innocent man may be too hurriedly blamed. I don't know – I would not have thought he looked like a murderer … I should like to tell what I do know, it is my duty.'

Beringar cast a brief glance at his wife for enlightenment, and Aline gave him a smile and the faintest of nods.

'If you are resolved on that,' he said, reassured, 'I will ask Brother Cadfael to escort you. And for the rest, you need have no anxieties about your own situation. It will be necessary for you to stay here until this matter is looked into, but naturally you will remain here in Aline's company, and you shall have every possible help in whatever dispositions you need to make.'

'I should like,' said Emma, 'to take my uncle's body back by the barge to Bristol for burial.' She had not considered, until then, that there would be no protector for her on the boat this time, only Roger Dod, whose mute but watchful and jealous devotion

was more than she could bear, Warin who would take care to notice nothing that might cause him trouble, and poor Gregory, who was strong and able of body but very dull of wit. She drew in breath sharply, and bit an uncertain lip, and the shadow came back to her eyes. 'At least, to send him back … His man of law there will take care of his affairs and mine.'

'I have spoken to the prior. Abbot Radulfus sanctions the use of an abbey chapel, your uncle's body can lie there when he is brought from the castle, and all due preparations will be made for his decent coffining. Ask for anything you want, it shall be at your disposal. I must summon your journeyman to attend at the castle this afternoon, too. How would you wish him to deal, concerning the fair? I will give him whatever instructions you care to send.'

She nodded understanding, visibly bracing herself again towards a world of shrewd daily business which had not ceased with the ending of a life. 'Be so kind as to tell him,' she said, 'to continue trading for the three days of the fair, as though his master still presided. My uncle would scorn to go aside from his regular ways for any danger or loss, and so will I in his name.' And suddenly, as freely and as simply as a small child, she burst into tears at last.

When Hugh was gone about his business, and Constance had withdrawn at Aline's nod, the two women sat quietly until Emma had ceased to weep, which she did as suddenly as she had begun. She wept, as some women have the gift of doing, without in the least defacing her own prettiness and without caring whether she did or no. Most lose the faculty, after the end of childhood. She dried her eyes, and looked up straightly at Aline, who was looking back at her just as steadily, with a serenity which offered comfort without pressing it.

'You must think,' said Emma, 'that I had no deep affection for my uncle. And indeed I don't know myself that you would be wrong. And yet I did love him, it has not been only loyalty and gratitude, though those came easier. He was a hard man, people said, hard to satisfy, and hard in his business dealings. But he was not hard to me. Only hard to come near. It was not his fault, or mine.'

'I think,' said Aline mildly, since she was being invited closer, 'you loved him as much as he would let you. As he *could* let you. Some men have not the gift.'

'Yes. But I would have liked to love him more. I would have done anything to please him. Even now I want to do everything as he would have wished. We shall keep the booth open as long as the fair lasts, and try to do it as well as he would have done. All that he had in hand, I want to see done thoroughly.' Her voice was resolute, almost eager. Master Thomas would certainly have approved the set of her chin and the spark in her eye. 'Aline, shall I not be a trouble to you by staying here? I – my uncle's men – there's one who likes me too well …

'So I had thought,' said Aline. 'You're most welcome here, and we'll not part with you until you can be sent back safely to Bristol, and your home. Not that I can find it altogether blameworthy in the young man to like you, for that matter,' she added, smiling.

'No, but I cannot like *him* well enough. Besides, my uncle would never have allowed me to be there on the barge without him. And now I have duties,' said Emma, rearing her head determinedly and staring the uncertain future defiantly in the face. 'I must see to the ordering of a fine coffin for him, for the journey home. There will be a master-carpenter, somewhere in the town?'

'There is. To the right, halfway up the Wyle, Master Martin Bellecote. A good man, and a good craftsman.

72

His lad was among these terrible rioters, as I hear,' said Aline, and dimpled indulgently at the thought, 'but so were half the promising youth of the town. I'll come in with you to Martin's shop.'

'No,' said Emma firmly. 'It will all be tedious and long at the sheriff's court, and you should not tire yourself. And besides, you have to buy your fine wools, before the best are taken. And Brother Cadfael – was that the name? – will show me where to find the shop. He will surely know.'

'There's very little to be known about this precinct and the town of Shrewsbury,' agreed Aline with conviction, 'that Brother Cadfael does not know.'

Cadfael received the abbot's dispensation to attend the hearing at the castle, and to escort the abbey's bereaved guest, without question. A civic duty could not be evaded, whether by secular or monastic. Radulfus had already shown himself both an austere but just disciplinarian and a shrewd and strong-minded business man. He owed his preferment to the abbacy as much to the king as to the papal legate, and valued and feared for the order of the realm at least as keenly as for the state of his own cure. Consequently, he had a use for those few among the brothers who shared his wide experience of matters outside the cloister.

'This death,' he said, closeted with Cadfael alone after Beringar's departure, 'casts a shadow upon our house and our fair. Such a burden cannot be shifted to other shoulders. I require of you a full account of what passes at this hearing. It was of me that the elders of the town asked a relief I could not grant. On me rests the load of resentment that drove those younger men to foolish measures. They lacked patience and thought, and they were to blame, but that does not absolve me. If the man's death has arisen out of my act, even though I could not act otherwise, I must know it,

for I have to answer for it, as surely as the man who struck him down.'

'I shall bring you all that I myself see and hear, Father Abbot,' said Cadfael.

'I require also all that you think, brother. You saw part of what happened yesterday between the dead man and the living youth. Is it possible that it could have brought about such a death as this? Stabbed in the back? It is not commonly the method of anger.'

'Not commonly.' Cadfael had seen many deaths in the open anger of battle, but he knew also of rages that had bred and festered into killings by stealth, with the anger as hot as ever, but turned sour by brooding. 'Yet it is possible. But there are other possibilities. It may indeed be what it first seems, a mere crude slaughter for the clothes on the body and the rings on the fingers, opportune plunder in the night, when no one chanced to be by. Such things happen, where men are gathered together and there is money changing hands.'

'It is true,' said Radulfus, coldly and sadly. 'The ancient evil is always with us.'

'Also, the man is of great importance in his trade and his region, and he may have enemies. Hate, envy, rivalry, are as powerful motives even as gain. And at a great fair such as ours, enemies may be brought together, far from the towns where their quarrels are known, and their acts might be guessed at too accurately. Murder is easier and more tempting, away from home.'

'Again, true,' said the abbot. 'Is there more?'

'There is. There is the matter of the girl, niece and heiress to the dead man. She is of great beauty,' said Cadfael plainly, asserting his right to recognise and celebrate even the beauty of women, though their enjoyment he had now voluntarily forsworn, 'and there are three men in her uncle's service, shut on

74

board a river barge with her. Only one of them old enough, it may be, to value his peace more. One, I think, God's simpleton, but not therefore blind, or delivered from the flesh. And one whole, able, every way a man, and enslaved to her. And this one it was who followed his master from the booth on the fairground, some say a quarter of an hour after him, some say a little more. God forbid I should therefore point a finger at an honest man. But we speak of possibilities. And will speak of them no more until, or unless, they become more than possibilities.'

'That is my mind, also,' said Abbot Radulfus, stirring and almost smiling. He looked at Cadfael steadily and long. 'Go and bear witness, brother, as you are charged, and bring me word again. In your report I shall set my trust.'

Emma had on, perforce, the same gown and bliaut she had worn the evening before, the gown dark blue like her eyes, but the tunic embroidered in many colours upon bleached linen. The only concession she could make to mourning was to bind up her great wealth of hair, and cover it from sight within a borrowed wimple. Nevertheless, she made a noble mourning figure. In the severe white frame her rounded, youthful face gained in concentrated force and meaning what it lost in pure grace. She had a look of single-minded gravity, like a lance in rest. Brother Cadfael could not yet see clearly where the lance was aimed.

When she caught sight of him approaching, she looked at him with pleased recognition, as the man behind the lance might have looked round at the fixed, partisan faces of his friends before the bout, but never shifted the focus of her soul's intent, which reached out where he could not follow.

'Brother Cadfael – have I your name right? It's

Welsh, is it not? You were kind, yesterday. Lady Beringar says you will show me where to find the master-carpenter. I have to order my uncle's coffin, to take him back to Bristol.' She was quite composed, yet still as simple and direct as a child. 'Have we time, before we must go to the castle?'

'It's on the way,' said Cadfael comfortably. 'You need only tell Martin Bellecote, whatever you ask of him he'll see done properly.'

'Everyone is being very kind,' she said punctiliously, like a well brought-up little girl giving due thanks. 'Where is my uncle's body now? I should care for it myself, it is my duty.'

'That you cannot yet,' said Cadfael. 'The sheriff has him at the castle, he must needs see the body for himself, and have the physician also view it. You need be put to no distress on that account, the abbot has given orders. Your uncle will be brought with all reverence to lie in the church here, and the brothers will make him decent for burial. I think he might well wish, could he tell you so now, that you should leave all to us. His care for you would reach so far, and your obedience could not well deny him.'

Cadfael had seen the dead man, and felt strongly that she should not have the same experience. Nor was it for her sake entirely that he willed so. The man she had respected and admired in his monumental dignity, living, had the right to be preserved for her no less decorously in death.

He had found the one argument that could deflect her absolute determination to take charge of all, and escape nothing. She thought about it seriously as they passed out at the gatehouse side by side, and he knew by her face the moment when she accepted it.

'But he did believe that I ought to take my full part, even in his business. He wished me to travel with him, and learn the trade as he knew it. This is the third such

76

journey I have made with him.' That reminded her that it must also be the last. 'At least,' she said hesitantly, 'I may give money to have Masses said for him, here where he died? He was a very devout man, I think he would like that.'

Well, her reserves of money might now be far longer than her reserves of peace of mind were likely to be; she could afford to buy herself a little consolation, and prayers are never wasted.

'That you may surely do.'

'He died unshriven,' she said, with sudden angry grief against the murderer who had deprived him of confession and absolution.

'Through no fault of his own. So do many. So have saints, martyred without warning. God knows the record without needing word or gesture. It's for the soul facing death that the want of shriving is pain. The soul gone beyond knows that pain for needless vanity. Penitence is in the heart, not in the words spoken.'

They were out on the highroad then, turning left towards the reflected sparkle that was the river between its green, lush banks, and the stone bridge over it, that led through the drawbridge turret to the town gate. Emma had raised her head, and was looking at Brother Cadfael along her shoulder, with faint colour tinting her creamy cheeks, and a sparkle like a shimmer of light from the river in her eyes. He had not seen her smile until this moment, and even now it was a very wan smile, but none the less beautiful.

'He was a good man, you know, Brother Cadfael,' she said earnestly. 'He was not easy upon fools, or bad workmen, or people who cheated, but he was a good man. Good to me! And he kept his bargains, and he was loyal to his lord ...' She had taken fire, for all the softness of her voice and the simplicity of her plea for him; it was almost as though she had been about to say 'loyal to his lord to the death!' She had that high,

heroic look about her, to be taken very seriously, even on that child's face.

'All which,' said Cadfael cheerfully, 'God knows, and needs not to be told. And never forget you've a life to live, and he'd want you to do him justice by doing yourself justice.'

'Oh, yes!' said Emma, glowing, and for the first time laid her hand confidingly on his sleeve. 'That's what I want! That's what I have most in mind!'

Chapter Two

At Martin Bellecote's shop, off the curve of the rising street called the Wyle, which led to the centre of the town, she knew exactly what she wanted for her dead, and ordered it clearly; more, she knew how to value a matching clarity and forth-rightness in the master-carpenter, and yet had time to be pleasantly distracted by the invasion of his younger children, who liked the look of her and came boldly to chatter and stare. As for the delinquent Edwy, sent home overnight after his tongue-lashing from Hugh Beringar, the youngster worked demurely with a plane in a corner of the shop, and was not too subdued to cast inquisitive glances of bright hazel eyes at the lady, and one impudent wink at Brother Cadfael when Emma was not noticing.

On the way through the town, up the steep street to the High Cross, and down the gentler slope beyond to the ramp which led up to the castle gateway, she fell into a thoughtful silence, putting in order her recollections. The shadow of the gate falling upon her serious face and cutting off the sunlight caused her eyes to dilate in awe; but the casual traffic of the watch here was no longer reminiscent of siege and battle, but easy and brisk, and the townspeople went in and out freely with their requests and complaints. The sheriff was a strong-minded, taciturn, able knight past fifty, and old in experience of both war and office, and while

he could be heavy-handed in crushing disorder, he was trusted to be fair in day to day matters. If he had not given the goodmen of the town much help in making good the dilapidations due to the siege, neither had he permitted them to be misused or heavily taxed to restore the damage to the castle. In the great court one tower was still caged in timber scaffolding, one wall shored up with wooden buttresses. Emma gazed, great-eyed.

There were others going the same way with them, anxious fathers here to bail their sons, two of the abbey stewards who had been assaulted in the affray, witnesses from the bridge and the jetty, all being ushered through to the inner ward, and a chill, stony hall hung with smoky tapestries. Cadfael found Emma a seat on a bench against the wall, where she sat looking about her with anxious eyes but lively interest.

'Look, there's Master Corbière!'

He was just entering the hall, and for the moment had no attention to spare for anyone but the hunched figure that slouched before him; blear-eyed but in his full wits today, going softly in awe of his irate lord, Turstan Fowler made his powerful form as small and unobtrusive as possible, and mustered patience until the storm should blow over. And what had he to do here, Cadfael wondered. He had not been on the jetty, and by the state in which he had been found near midnight, his memories of yesterday should in any case be vague indeed. Yet he must have something to say to the purpose, or Corbière would not have brought him here. By his mood last night, he had meant to leave him locked up all day, to teach him better sense.

'Is this the sheriff?' whispered Emma.

Gilbert Prestcote had entered, with a couple of lawmen at his elbows to advise him on the legalities. This was no trial but it rested with him whether the rioters would go home on their own and their sires'

bond to appear at the assize, or be held in prison in the meantime. The sheriff was a tall, spare man, erect and vigorous, with a short black beard trimmed to a point, and a sharp and daunting eye. He took his seat without ceremony, and a sergeant handed him the list of names of those in custody. He raised his eyebrows ominously at the number of them.

'All these were taken in riot?' He spread the roll on his table and frowned down at it. 'Very well! There is also the graver matter of the death of Master Thomas of Bristol. At what hour was the last word we have of Master Thomas alive and well?'

'According to his journeyman and his watchman, he left his booth on the horse-fair, intending to return to his barge, more than an hour past the Compline bell. That is the last word we have. His man Roger Dod is here to testify that the hour was rather more than a quarter past nine of the evening and the watchman bears that out.'

'Late enough,' said the sheriff, pondering. 'The fighting was over by then, and Foregate and fairground quiet. Hugh, prick me off here all those who were then already in custody. Whatever their guilt for damages to goods and gear, they cannot have had any hand in this murder.'

Hugh leaned to his shoulder, and ran a rapid hand down the roster. 'It was a sharp encounter, but short. We had it in hand very quickly, they never reached the end of the Foregate. This man was picked up last, it might be as late as ten, but in an ale-house and very drunk, and the ale-wife vouches for his having been there above an hour. A respectable witness, she was glad to get rid of him. But he's clear of the killing. This one crept back to the bridge a little later, and owned to having been one among the rabble, but we let him home, for he's very lame, and there are witnesses to all his moves since before nine. He's here to answer for his

part in the muster, as he promised. I think you may safely write him clear of any other blame.'

'It leaves but one,' said Prestcote, and looked up sharply into Beringar's face.

'It does,' said Hugh, and committed himself to nothing further.

'Very well! Have in all the rest, but keep him aside. Let us hold these two matters apart, and deal with the lesser first.'

Into the space roped off along one side the hall, the sheriff's officers herded their prisoners, a long file of sullenly sheepish young men, bruised, dishevelled and sorry for themselves now, but still nursing the embers of a genuine resentment. There were some torn coats among them, and a purple eye or two, and the lingering signs of bloody noses and battered crowns, and a night on the stones of indifferently swept cells had done their best clothes, donned for dignified battle as knights case themselves in ceremonial armour, no good at all. There would be indignant mothers scolding bitterly as they scrubbed and mended, or here and there a young wife doing the nagging on behalf of all women. The offenders stood in line doggedly, set their jaws, and braced themselves to endure whatever might follow.

Prestcote was thorough. Plainly he was preoccupied with the more serious evil, and little disposed to fulminate overmuch about this civic discord, which in the end had done comparatively little harm. So though he called every culprit separately, and had him answer for his own part in the affray, he got through them rapidly and reasonably. Most of them freely owned that they had taken part, maintained that the intention had been entirely lawful and peaceable, and the disintegration later had been unintentional and none of their making. Several bore witness that they had been with Philip Corviser on the jetty, and told how he

82

had been assaulted, thus letting loose the riot that followed. Only one here and there sought to prove that he had never so much as overset one trestle under a stall, nor even been on the abbey side of Severn that evening. And those few were already committed deep on the evidence of law-abiding citizens.

Agitated fathers, vengeful rather than doting, came forward to claim each dejected hero, pledged attendance at the assize, and offered surety for the pledge. The lame lad was lectured perfunctorily, and dismissed without penalty. Two who had been particularly voluble in asserting that they were elsewhere at the time, and unjustly accused, were returned to their prison for a day or two, to reconsider the nature of truth.

'Very well!' said Prestcote, dusting his hands irritably. 'Clear the hall, but for those who have evidence to give concerning Master Thomas of Bristol. And bring in Philip Corviser.'

The line of young men had vanished, hustled out and shepherded away by loyal but exasperated families. At home they would have to sit and nurse sore heads and sore hearts while fathers hectored and dames wept, pouring out on them all the fear and worry they had suffered on their behalf. Emma looked after the last of them with round, sympathetic eyes, as he was haled away by the ear by a diminutive mother half his size, and shrill as a jay. Poor lad, he needed no other punishment, he was drowning in mortification already.

She turned about, and there where his fellows had been, but monstrously alone in the middle of that stony wall, was Philip Corviser.

He gripped the rope with both hands, and stood rigidly erect, neck as stiff as a lance, though for the rest he looked as if his flesh might melt and droop off the bone, he was so haggard. His extreme pallor, which

Cadfael knew for what raw wine can do to the beginner, the day after his indulgence, Emma almost certainly took for the fruit of dire injury and great anguish of mind. She paled in reflection, staring piteously, though he was nothing to her, except that she had seen him struck down, and been afraid he might not rise again.

For all his efforts, he was a sorry figure. His best cotte was torn and soiled, and worse, speckled with drops of blood under his left ear, and vomit about the skirts. He mustered his gangling limbs gallantly but somewhat uncertainly, and his harmless, sunburned face, unshaven now and ashen under its tan, blushed to an unbecoming and unexpected purple when he caught sight of his father, waiting with laboured patience among the onlookers. He did not look that way again, but kept his bruised brown eyes fixed upon the sheriff.

He answered to his name in a voice too loud, from nervous defiance, and agreed to the time and place of his arrest. Yes, he had been very drunk, and hazy about his movements, and even about the circumstances of his arrest, but yes, he would try to answer truthfully to what was charged against him.

There were several witnesses to testify that Philip had been the originator and leader of the whole enterprise which had ended so ignominiously. He had been in the forefront when the angry young men crossed the bridge, he had given the signal that sent some of the party ahead along the Foregate, while he led a handful down to the riverside, and entered into loud argument with the merchants unloading goods there. Thus far all accounts tallied, but from then on they varied widely. Some had the youths beginning at once to toss merchandise into the river, and were certain that Philip had been in the thick of the battle. One or two of the aggrieved merchants alleged with

righteous indignation that he had assaulted Master Thomas, and so began the whole turmoil. Since they would all have their say, Hugh Beringar had held back his preferred witnesses until last.

'My lord, as to the scene by the river, we have here the niece of Master Thomas, and two men who intervened, and afterwards helped to rescue much of what had been cast into the river: Ivo Corbière of Stanton Cobbold, and Brother Cadfael of the abbey, who was assisting a Welsh-speaking trader. There were no others so close to the affair. Will you hear Mistress Vernold?'

Philip had not realised until that moment that she was present. The mention of her caused him to look round wildly, and the sight of her stepping shyly forward to stand before the sheriff's table brought out a deep and painful blush, that welled out of the young man's torn collar and mounted in a great wave to his red-brown hair. He averted his eyes from her, wishing, thought Cadfael, for the floor to open and swallow him up. It would not have mattered so much looking a piteous object to others, but before her he was furious and ashamed. Not even the thought of his father's mortification could have sunk his spirits so low. Emma, after one rapid glance, sympathetic enough, had also turned her eyes away. She looked only at the sheriff, who returned her straight gaze with concern and compunction.

'Was it needful to put Mistress Vernold to this distress, at such a time? Madam, you could well have been spared an appearance here, the lord Corbière and the good brother would have been witness enough.'

'I wished to come,' said Emma, her voice small but steady. 'Indeed I was not pressed, it was my own decision.'

'Very well, if that is your wish. You have heard these

85

varying versions of what happened. There seems little dispute until these disturbers of the peace came down to the jetty. Let me hear from you what followed.'

'It is true that young man was the leader. I think he addressed himself to my uncle because he seemed the most important merchant then present, but he spoke high to be heard by all the rest. I cannot say that he uttered any threats, he only stated that the town had a grievance, and the abbey was not paying enough for the privilege of the fair, and asked that we, who come to do business here, should acknowledge the rights of the town, and pay a tithe of our rents and tolls to the town instead of all to the abbey. Naturally my uncle would not listen, but stood firm on the letter of the charter, and ordered the young men out of his way. And when he – the prisoner here – would still be arguing, my uncle turned his back and shrugged him off. Then the young man laid a hand on his arm, wanting to detain him still, and my uncle, who had his staff in his hand, turned and struck out at him. Thinking, I suppose, that he intended him offence or injury.'

'And did he not?' The sheriff's voice indicated mild surprise.

She cast one brief glance at the prisoner, and one in quest of reassurance at Brother Cadfael, and thought for a moment. 'No, I think not. He was beginning to be angry, but he had not said any ill word, or made any threatening movement. And my uncle, of course in alarm, hit hard. It felled him, and he lay in a daze.' This time she did turn and look earnestly at Philip, and found him staring at her wide-eyed. 'You see he is marked. His left temple.' Dried blood had matted the thick brown hair.

'And did he then attempt retaliation?' asked Prestcote.

'How could he?' she said simply. 'He was more than

half stunned, he could not rise without help. And then all the others began to fight, and to throw things into the river. And Brother Cadfael came and helped him to his feet and delivered him to his friends, and they took him away. I am sure he could not have walked unaided. I think he did not know what he was doing, or how he came to such a state.'

'Not then, perhaps,' said Prescote reasonably. 'But later in the evening, somewhat recovered, and as he has himself admitted, very drunk, he may well have brooded on a revenge.'

'I can say nothing as to that. My uncle would have struck him again, and might have done him desperate hurt if I had not stopped him. That is not his nature,' she said firmly, 'it was most unlike him, but he was in a rage, and confused. Brother Cadfael will confirm what I say.'

'At all points,' said Brother Cadfael. 'It is a perfectly balanced and just account.'

'My lord Corbière?'

'I have nothing to add,' said Ivo, 'to what Mistress Vernold has so admirably told you. I saw the prisoner helped away by his fellows, and what became of him after that I have no knowledge. But here is a man of mine, Turstan Fowler, who says he did see him later in the evening, drinking in an ale-house at the corner of the horse-fair. I must say,' added Ivo with resigned disgust, 'that his own recollection of the night's events ought to be as hazy as the prisoner's, for we took him up dead drunk past eleven, and by the look of him he had been in the same state some time then. I had him put into a cell in the abbey overnight. But he claims his head is clear now, and he knows what he saw and heard. I thought it best he should speak here for himself.'

The archer edged forward sullenly, peering up under thick frowning brows, as though his head still

rang.

'Well, what is it you claim to know, fellow?' asked Prestcote, eyeing him narrowly.

'My lord, I had no call to be out of the precinct at all, last night, my lord Corbière had given me orders to stay within. But I knew he would spend the evening looking the ground over, so I ventured. I got my skinful at Wat's tavern, by the north corner of the horse-fair. And this fellow was there, drinking fit to beat me, and I'm an old toper, and can carry it most times. The place was full, there must be others can tell you the same. He was nursing his sore head, and breathing fire against the man that gave it him. He swore he'd be up with him before the night was out. And that's all the meat of it, my lord.'

'At what hour was this?' asked Prestcote.

'Well, my lord, I was still firm on my feet then, and clear in my mind, and that I certainly was not later in the evening. It must have been somewhere halfway between eight and nine. I should have borne my drink well enough if I had not gone from ale to wine, and then to a fierce spirit, and that last was what laid me low, or I'd have been back within the wall before my lord came home, and escaped a night on the stones.'

'It was well earned,' said Prestcote dryly. 'So you took yourself off to sleep off your load – when?'

'Why, about nine, I suppose, my lord, and was fathoms deep soon after. Troth, I can't recall where, though I remember the inn. They can tell you where I was found who found me.'

At this point it dawned abruptly upon Brother Cadfael that by pure chance this whole interrogation, since Philip had been brought in, had been conducted without once mentioning the fact that Master Thomas at this moment lay dead in the castle chapel. Certainly the sheriff had addressed Emma in tones of sympathy and consideration appropriate to her newly-orphaned

state, and her uncle's absence might in itself be suggestive, though in view of the importance of his business at the fair, and the fact that Emma had once, at least, referred to him in the present tense, a person completely ignorant of his death would hardly have drawn any conclusion from these hints, unless he had all his wits about him. And Philip had been all night in a prison cell, and haled out only to face this hearing, and moreover, was still sick and dulled with his drinking, his broken head and his sore heart, and in no case to pick up every inference of what he heard. No one had deliberately laid a trap for him, but for all that, the trap was there, and it might be illuminating to spring it.

'So these threats you heard against Master Thomas,' said Prestcote, 'can have been uttered only within an hour, probably less, of the time when the merchant left his booth to return alone to his barge. The last report we have of him.'

That was drawing nearer to the spring, but not near enough. Philip's face was still drawn, resigned and bewildered, as though they had been talking Welsh over his head. Brother Cadfael struck the prop clean away; it was high time.

'The last report we have of him *alive*,' he said clearly.

The word might have been a knife going in, the slender kind that is hardly felt for a moment, and then hales after it the pain and the injury. Philip's head came up with a jerk, his mouth fell open, his bruised eyes rounded in horrified comprehension.

'But it must be remembered,' continued Cadfael quickly, 'that we do not know the hour at which he died. A body taken from the water may have entered it at any time during the night, after *all* the prisoners were in hold, and all honest men in bed.'

It was done. He had hoped it would settle the issue of guilt and innocence, at least to his satisfaction, but

now he still could not be quite sure the boy had not known the truth already. How if he had only held his peace and listened to the ambiguous voices, and been in doubt whether Master Thomas's corpse had yet been found? On the face of it, if he had had any hand in that death, he was a better player than any of the travelling entertainers who would be plying their trade among the crowds this evening. His pallor, from underdone dough, had frozen into marble, he tried to speak and swallowed half-formed words, he drew huge breaths into him, and straightened his back, and turned great, shocked eyes upon the sheriff. On the face of it – but every face can dissemble if the need is great enough.

'My lord,' pleaded Philip urgently, when he had his voice again, 'is this truth? Master Thomas of Bristol is dead?'

'Known or unknown to you,' said Prestcote dryly, '– and I hazard no judgment – it is truth. The merchant is dead. Our main purpose here now is to examine how he died.'

'Taken from the water, the monk said. Did he drown?'

'That, if you know, you may tell us.'

Abruptly the prisoner turned his back upon the sheriff, took another deep breath into him, and looked directly at Emma, and from then on barely took his eyes from her, even when Prestcote addressed him. The only judgment he cared about was hers.

'Lady, I swear to you I never did your uncle harm, never saw him again after they hauled me away from the jetty. What befell him I do not know, and God knows I'm sorry for your loss. I would not for the world have touched him, even if we had met and quarrelled afresh, knowing he was your kinsman.'

'Yet you were heard threatening harm to him,' said the sheriff.

'It may be so. I cannot drink, I was a fool ever to try that cure. I recall nothing of what I said, I make no doubt it was folly, and unworthy. I was sore and bitter. What I set out to do was honest enough, and yet it fell apart. All went to waste. But if I talked violence, I did none. I never saw the man again. When I turned sick from the wine I left the tavern and went down to the riverside, away from the boats, and lay down there until I made shift to drag myself back to the town. I admit to the trouble that arose out of my acts, and all that has been said against me, all but this. As God sees me, I never did your uncle any injury. Speak, and say you believe me!'

Emma gazed at him with parted lips and dismayed eyes, unable to say yes or no to him. How could she know what was true and what was lies?

'Let her be,' said the sheriff sharply. 'It is with us you have to deal. This matter must be probed deeper than has been possible yet. Nothing is proven, but you stand in very grave suspicion, and it is for me to determine what is to be done with you.'

'My lord,' ventured the provost, who had kept his mouth tightly shut until now, against great temptation, 'I am prepared to stand surety for my son to whatever price you may set, and I guarantee he shall be at your disposal at the assize, and at whatever time between when you may need to question him. My honour has never been in doubt, and my son, whatever else, has been known as a man of his word, and if he gives his bond here he will keep it, even without my enforcement. I beg your lordship will release him home to my bail.'

'On no terms,' said Prestcote decidedly. 'The matter is too grave. He stays under lock and key.'

'My lord, if you so order, under lock and key he shall be, but let it be in my house. His mother –'

'No! Say no more, you must know it is impossible. He

91

stays here in custody.'

'There is nothing against him in the matter of this death,' offered Corbière generously, 'as yet, that is, except my rogue's witness of his threats. And thieves do haunt such gatherings as the great fairs, and if they can cut a man out from his fellows, will kill him for the clothes on his back. And surely the fact that the body was stripped accords better with just such a foul chance crime for gain? Vengeance has nothing to feed on in a bundle of clothing. The act is all.'

'True,' agreed Prestcote. 'But supposing a man had killed in anger, perhaps simply gone too far in an assault meant only to injure, he might be wise enough to strip his victim, to make it appear the work of common robbers, and turn attention away from himself. There is much work to be done yet in this case, but meantime Corviser must remain in hold. I should be failing in my duty if I turned him loose, even to your care, master provost.' And the sheriff ordered, with a motion of his hand: 'Take him away!'

Philip was slow to move, until the butt of a lance prodded him none too gently in the side. Even then he kept his chin on his shoulder for some paces, and his eyes desperately fixed upon Emma's distressed and doubting face. 'I did not touch him,' he said, plucked forcibly away towards the door through which his guards had brought him. 'I pray you, believe me!' Then he was gone, and the hearing was over.

Out in the great court they paused to draw grateful breath, released from the shadowy oppression of the hall. Roger Dod hovered, with hungry eyes upon Emma.

'Mistress, shall I attend you back to the barge? Or will you have me go straight back to the booth? I had Gregory go there to help Warin, while I had to be absent, but trade was brisking up nicely, they'll be hard

pushed by now. If that's what you want? To work the fair as he'd have worked it?'

'That is what I want,' she said firmly. 'To do all as he would have done. You go straight back to the horse-fair, Roger. I shall be staying with Lady Beringar at the abbey for this while, and Brother Cadfael will escort me.'

The journeyman louted, and left them, without a backward glance. But the very rear view of him, sturdy, stiff and aware, brought back to mind the intensity of his dark face and burning, embittered eyes. Emma watched him go, and heaved a helpless sigh.

'I am sure he is a good man, I know he is a good servant, and has stood loyally by my uncle many years. So he would by me, after his fashion. And I do respect him, I must! I think I could like him, if only he would not want me to love him!'

'It's no new problem,' said Cadfael sympathetically. 'The lightning strikes where it will. One flames, and the other remains cold. Distance is the only cure.'

'So I think,' said Emma fervently. 'Brother Cadfael, I must go to the barge, to bring away some more clothes and things I need. Will you go with me?'

He understood at once that this was an opportune time. Both Warin and Gregory were coping with customers at the booth, and Roger was on his way to join them. The barge would be riding innocently beside the jetty, and no man aboard to trouble her peace. Only a monk of the abbey, who did not trouble it at all. 'Whatever you wish,' he said. 'I have leave to assist you in all your needs.'

He had rather expected that Ivo Corbière would come to join her once they were out of the hall, but he did not. It was in Cadfael's mind that she had expected it, too. But perhaps the young man had decided that it was hardly worthwhile making a threesome with the desired lady and a monastic attendant, who clearly had

93

his mandate, and would not consent to be dislodged. Cadfael could sympathise with that view, and admire his discretion and patience. There were two days of the fair left yet, and the great court of the abbey was not so great but guests could meet a dozen times a day. By chance or by rendezvous!

Emma was very silent on the way back through the town. She had nothing to say until they emerged from the shadow of the gate into full sunlight again, above the glittering bow of the river. Then she said suddenly: 'It was good of Ivo to speak so reasonably for the young man.' And on the instant, as Cadfael flashed a glance to glimpse whatever lay behind the words, she flushed almost as deeply as the unlucky lad Philip had blushed on beholding her a witness to his shame.

'It was very sound sense,' said Cadfael, amiably blind. 'Suspicion there may be, but proof there's none, not yet. And you set him a pace in generosity he could not but admire.'

The flush did not deepen, but it was already bright as a rose. On her ivory, silken face, so young and unused, it was touching and becoming.

'Oh, no,' she said, 'I only told simply truth. I could do no other.' Which again was simple truth, for nothing in her life thus far had corrupted her valiant purity. Cadfael had begun to feel a strong fondness for this orphan girl who shouldered her load without timidity or complaint, and still had an open heart for the burdens of others. 'I was sorry for his father,' she said. 'So decent and respected a man, to be denied so. And he spoke of his wife … she will be out of her wits with worry.'

They were over the bridge, they turned down the green path, trodden almost bare at this busy, hot time, that led to the riverside and the long gardens and orchards of the Gaye. Master Thomas's deserted barge nestled into the green bank at the far end of the jetty,

close-moored. One or two porters laboured along the boards with fresh stocks from the boats, shouldered them, and tramped away up the path to replenish busy stalls. The riverside lay sunlit, radiantly green and blue, and almost silent, but for the summer sounds of bees drunkenly busy among the late summer flowers in the grass. Almost deserted, but for a solitary fisherman in a small boat close under the shadow of the bridge; a comfortable, squarely-built fisherman stripped to shirt and hose, and bristling thornily with black curls and black bush of beard. Rhodri ap Huw clearly trusted his servant to deal profitably with his English customers, or else he had already sold out all the stock he had brought with him. He looked somnolent, happy, almost eternal, trailing his bait along the current under the archway, with an occasional flick of a wrist to correct the drift. Though most likely the sharp eyes under the sleepy eyelids were missing nothing that went on about him. He had the gift, it seemed, of being everywhere, but everywhere disinterested and benevolent.

'I will be quick,' said Emma, with a foot on the side of the barge. 'Last night Constance lent me all that I needed, but I must not continue a beggar. Will you step aboard, brother? You are welcome! I'm sorry to be so poor a hostess.' Her lips quivered. He knew the instant when her mind returned to her uncle, lying naked and dead in the castle, a man she had revered and relied on, and perhaps felt to be eternal in his solidity and self-confidence. 'He would have wished me to offer you wine, the wine you refused last night.'

'For want of time only,' said Cadfael placidly, and hopped nimbly over on to the barge's low deck. 'You go get what you need, child, I'll wait for you.'

The space aboard was well organised, the cabin aft rode low, but the full width of the hull, and though Emma had to stoop her neat head to enter, stepping

down to the lower level within, she and her uncle would have had room within for sleeping. Little to spare, yet enough, where no alien or suspect thing might come. But taut, indeed, when she was short of her natural protector, with three other men closely present on deck outside. And one of them deeply, hopelessly, in love. Uncles may not notice such glances as his, where their own underlings are concerned.

She was back, springing suddenly to view in the low doorway. Her eyes had again that look of shock and alarm, but now contained and schooled. Her voice was level and low as she said: 'Someone has been here! Someone strange! Someone has handled everything we left here on board, pawed through my linen and my uncle's, too, turned every board or cover. I do not dream, Brother Cadfael! It is true! Our boat has been ransacked while it was left empty. Come and see!'

It was without guile that he asked her instantly: 'Has anything been taken?'

Still possessed by her discovery, and unguardedly honest, Emma said: 'No!'

Chapter Three

Everything in the boat, and certainly in the small cabin, seemed to Cadfael to be in immaculate order, but he did not therefore doubt her judgment. A girl making her third journey in this fashion, and growing accustomed to making the best use of the cramped space, would know exactly how she had everything folded and stowed, and the mere disturbance of a fold, the crumpling of a corner in the neat low chest under her bench-bed would be enough to alert her, and betray the intervention of another hand. But the very attempt at perfect restoration was surprising. It argued that the interloper had had ample time at his disposal, while all the crew were absent. Yet she had said confidently that nothing had been stolen.

'You are sure? You've had little time to examine everything here. Best look round thoroughly and make sure, before we report this to Hugh Beringar.'

'Must I do that?' she asked, a little startled, even, he thought, a little dismayed. 'If there's no harm? They are burdened enough with other matters.'

'But do you not see, child, that this comes too aptly on the other? Your uncle killed, and now his barge ransacked ...'

'Why, there can surely be no connection,' she said quickly. 'This is the work of some common thief.'

'A common thief who took nothing?' said Cadfael.

'Where there are any number of things worth the taking!'

'Perhaps he was interrupted ...' But her voice wavered into silence, she could not even convince herself.

'Does it look so to you? I think he must have been through all your belongings at leisure, to leave them so neat for you. And removed himself only when he was satisfied.' But of what? That what he wanted was not there?

Emma gnawed a dubious lip, and looked about her thoughtfully. 'Well, if we must report it ... You're right, I spoke too soon, perhaps I should go through everything. No use telling him but half a tale.'

She settled down methodically to take out every item of clothing and equipment from both chests, laying them out on the beds, even unfolding those which showed, to her eyes at least, the most obvious signs of handling, and refolding them to her own satisfaction. At the end of it she sat back on her heels and looked up at Cadfael, thoughtfully frowning.

'Yes, there have been some things taken, but so cunningly. Small things that would never have been missed until we got home. There's a girdle of mine missing, one with a gold clasp. And a silver chain. And a pair of gloves with gold embroidery. If my thumbs had not pricked when I came in here, I should not have missed them, for I shouldn't have wanted to wear any of them. What could I want with gloves in August? I bought them all in Gloucester, on the way up the river.'

'And of your uncle's belongings?'

'I think there is nothing missing. If some moneys were left here, certainly none are here now, but his strong-box is at the booth. He never carried valuables on such journeys as this, except the rings he always wore. I should not have had such rich trifles here

myself, if I had not but newly bought them.'

'So it seems,' said Cadfael, 'whoever took the opportunity of stepping aboard boldly, to see what he could pick up, had the wit to take only trifles he could slip in his sleeve or his pouch. That makes good sense. However, naturally it was done, he'd be likely to cause some curiosity if he stepped ashore with his arms full of your uncle's gowns and shirts.'

'And we must trouble Hugh Beringar and the sheriff over so trivial a loss?' wondered Emma, jutting a doubtful lip. 'It seems a pity, when he has so many graver matters on his mind. And you see this is only an ordinary, vulgar filching, because the boat was left empty a while. Small creatures of prey have an eye to such chances.'

'Yes, we must,' said Cadfael firmly. 'Let the law be the judge whether this has anything to do with your uncle's death or no. That's not for us to say. You find what you need to take with you, and we'll go together and see him, if he's to be found at this hour.'

Emma put together a fresh gown and tunic, stockings and shift and other such mysteries as girls need, with a composure which Cadfael found at once admirable and baffling. The immediate discovery of the invasion of her possessions had startled and disturbed her, but she had come to terms with it very quickly and calmly, and appeared perfectly indifferent to the loss of her finery. He was just considering how odd it was that she should be so anxious to disconnect this incident from her uncle's death, when she herself, in perverse and unthinking innocence, restored the link.

'Well, at any rate,' said Emma, gathering her bundle together neatly in the skirt of the gown, and rising nimbly from her knees, 'no one can dare say that the provost's son was to blame for this. He's safe in a cell in the castle, and the sheriff himself can be his witness this time.'

Hugh Beringar had shrugged off his duties to enjoy at least the evening meal with his wife. Mercifully the first day of the fair had passed so far without further incident, no disorders, no quarrels, no accusations of cheating or overcharging, no throat-cutting or price-cutting, as though the uproar of the previous evening, and its deadly result, had chastened and subdued even the regular offenders. Trade was thriving, rents and tolls bringing in a high revenue for the abbey, and sales seemed set to continue peacefully well into the night.

'And I have bought some spun wool,' said Aline, delighted with her day's shopping, 'and some very fine woollen cloth, so soft – feel it! And Constance chose two beautiful fleeces from Cadfael's Welsh merchant, she wants to card and spin them herself for the baby. And I changed my mind about a cradle, for I saw nothing in the fair to match what Martin Bellecote can do. I shall go to him.'

'The girl is not back yet?' said Hugh, mildly surprised. 'She left the castle well before me.'

'She'll have gone to bring some things from the barge. She had nothing with her last night, you know. And she was going to Bellecote's shop, too, to bespeak the coffin for her uncle.'

'That she'd done on the way,' said Hugh, 'for Martin came to the castle about the business before I left. They'll be bringing the body down to the chapel here before dark.' He added appreciatively: 'A fair-minded lass, our Emma, as well as a stout-hearted one. She would not have that fool boy of Corviser's turned into the attacker, even for her uncle's sake. A straight tale as ever was. He opened civilly, was brusquely received, made the mistake of laying hand on the old man, and was felled like a poled ox.'

'And what does he himself say?' Aline looked up intently from the bolt of soft stuff she was lovingly

stroking.

'That he never laid eyes on Master Thomas again, and knows no more about his death than you or I. But there's that falconer of Corbière's says he was breathing fire and smoke against the old man in Wat's tavern well into the evening. Who knows! The mildest lamb of the flock – but that's not his reputation! – may be driven to clash foreheads when roused, but the knife in the back, somehow – that I doubt. He had no knife on him when he was taken up at the gate. We shall have to ask all his companions if they saw such a thing about him.'

'Here is Emma,' said Aline, looking beyond him to the doorway.

The girl came in briskly with her bundle, Brother Cadfael at her shoulder. 'I'm sorry to have been so long,' said Emma, 'but we had reason. Something untoward has happened – oh, it is not so grave, no great harm, but Brother Cadfael says we must tell you.'

Cadfael forbore from urging, stood back in silence, and let her tell it in her own way, and a very flat way it was, as though she had no great interest in her reported loss. But for all that, she described the bits of finery word for word as she had described them to him, and went into greater detail of their ornaments. 'I did not wish to bother you with such trumpery thefts. How can I care about a lost girdle and gloves, when I have lost so much more? But Brother Cadfael insisted, so I have told you.'

'Brother Cadfael was right,' said Hugh sharply. 'Would it surprise you, child, to know that we have had not one complaint of mispractice or stealing or any evil all this day, touching any other tradesman at the fair? Yet one threat follows another where your uncle's business is concerned. Can that truly be by chance? Is there not someone here who has no interest in any other, but all too much in him?'

'I knew you would think so,' she said, sighing helplessly. 'But it was only by chance that our barge was left quite unmanned all this afternoon, by reason of Roger being needed with the rest of us at the castle. I doubt if there was another boat there unwatched. And common thieves have a sharp eye out for such details. They take what they can get.'

It was a shrewd point, and clearly she was not the girl to lose sight of any argument that could serve her turn. Cadfael held his peace. There would be a time to discuss the matter with Hugh Beringar, but it was not now. The questions that needed answers would not be asked of Emma; where would be the use? She had been born with all her wits about her, and through force of circumstances she was learning with every moment. But why was she so anxious to have this search of her possessions shrugged aside as trivial, and having no bearing on Master Thomas's murder? And why had she stated boldly, in the first shock of discovery, indeed without time to view the field in any detail, that nothing had been taken? As though, disdaining the invasion, she had good reason to know that it had been ineffective?

And yet, thought Cadfael, studying the rounded resolute face, and the clear eyes she raised to Hugh's searching stare, I would swear this is a good, honest girl, no way cheat or liar.

'You'll not be needing me,' he said, 'Emma can tell you all. It's almost time for Vespers, and I have still to go and speak with the abbot. There'll be time later, Hugh, after supper.' Abbot Radulfus was a good listener. Not once did he interrupt with comment or question, as Brother Cadfael recounted for him all that had passed at the sheriff's hearing and the unexpected discovery at the barge afterwards. At the end of it he sat for a brief while in silence still, pondering what he had heard.

'So we now have one unlawful act of which the man charged cannot possibly be guilty, whatever may be the truth concerning the other. What do you think, does this tend to weaken the suspicion against him, even on the charge of murder?'

'It weakens it,' said Cadfael, 'but it cannot clear him. It may well be true, as Mistress Vernold believes, that the two things are no way linked, the filching from the barge a mere snatch at what was available, for want of a watchman to guard it. Yet two such assaults upon the same man's life and goods looks like methodical purpose, and not mere chance.'

'And the girl is now a guest within our halls,' said Radulfus, 'and her safety our responsibility. Two attacks upon one man's life and goods, you said. How if there should be more? If a subtle enemy is pursuing some private purpose, it may not end with this afternoon's violation, as we have seen it did not end with the merchant's death. The girl is in the care of the deputy sheriff, and could not be in better hands. But like them, she is a guest under our roof. I do not want the brothers of our community distracted from their devotions and duties, or the harmony of our services shaken, I would not have these matters spoken of but between you and me, and of course as is needful to aid the law. But you, Brother Cadfael, have already been drawn in, you know the whole state of the case. Will you have an eye to what follows, and keep watch on our guests? I place the interests of the abbey in your hands. Do not neglect your devotional duties, unless you must, but I give you leave to go in and out freely, and absent yourself from offices if there is need. When the fair ends, our halls will empty, our tenant merchants depart. It will be out of our hands then to protect the just or prevent the harm that threatens from the unjust. But while they are here, let us do what we can.'

'I will undertake what you wish, Father Abbot,' said Cadfael, 'to the best I may.'

He went to Vespers with a burdened heart and a vexed mind, but for all that, he was glad of the Abbot's charge. It was, in any case, impossible to give up worrying at so tangled a knot, once it had presented itself to his notice, even apart from the natural concern he felt for the girl, and there was no denying that the Benedictine round, dutifully observed, did limit a man's mobility for a large part of the day.

Meantime, he drove the affairs of Emma Vernold from his thoughts with a struggle that should have earned him credit in heaven, and surrendered himself as best he could to the proper observance of Vespers. And after supper he repaired to the cloister, and was not surprised to find Hugh Beringar there waiting for him. They sat down together in a corner where the evening breeze coiled about them very softly and gratefully, and the view into the garth was all emerald turf and pale grey stone, and azure sky melting into green, through a fretwork of briars blowsy with late, drunken-sweet roses.

'There's news in your face,' said Cadfael, eyeing his friend warily. 'As though we have not had enough for one day!'

'And what will you make of it?' wondered Hugh. 'Not an hour ago a lad fishing in Severn hooked a weight of sodden cloth out of the water. All but broke his line, so he let it back in, but was curious enough to play it to shore until he could take it up safely. A fine, full woollen gown, made for a big man, and one with money to spend, too.' He met Cadfael's bright, alerted eyes, rather matching certainties than questioning. 'Yes, what else? We did not trouble Emma with it – who would have the heart! She's drawing Aline a pattern for an embroidered hem for an infant's robe, one she

104

got from France. They have their heads together like sisters. No, we fetched Roger Dod to swear to it. It's Master Thomas's gown, no question. We're poling down the banks now after hose and shirt. To any wandering thief that gown was worth a month's hunting.'

'So no such leech would have thrown it away,' said Cadfael.

'Never!'

'There were also rings taken from his fingers. But rings, I suppose, might be too good to discard, even to prove that this was a murder for hate, not for gain. Rings would sink even if hurled into the Severn. So why hurl them?'

'As usual,' said Hugh, elevating thin black brows, 'you're ahead of me rather than abreast. On the face of it, this was a killing for private malice. So while we examine it, Ivo Corbière very sensibly points out that a murderer so minded would not have stayed to strip the body and put it into the river, but left it lying, and made off as fast as he could. Vengeance, he says rightly, has nothing to feed on in a bundle of clothing. The act is all! And that moved my sheriff to remark that the same thought might well have occurred to the murderer, and caused him to strip his victim naked for that very reason, a hoodwink for the law. Now we drag out of the river the dead man's gown. And where does that leave you and me, my friend?'

'In two minds, or more,' said Cadfael ruefully. 'If the gown never had been found, the notion of common robbery would have held its ground and told in young Corviser's favour. Is it possible that what was said in the sheriff's court put that thought into someone's mind for the first time, and drove him to discard the gown where it was likely to be found? There's one person it would suit very well to have the case against your prisoner strengthened, and that's the murderer

himself. Supposing yon fool boy is not the murderer, naturally.'

'True, half a case can come to look almost whole by the addition of one more witness. But what a fool your man would be, to toss the gown away for proof the killing was not for robbery, thus turning suspicion back upon Philip Corviser, and then creep aboard the barge and steal, when Philip Corviser is in a cell in the castle, and manifestly out of the reckoning.'

'Ah, but he never supposed the theft would be discovered until the barge was back in Bristol, or well on the way. I tell you, Hugh, *I* could see no trace of an alien hand anywhere among those stores on deck or the chattels in the cabin, and Emma herself said she would not have missed the lost things until reaching home again. They were bought on this journey, she had no intention of wearing them. Nothing obvious was stolen, she had almost reached the bottom of her chest before she found out these few bits of finery were gone. But for her sharp eye for her own neat housekeeping, she would not have known the boat had been visited.'

'Yet robbery points to two separate villains and two separate crimes,' pointed out Hugh with a wry smile, 'as Emma insists on believing. If hate was the force behind the man's death, why stoop to pilfer from him afterwards? But do *you* believe the two things are utterly separate? I think not!'

'Strange chances do jostle one another sometimes in this world. Don't put it clean out of mind, it may still be true. But I cannot choose but believe that it's the same hand behind both happenings, and the same purpose, and it was neither theft nor hatred, or the death would have ended it.'

'But Cadfael, in heaven's name, what purpose that demanded a man's death could get satisfaction afterwards from stealing a pair of gloves, a girdle and a

chain?'

Brother Cadfael shook his head helplessly, and had no answer to that, or none that he was yet prepared to give.

'My head spins, Hugh. But I have a black suspicion it may not be over yet. Abbot Radulfus has given me his commission to have an eye to the matter, for the abbey's sake, and permission to go in and out as I see fit for the purpose. It's as the back of his mind that if there's some malignant plot in hand against the Bristol merchant, his niece may not be altogether safe, either. If Aline can keep her at her side, so much the better. But I'll be keeping a watchful eye on her, too.' He rose, yawning. 'Now I must be off to Compline. If I'm to scamp my duties tomorrow, let me at least end today well.'

'Pray for a quiet night,' said Hugh, rising with him, 'for we've not the men to mount patrols through the dark hours. I'll take one more turn along the Foregate with my sergeant, as far as the horse-fair, and then I'm for my bed. I saw little enough of it last night!'

The night of the first of August, the opening day of Saint Peter's Fair, was warm, clear, and quiet enough. Traders along the Foregate kept their stalls open well into the dark hours, the weather being so inviting that plenty of customers were still abroad to chaffer and bargain. The sheriff's officers withdrew into the town, and even the abbey servants, left to keep the peace if it were threatened, had little work to do. It was past midnight when the last lamps and torches were quenched, and the night's silence descended upon the horse-fair.

Master Thomas's barge rocked very softly to the motion of the river. Master Thomas himself lay in a chapel of the abbey, decently shrouded, and in his workshop in the town Martin Bellecote the master-carpenter worked late upon the fine, lead-lined coffin

107

Emma had ordered from him. And in a narrow and dusty cell in the castle, Philip Corviser tossed and turned and nursed his bruises on a thin mattress of straw, and could not sleep for fretting over the memory of Emma's doubting, pitying face.

The Second Day of the Fair

Chapter One

The second day of the fair dawned brilliantly, a golden sun climbing, faint mist hanging like a floating veil over the river. Roger Dod rose with the dawn, shook Gregory awake, rolled up his brychan, washed in the river, and made a quick meal of bread and small ale before setting off along the Foregate to his master's booth. All along the highroad traders were clambering out of their cloaks, yawning and stretching, and setting out their goods ready for the day's business. Roger exchanged greetings with several of them as he passed. Where so many were gathered at close quarters, even a dour and silent man could not help picking up acquaintance with a few of his fellows.

The first glimpse of Master Thomas's booth, between the busy stirrings of its neighbours, brought a scowl to Roger's brown and a muttered oath to his tongue, for the wooden walls were still fast closed. Every hatch still sealed, and the sun already climbing! Warin must be fast asleep, inside there. Roger hammered on the front boards, which should by this hour have been lowered trimly on to their trestles, and set out with goods for sale. He got no response from within.

'Warin!' he bellowed. 'Devil take you, get up and let me in!'

No reply, except that several of the neighbours had

turned curiously to listen and watch, abandoning their own activities to attend to this unexpected clamour.

'Warin!' bawled Roger, and thumped again vigorously. 'You idle swine, what's come to you?'

'I did wonder,' said the cloth-merchant next door, pausing with a bolt of flannel in his arms. 'There's been no sign of him. A sound sleeper, your watchman!'

'Hold hard!' The armourer from the other side leaned excitedly over Roger's shoulder, and fingered the edge of the wooden door. 'Splinters, see?' Beside the latch the boards showed a few pale threads, hardly enough to be seen, and at the thrust of his hand the door gave upon a sliver of darkness. 'No need to hammer, the way in is open. A knife has been used on this!' said the armourer, and there fell a momentary silence.

'Pray God that's all it's been used on!' said Roger in an appalled whisper, and thrust the door wide. He had a dozen of them at his back by then; even the Welshman Rhodri ap Huw had come rolling massively between the stalls to join them, sharp black eyes twinkling out of the thicket of his hair and beard, though what he made of the affair, seeing he spoke no English, no one stopped to consider.

From the darkness within welled the warm scent of timber, wine and sweetmeats, and a faint, strange sound like the breathy grunting of a dumb man. Roger was propelled forward into the dimness by the eager helpers crowding at his back, all agape with curiosity. The stacked bales and small casks of wine took shape gradually, after the brief blindness of entering this dark place from sunlight. Everything stood orderly and handy, just as it had been left overnight, and of Warin there was no sign, until Rhodri ap Huw, ever practical, unbolted the front hatch and let it down, and the brightness of the morning came flooding in.

Stretched along the foot of the same front wall,

where Rhodri must almost have set foot on him, Warin lay rolled in his own cloak and tied at elbows, knees and ankles with cords, so tightly that he could barely wriggle enough to make the folds of cloth rustle. There was a sack drawn over his head, and a length of linen dragged the coarse fibres into his mouth and was secured behind his neck. He was doing his best to answer to his name, and at least his limited jerkings and muted grunts made it plain that he was alive.

Roger uttered a wordless yell of alarm and indignation, and fell on his knees, plucking first at the linen band that held the sack fast. The coarse cloth was wet before with spittle, and the mouth within must be clogged and stung with ropey fibres, but at least the poor wretch could breathe, his strangled grunts were trying to form words long before the linen parted, and let him spit out his gag. Still beneath his sack, his hoarse croak demanded aggrievedly: 'Where were you so long, and me half-killed?'

A couple of pairs of willing hands were at work on the other bonds by that time, all the more zealously now they had heard him speak, and indeed complain, in such reassuringly robust tones. Warin emerged gradually from his swaddlings, unrolled unceremoniously out of the cloak so that he ended face-down on the ground, and still incoherently voluble. He righted himself indignantly, but so spryly that it was plain he had no broken bones, no painful injuries, and had not even suffered overmuch from the cramps of his bonds. He looked up from under his wild grey thatch of hair, half defensive and half accusing, glaring round the circle of his rescuers as though they had been responsible for his hours of discomfort.

'Late's better than never!' he said sourly, and hawked, and spat out fibres of sacking. 'What took you so long? Is everybody deaf? I've been kicking here half the night!'

Half a dozen hands reached pleasurably to hoist him to his feet and sit him down gently on a cask of wine. Roger stood off and let them indulge their curiosity, scowling blackly at his colleague meantime. There was no damage done, not a scratch on the old fool! The first threat, and he had crumpled into a pliable rag.

'For God's sake, what happened to you? You had the booth sealed. How could any man break in here, and you not know? There are other merchants sleep here with their wares, you had only to call.'

'Not all,' said the cloth-merchant fairly. 'I myself lie at a tavern, so do many. If your man was sound asleep, as he well might be with all closed for the night …'

'It was long past midnight,' said Warin, scrubbing aggrievedly at his chafed ankles. 'I know because I heard the little bell for Matins, over the wall, before I slept. Not a sound after, until I awoke as that hood came over my head. They rammed the stuff into my mouth. I never saw face or form, they rolled me up like a bale of wool, and left me tied.'

'And you never raised a cry!' said Roger bitterly. 'How many were they? One or more?'

Warin was disconcerted, and wavered, swaying either way. 'I think two. I'm not sure …'

'You were hooded, but you could hear. Did they talk together?'

'Yes, now I recall there was some whispering. Not that I could catch any words. Yes, they were two. There was moving about of casks and bales here, that I know …'

'For how long? They durst not hurry, and have things fall and rouse the fairground,' said the armourer reasonably. 'How long did they stay?'

Warin was vague, and indeed to a man blindfolded and tied by night, time might stretch out like unravelled thread. 'An hour, it might be.'

'Time enough to find whatever was of most value

here,' said the armourer, and looked at Roger Dod, with a shrug of broad shoulders. 'You'd better look about you, lad, and see what's missing. No need to trouble for anything so weighty as casks of wine, they'd have needed a cart for those, and a cart in the small hours would surely have roused someone. The small and precious is what they came for.'

But Roger had already turned his back on his rescued fellow, and was burrowing frantically among the bales and boxes stacked along the wall. 'My master's strong-box! I built it in behind here, out of sight ... Thank God I took the most of yesterday's gains back to the barge with me last night, and have them safe under lock and key, but for all that, there was a good sum left in it. And all his accounts, and parchments ...'

He was thrusting boxes and bags of spices aside in his haste, scenting the air, pushing out of his way wooden caskets of sugar confections from the east, come by way of Venice and Gascony, and worth high prices in any market. 'Here, against the wall ...'

His hands sank helplessly, he stood staring in dismay. He had bared the boards of the booth; goods stood piled on either side, and between them, nothing. Master Thomas's strong-box was gone.

Brother Cadfael had taken advantage of the early hours to put in an hour or two of work with Brother Mark in the herb-gardens, while he had no reason to anticipate any threat to Emma, for she was surely still asleep in the guest-hall with Constance, and out of reach of harm. The morning was clear and sunny, the mist just lifting from the river, shot through with oblique gold, and Mark sang cheerfully about his weeding, and listened attentively and serenely as Cadfael instructed him in all particulars of the day's work.

'For I may have to leave all things in your hands. And so I can, safely enough, I know, if I should chance to be called away.'

'I'm well taught,' said Brother Mark, with his grave smile, behind which the small spark of mischief was visible only to Cadfael, who had first discovered and nurtured it. 'I know what to stir and what to let well alone in the workshop.'

'I wish I could be as sure of my part outside it,' said Cadfael ruefully. 'There are brews among us that need just as sure a touch, boy, and where to stir and where to let be is puzzling me more than a little. I'm walking a knife-edge, with disastrous falls on either side. I know my herbs. They have fixed properties, and follow sacred rules. Human creatures do not so. And I cannot even wish they did. I would not have one scruple of their complexity done away, it would be lamentable loss.'

It was time to go to Prime. Brother Mark stooped to rinse his hands in the butt of water they kept warming through the day, to be tempered for the herbs at the evening watering. 'It was being with you made me know that I want to be a priest,' he said, speaking his mind as openly as always in Cadfael's company.

'I had never the urge for it,' said Cadfael absently, his mind on other matters.

'I know. That was the one thing wanting. Shall we go?'

They were coming out from Prime, and the lay servants already mustering for their early Mass, when Roger Dod came trudging in at the gatehouse, out of breath, and with trouble plain to be read in his face.

'What, again something new?' sighed Cadfael, and set off to intercept him before he reached the guest-hall. Suddenly aware of this square, sturdy figure bearing down on him with obvious purpose,

116

Roger checked, and turned an anxious face. His frown cleared a little when he recognised the same monk who had accompanied the deputy sheriff in the vain search for Master Thomas, on the eve of Saint Peter. 'Oh, it's you, brother, that's well! Is Hugh Beringar within? I must speak to him. We're beset! Yesterday the barge, and now the booth, and God knows what's yet to come, and what will become of us before ever we get away from this deadly place. My master's books gone – money and box and all! What will Mistress Emma think? I'd rather have had my own head broke, if need be, than fail her so!'

'What's this talk of broken heads?' asked Cadfael, alarmed. 'Whose? Are you telling me there've been thieves ransacking your booth now?'

'In the night! And the strong-box gone, and Warin tied up hand and foot with a throatful of sacking, and nobody heard sound while they did it. We found him not half an hour ago …'

'Come!' said Cadfael, grasping him by the sleeve and setting off for the guest-hall at a furious pace. 'We'll find Hugh Beringar. Tell your tale once, and save breath!'

In Aline's apartments the women were only just out of bed, and Hugh was sitting over an early meal in shirt and hose, shoeless, when Cadfael rapped at the door, and cautiously put his head in.

'Your pardon, Hugh, but there's news. May we come in?'

Hugh took one look at him, recognised the end of his ease, and bade them in resignedly.

'Here's one has a tale to tell,' said Cadfael. 'He's new come from the horse-fair.'

At sight of Roger, Emma came to her feet in astonishment and alarm, the soft, bemused bloom of sleep gone from her eyes, and the morning flush from her cheeks. Her black hair, not yet braided, swung in a

glossy curtain about her shoulders, and her loose undergown was ungirdled, her feet bare. 'Roger, what is it? What has happened now?'

'More theft and roguery, mistress, and God knows I can see no reason why all the rascals in the shire should pick on us for prey.' Roger heaved in deep breath, and launched headlong into his complaint. 'This morning I go to the stall as usual, and find it all closed, and not a sound or a word from within for all my shouting and knocking, and then come some of the neighbours, wondering, and one sees that the inside bar has been hoisted with a knife – and a marvellous thin knife it must have been. And we go in and find Warin rolled up like baggage in his own cloak, and fast tied, and his mouth stuffed with sacking – a bag over his head, fit to choke him ...'

'Oh, no!' breathed Emma in a horrified whisper, and pressed a fist hard against trembling lips. 'Oh, poor Warin! He's not ... oh, not dead ...?'

Roger gave vent to a snort of contempt. 'Not he! alive and fit as a flea, barring being stiff from the cords. How he could sleep so sound as not to hear the fumbling with the latch, nor even notice when the door was opened, there's no guessing. But if he did hear, he took good care not to give the robbers any trouble. You know Warin's no hero. He says he was only shook awake when the sack went over his head, and never saw face nor form, though he thinks there were two of them, for there was some whispering. But as like as not he heard them come, but chose not to, for fear they'd slip the knife in his ribs.'

Emma's colour had warmed into rose again. She drew a deep breath of thankfulness. 'But he's safe? He's taken no harm at all?' She caught Aline's sympathetic eye, and laughed shakily with relief. 'I *know* he is not brave. I'm *glad* he is not! Nor very clever nor very industrious, either, but I've known him since I

118

was a little girl, he used to make toys for me, and willow whistles. Thank God he is not harmed!'

'Not a graze! I wish,' said Roger, his eyes burning jealously upon her childish morning beauty, not yet adorned and needing no adornment, 'I wish to God I'd stayed there to be watchman myself, they'd not have broken in there unscathed, and found everything handed over on a platter.'

'But then you might have been killed, Roger. I'm glad you were *not* there, you'd surely have put up a fight and come to harm. What, against two, and you unarmed? Oh, no, I want no man hurt to protect my possessions.'

'What followed?' asked Hugh shortly, stamping his feet into his shoes and reaching for his coat. 'You've left him there to mind the stall? Is he fit?'

'As you or me, my lord. I'll send him to you to tell his own tale when I get back.'

'No need, I'm coming with you to view the place and the damage. Finish your tale. They'll scarcely have left empty-handed. What's gone with them?'

Roger turned devoted, humble, apologetic eyes upon Emma. 'Sorrow the day, mistress, my master's strong-box is gone with them!'

Brother Cadfael was watching Emma's face just as intently as was her hopeless admirer, and it seemed to him that in the pleasure of knowing that her old servant had survived unharmed, she was proof against all other blows. The loss of the strong-box she received with unshaken serenity. In these surroundings, safe from any too pressing manifestation of his passion, she was even moved to comfort Roger. A kindhearted girl, who did not like to see any of her own people out of sorts with his competence and his self-respect.

'You must not feel it so sharply,' she said warmly. 'How could you have prevented? There is no fault attaches to you.'

119

'I took most of the money back to the barge with me last night,' pleaded Roger earnestly. 'It's safe locked away, there's been no more tampering there. But Master Thomas's account books, and some parchments of value, and charters ...'

'Then there will be copies,' said Emma firmly. 'And what is more, if they took the box, supposing it to be full of money, they'll keep what money was left there, and most likely discard the box and the parchments, for what use can they make of those? We may get most of it back, you will see.'

Not merely a kind girl, but a girl of sense and fortitude, who bore up nobly under her losses. Cadfael looked at Hugh, and found Hugh looking at him, just as woodenly, but with one lively eyebrow signalling slightly sceptical admiration.

'Nothing is lost,' said Emma firmly, 'of any value to compare with a life. Since Warin is safe, I cannot be sad.'

'Nevertheless,' said Hugh with deliberation, 'it might be well if one abbey sergeant stood guard on your booth until the fair is over. For it does seem that all the misfortunes that should by rights be shared among all the abbey's clients are falling solely upon you. Shall I ask Prior Robert to see to it?'

She looked down, wary and thoughtful, for a moment, and then lifted deep blue eyes wide and clear as the sky, and a degree more innocent than if they had but newly opened on the world. 'It's kind of you,' she said, 'but surely everything has now been done to us. I don't think it will be necessary to set a guard upon us now.'

Hugh came to Cadfael's workshop after the midday meal, leaving Emma in Aline's charge, helped himself to a horn of wine from Cadfael's private store, and settled down on the bench under the eaves, on the

shady side. The fragrance of the herbs lay like a sleepy load on the air within the pleached hedges, and set him yawning against his will and his mood, which was for serious discussion. They were well away from the outer world here, the busy hum of the marketplace drifted to them only distantly and pleasantly, like the working music of Brother Bernard's bees. And Brother Mark, weeding the herb-beds with delicate, loving hands, habit kilted to his knees, was no hindrance at all to their solitude.

'A separate creature,' said Brother Cadfael, eyeing him with detached affection 'My priest, my proxy. I had to find some way of evading the fate that closed on me. There goes my sacrificial lamb, the best of the flock.'

'Some day he will take *your* confession,' said Hugh, watching Mark pluck out weeds as gently as though he pitied them, 'and you'll be a lost man, for he'll know every evasion.' He sipped wine, drew it about his mouth thoughtfully, swallowed it and sat savouring the after-taste for a moment. 'This fellow Warin had little to add,' he said then. 'What do you say now? This *cannot* be chance.'

'No,' agreed Cadfael, propping the door of his workshop wide to let in the air, and coming to sit beside his friend, 'it cannot be chance. The man is killed, stripped, his barge searched, his booth searched. Not a soul besides, at this fair where there are several as wealthy, has suffered any attack or any loss. No, there is nothing done at hazard here.'

'What, then? Expound! The girl claimed there were things stolen from the barge. Now something positive, a strong-box, the single portable thing in the booth that might confidently be supposed to hold valuables, is demonstrably stolen from this last assault. If these are not simple thefts, what are they? Tell me!'

'Stages in a quest,' said Cadfael. 'It seems to me

there's a hunt afoot for something. I do not know what, but some quite single, small thing, and precious, which was, or was thought to be, in the possession of Master Thomas. On the night he came here he was murdered, and his body stripped. The first search. And it was fruitless, for the next day his barge was visited and ransacked. The second search.'

'Not altogether fruitless this time,' said Beringar dryly, 'for we know on the best authority, do we not, that whoever paid that visit left the richer by three things, a silver chain, a girdle with a gold clasp, and a pair of embroidered gloves.'

'Hmmm!' Cadfael twitched his brown nose doubtfully between finger and thumb, and eyed the young man sidewise.

'Oh, come!' said Hugh indulgently, and flashed his sudden smile. 'I may not stumble on these subtleties as quickly as you, but since knowing you I've had to keep my wits about me. The lady has a bold mind and an excellent memory, and I have no hope in the world of getting her to make a mistake in one detail of the embroidery on those lost gloves, but for all that, I doubt if they ever existed.'

'You might,' Cadfael suggested, though without much hope, 'try asking her outright what it is she's hiding.'

'I did!' owned Hugh, ruefully grinning. 'She opened great, hurt eyes at me, and could not understand me! She knows nothing, she's hiding nothing, she has nothing to tell more than she's already told, and every word of that is truth. But for all that, and however angelically, the girl's lying. What was it stuck in your craw, and brought you up against the same shock before ever it dawned upon me?'

'I should be sorry,' said Cadfael slowly, 'if anything I have done or said made you think any evil of the girl, for I think none.'

'Neither do I, you need not fear it. But I do think she may be meddling in something she would do better to let well alone, and I would rather, as you would, as Abbot Radulfus would, that no harm should come to her under our care. Or ever, for that matter. I like her well.'

'When we went together to the barge,' said Cadfael, 'and she took no more than a minute within to cry out that someone had been there, pawing through all their belongings, I never doubted she was telling truth. Women know how they leave things, it needs only a wrong fold to betray an alien hand, and certainly it shocked and startled her, that was no feigning. Nor was it the next moment, when I asked if anything had been taken, and without pause for thought, she said: "No!" An absolute no, I would say even triumphant. I thought little of it, then, but urged her to look thoroughly and make sure. When I said she must report the matter, she thought again, and took pains to discover that indeed a few things had been stolen. I think she regretted that ever she had cried out in the first place, but if the law must know of it, she would ensure that it was accepted as a trivial theft by some common pickpurse. Truth is what she told unguardedly, with that scornful "no" of hers. Afterwards she made to undo the effect by lying, and for one not by nature a liar she did it well. But for all that, I think, like you, those pretty things of hers never existed, or never were aboard the barge.'

'Still remains the question,' said Hugh, considering, 'of why she was so sure in the first place that nothing had been taken.'

'Because,' said Cadfael simply, 'she knew what the thief must have come looking for, and she knew he had not found it, because she knew it was not there to be found. The second search was also vain. Whatever it may be, it was not on Master Thomas's person, which

was clearly the most likely place, nor was it on his barge.'

'Hence this third search! So now divine for me, Cadfael, whether this third attempt has succeeded or no. The merchant's strong-box is vanished – again a logical place to keep something so precious. Will this be the end of it?' Cadfael shook his head emphatically. 'This attempt has fared no better than the others,' he said positively. 'You may take that as certain.'

'How can you be so sure of it?' demanded Hugh curiously.

'You saw all that I saw. She does not care a farthing for the loss of the strong-box! As soon as she knew that the man Warin was unhurt, she took everything else calmly enough. Whatever it is the unknown is seeking, she knew it was not in the barge, and she knew it was not in the booth. And I can think of only one reason why she should know so well where it is *not*, and that is that she knows equally well where it *is*.'

'Then the next possibility the enemy will be considering,' said Hugh with conviction, 'is where *she* is – on her person or in some hiding-place only she knows of. Well, we'll keep a vigilant eye on Emma, between us. No,' said Hugh reflectively, 'I cannot imagine any evil of her, but neither can I imagine how she can be tangled in something grim enough to bring about murder, violence and theft, nor why, if she knows herself to be in danger and in need of help, she won't speak out and ask for it. Aline has tried her best to get her to confide, and the girl remains all sweetness and gratitude, but lets no word drop of any burden she may be carrying. And you know Aline, she draws out confidences without ever asking a probing question, and whoever can resist her is beyond the reach of the rest of us …'

'I'm glad to see you so fond a husband,' said Cadfael approvingly.

'So you should be, it was you tossed the girl into my arms in the first place. You'd best be worrying now about what manner of father I shall make! And you might put in a prayer for me on the issue, some time when you're on your knees. No, truly, Cadfael … I wonder about this girl. Aline likes her, and that's recommendation enough. And she seems to like Aline – no, more than like! Yet she never lets down her veils. When she seems most to cherish my most cherishable lady, she is also more careful not to let slip one unguarded word about her own situation.'

Brother Cadfael saw no paradox there. 'So she would be, Hugh,' he said gravely. 'If she feels herself to be in danger, the last thing she will do is to draw in beside her someone she values and likes. By every means in her power – and I think she is a clever and resourceful girl – she will stand off her friends from any share in what she is about.'

Beringar considered that long and sombrely, nursing his empty horn. 'Well, all we can do is hedge her about thick enough to stand off, likewise, whatever move may be made against her.'

It had not occurred to him, it was only now insinuating itself into Cadfael's thoughts, that the next decisive move might come from Emma herself, rather than being made against her. A piece of this mystery, apparently the vital piece, she had in her hands; if any use was to be made of it, it might well be at her decree.

Hugh set aside his drinking-horn and rose, brushing the summer dust from his cotte. 'Meantime, the sheriff is left with a murder on his hands, and I tell you, Cadfael, that affair now looks less than ever like a drunken revenge by an aggrieved youth of the town – though to tell truth, it never did look too convincing, even if we could not discard it out of hand.'

'Surely there's good ground now for letting the provost bail his lad out and take him home?' said

Cadfael, encouraged. 'Of all the young men around this town, Philip must be the clearest from any suspicion of this last outrage, or the raid on the barge, either. The gaoler who turns the key on him can witness where *he*'s been all this while, and swear he never left it.'

'I'm off to the castle now,' said Hugh. 'I can't vouch for the sheriff, but I'll certainly speak a word in his ear, and in the provost's, too. It's well worth making the approach.'

He looked down, flashing out of his preoccupation with a sudden mischievous smile, combed the fingers of one hand through the hedge of bushy greying hair that rimmed Cadfael's sunburned tonsure, leaving it bristling like thorn-bushes, snapped a finger painfully against the nut-brown dome between, and took his departure with his usual light stride and insouciant bearing, which the unwary mistook for the mark of a frivolous man. Such small indulgences he was more likely to permit himself, strictly with friends, when he was engaged on something more than usually grave.

Cadfael watched him go, absently smoothing down the warlike crest Hugh had erected. He supposed he had better be stirring, too, and hand over charge here to Brother Mark until evening. It would not do to take his eyes off Emma for any length of time, and Aline, to please a solicitous husband, consented to doze for an hour or two in the afternoon, for the sake of the child. Grandchildren by proxy, Cadfael reflected, might be a rare and pleasurable recompense for a celibate prime. As for old age, he had not yet begun to think about it; no doubt it had its own alleviations.

Chapter Two

For all I said,' Emma mused aloud, putting fine stitches into a linen band for an infant's cap, in the lofty midday light in the window of Aline's bedchamber, 'I do grieve for those gloves of mine. Such fine leather, supple and black, and a wealth of gold in the embroidery. I never bought such expensive ones before.' She reached the end of her seam, and snipped off the thread neatly. 'They say there's a very good glover has a stall in the fair,' she said, smoothing her work. 'I thought I might take a look at his wares, and see if he has anything as fine as those I've lost. They tell me he's well known in Chester, and the countess buys from him. I think perhaps I'll walk along the Foregate this afternoon, and see what he has. What with all these upsets, I've hardly seen anything of the fair.'

'A good idea,' said Aline. 'Such a fine day, we should not be spending it here within doors. I'll come with you.'

'Oh, no, you should not,' protested Emma solicitously. 'You have not had your sleep this afternoon. No need to keep me company that short way. I should be distressed if you tired yourself on my account.'

'Oh, folly!' said Aline cheerfully. 'I am so healthy I shall burst if I have too little to do. It's Constance and Hugh who want to make an invalid of me, just because I'm in a woman's best and happiest estate. And Hugh is

gone to the sheriff, and Constance is visiting with a cousin of hers in the Wyle, so who's to fret? I'll slip on my shoes, and we'll go. I should like to buy a box of those sugared fruits your uncle brought from the east. We'll do that, too.'

It seemed that Emma had, after all, lost her taste for the expedition. She sat stroking the embroidered band she had just finished, and eyed the shape of linen cut for the crown. 'I don't know – I should finish this, perhaps. After tomorrow there may be no choice, and I should be sorry to leave it for someone else to finish. As for the candied fruits, I'll ask Roger to bring you a box, when he comes again this evening to tell me how the day has gone. Tomorrow it will be here.'

'That's kind,' said Aline, slipping on her shoes none the less, 'but he could hardly try on a pair of gloves for you, or choose with your eye. So let's go and see for ourselves. It won't take long.'

Emma sat hesitating, but whether in a genuine endeavour to make up her mind, or in search of a way of extricating herself from an unsatisfactory situation, Aline could not be sure. 'Oh, no, I should not! How can I give my mind to such vanity, at a time like this! I'm ashamed that I ever thought of it. My uncle dead, and here am I yearning after trumpery bits of finery. No, I won't be so shallow. Let me at least go on with my work for the child, instead of thinking only of my own adornment.' And she picked up the cut linen. Aline noted that the hand holding it trembled a little, and wondered whether to persist. Plainly the girl wanted to go forth for some purpose of her own, but would not go unless it could be alone. And alone, said Aline firmly to herself, she certainly shall not go, if I can prevent.

'Well,' she said doubtfully, 'if you're determined to be so penitential, I won't play the devil and tempt you. And I'm the gainer, your sewing is so fine, I could

128

never match it. Who taught you so well?' She slipped off her soft leather shoes, and sat down again. Something, at least, she had learned, better to let well alone now. Emma welcomed the change of subject eagerly. Of her childhood she would talk freely.

'My mother was a famous embroidress. She began to teach me as soon as I could manage a needle, but she died when I was only eight, and Uncle Thomas took me in. We had a housekeeper, a Flemish lady who had married a Bristol seaman, and been widowed when his ship was lost, and she taught me everything she knew, though I could never equal her work. She used to make altar cloths and vestments for the church, such beautiful things ...'

So a plain pair of good black gloves, thought Aline, would have done well enough for you at any time, since you could have adorned them to your own fancy. And those who can do such things exquisitely, seldom prefer the work of others.

It was not difficult to keep Emma talking, but for all that, Aline could not help wondering what was going through the girl's mind, and how soon, and how cunningly, she would make the next bid to slip away solitary about her mysterious business. But as it fell out, she need not have troubled, for late in the afternoon came a lay brother from the gatehouse, to announce that Martin Bellecote had brought down Master Thomas's coffin, and desired permission to proceed with his business. Emma rose instantly, laying down her sewing, her face pale and intent. If there was one thing certain, it was that no other matter, however urgent, would take her away from the church until her uncle was decently coffined and sealed down for his journey home, and prayers said for his repose, as later she would attend the first Mass for him. Whatever he had been to others, he had been uncle and father and friend to his orphaned kinswoman, and no reverence,

129

no tribute, would be omitted from his obsequies.

'I will come myself,' said Emma. 'I must say farewell to him.' She had not yet seen him, dead, but the brothers, long expert in the gentle arts that reconcile life to death, would have made sure that she would be able to remember him without distress.

'Shall I come with you?' offered Aline.

'You are very good, but I would rather go alone.'

Aline followed as far as the great court, and watched the little procession cross to the cloister, Emma walking beside the handcart on which Martin and his son wheeled the coffin. When they had lifted the heavy box and carried it in by the south door of the church, with Emma following, Aline stood for some minutes looking about her. At this hour most of the guests and many of the lay servants were out at the fair, only the brothers went about their business as usual. Through the wide gate of the distant stable-yard she could see Ivo Corbière's young groom rubbing down a pony, and the archer Turstan Fowler sitting on a mounting-block, whistling as he burnished a saddle. Sober and recovered from his debauch, he was a well-set-up and comely fellow, with the open face of one who has not a care in the world. Evidently he was long since forgiven, and back in favour.

Brother Cadfael, coming from the gardens, saw her still gazing pensively towards the church. She smiled at sight of him.

'Martin has brought the coffin. They are within there, she'll think of nothing else now. But, Cadfael, she intends to give us all the slip when she can. She has tried. She would see, she said, if the glover at the fair has something to take the place of the ones she lost. But when I said I would go with her, no, that would not do, she gave up the idea.'

'Gloves!' murmured Brother Cadfael, scrubbing thoughtfully at his chin. 'Strange, when you think of it,

130

that it should be gloves she has on her mind, in the middle of summer.'

Aline was in no position to follow that thought, she took it at its surface meaning. 'Why strange? We know there were some stolen from her, and here we are at one of the few fairs where rare goods are to be bought, it follows naturally enough. But of course the glover is only a handy excuse.'

Cadfael said no more then, but he went away very thoughtfully towards the cloister. The strange thing was not that a girl should want to replace, while chance offered, a lost piece of finery. It was rather that when she was suddenly confronted by the need to pass off as simple robbery a raid she knew to be something very different, one of the articles she claimed to have lost should be a thing so inappropriate to the season that she felt obliged to account for it by saying she had newly bought it in Gloucester on the journey. Why gloves, unless she had gloves running in her mind already for another reason? Gloves? Or glovers?

In the transept chapel Martin Bellecote and his young son set up the heavy coffin on a draped trestle, and reverently laid the body of Master Thomas of Bristol within it. Emma stood looking down at her uncle's dead face for a long time, without tears or words. It would not be painful, she found, to remember him thus, dignified and remote in death, the bones of his cheeks and brow and jaw more strongly outlined than in life, his florid flesh contracted and paled into waxen austerity. Now at the last moment she wanted to give him something to take with him into his grave, and realised that in the buffeting of these two days she had not been able to think clearly enough to be ready for the parting. Not the fact of death, but the absolute need of some ceremonial tenderness, separate from the public rites, suddenly seemed to her overwhelmingly important.

'Shall I cover him?' asked Martin Bellecote gently.

Even so soft a sound startled her. She looked round almost wonderingly. The man, large, comely and calm, waited her orders without impatience. The boy, grave and silent, watched her with huge hazel eyes. From her four years' superiority over him she pondered whether so young a creature should be doing this office, and then she understood that those eyes were preoccupied rather with her living self than with the dead, and the vigorous, flowing sap in him reached up towards light and life as to the sun, and recognised shadow only by virtue of its neighbouring brightness. That was right and good.

'No, wait just a moment,' she said. 'I'll come back!'

She went quickly out into the sunlight, and looked about her for the path that led into the gardens. The green lines of a hedge and the crowns of trees within drew her, she came into a walk where flowers had been planted. The brothers were great gardeners, and valued food crops for good reason, but they had time also for roses. She chose the one bush that bore a bloom like no other, pale yellow petals shading into rose at the tips, and plucked one flower only. Not the buds, not even the one perfect globe, but a wide-open bloom just beyond its prime but still unflawed. She took it back, hurrying, into the church with her. He was not young, not even at his zenith, but settling into his autumn, and this was the rose for him.

Brother Cadfael had watched her go, he watched her come again, and followed her into the chapel, but held aloof in the shadows. She brought her single flower and laid it in the coffin, beside the dead man's heart.

'Cover him now,' she said, and stood well back to let them work in peace. When it was done, she thanked them, and they withdrew and left her there, as clearly was her wish. So, just as silently, did Brother Cadfael

Emma remained kneeling on the stones of the transept, unaware of discomfort, a great while, her eyes wide open all that time upon the closed coffin, on its draped stand before the altar. To lie thus in the church of a great abbey, to have a special Mass sung for him, and then to be taken home in a grand coffin for burial with still further rites, surely that was glory, and he would have liked it. All was to be done as he would have liked. All! He would be pleased with her.

She knew her duty; she said prayers for him, a great many prayers, because the form was blessedly laid down, and her mind could range while her lips formed the proper words. She would do what he had wanted done, what he had half-confided to her, as he had to no other. She would see his task completed, and he would rest, pleased with her. And then ... she had hardly looked beyond, but there was a great, summer-scented breeze blowing through her spirit, telling her she was young and fair, and wealthy into the bargain, and that boys like the coffin-maker's young son looked upon her with interest and pleasure. Other young men, too, of less green years ...

She rose from her knees at last, shook out her crumpled skirts, and walked briskly out of the chapel into the nave of the church, and rounding the clustered stone pillars at the corner of the crossing, came face to face with Ivo Corbière.

He had been waiting, silent and motionless, in his shadowy corner, refraining even from setting foot in the chapel until her vigil was over, and the resolution with which she had suddenly ended it flung her almost into his arms. She uttered a startled gasp, and he put out reassuring hands to steady her, and was in no haste to let go. In this dim place his gold head showed darkened to bronze, and his face, stooped over her solicitously, was so gilded by the summer that it had almost the same fine-metal burnishing.

'Did I alarm you? I'm sorry! I didn't want to disturb you. They told me at the gatehouse that the master-carpenter had come and gone, and you were here. I hoped if I waited patiently I might be able to talk with you. If I have not pressed my attentions on you until now,' he said earnestly, 'it is not because I haven't thought of you. Constantly!'

Her eyes were raised to his face with a fascinated admiration she would never have indulged in full light, and she quite forgot to make any move to withdraw herself from his hold. His hands slid down her forearms, but halted at her hands, and the touch, by mutual consent, became a clasp.

'Almost two days since I've spoken with you!' he said. 'It's an age, and I've grudged it, but you were well-friended, and I had no right ... But now that I have you, let me keep you for an hour! Come out and walk in the gardens. I doubt if you've even seen them yet.'

They went out together into the sunlight, through the cloister garth and out into the bustle and traffic of the great court. It was almost time for Vespers, the quietest hours of the afternoon now spent, the brothers gathering gradually from their dispersed labours, guests returning from the fairground and the riverside. It was a gratifying thing to walk through this populous place on the arm of a nobleman, lord of a modest honour scattered through Cheshire and Shropshire. For the daughter of craftsmen and merchants, a very gratifying thing! They sat down on a stone bench in the flower-garden, on the sunny side of the pleached hedge, with the heady fragrance of Brother Cadfael's herbarium wafted to them in drunken eddies on a soft breeze.

'You will have troublesome dispositions to make,' said Corbière seriously. 'If there is anything I can arrange for you, let me know of it. It will be my

pleasure to serve you. You are taking him back to Bristol for burial?'

'It's what he would have wished. There will be a Mass for him in the morning, and then we shall carry him back to his barge for the journey home. The brothers have been kindness itself to me.'

'And you? Will you also return with the barge?'

She hesitated, but why not confide in him? He was considerate and kind, and quick to understand. 'No, it would be – unwise. While my uncle lived it was very well, but without him it would not do. There is one of our men – I must say no evil of him, for he has done none, but ... He is too fond. Better we should not travel together. But neither do I want to offer him insult, by letting him know he is not quite trusted. I've told him that I must remain here a few days, that I may be needed if the sheriff has more questions to ask, or more is found out about my uncle's death.'

'But then,' said Ivo with warm concern, 'what of your own journey home? How will you manage?'

'I shall stay with Lady Beringar until we can find some safe party riding south, with women among them. Hugh Beringar will advise me. I have money, and I can pay my way. I shall manage.'

He looked at her long and earnestly, until his gravity melted into a smile. 'Between all your well-wishers, you will certainly reach your home without mishap. I'll be giving my mind to it, among the rest. But now let's forget, for my sake, that there must be a departure, and make the most of the hours while you are still here.' He rose, and took her by the hand to draw her up with him. 'Forget Vespers, forget we're guests of an abbey, forget the fair and the business of the fair, and all that such things may demand of you in future. Think only that it's summer, and a glorious evening, and you're young, and have friends ... Come down with me past the fish-ponds, as far as the brook. That is

135

all abbey land, I wouldn't take you beyond.'

She went with him gratefully, his hand cool and vital in hers. By the brook below the abbey fields it was cool and fresh and bright, full of scintillating light along the water, and birds dabbling and singing, and in the pleasure of the moment she almost forgot all that lay upon her, so sacred and so burdensome. Ivo was reverent and gentle, and did not press her too close, but when she said regretfully that it was time for her to go back, for fear Aline might be anxious about her, he went with her all the way, her hand still firmly retained in his, and presented himself punctiliously before Aline, so that Emma's present guardian might study, accept and approve him. As indeed she did.

It was charmingly and delicately done. He made himself excellent company for as long as was becoming on a first visit, invited and deferred to all Aline's graceful questions, and withdrew well before he had even drawn near the end of his welcome.

'So that's the young man who was so helpful and gallant when the riot began,' said Aline, when he was gone. 'Do you know, Emma, I do believe you have a serious admirer there.' A wooer gained, she thought, might come as a blessed counter-interest to a guardian lost. 'He comes of good blood and family,' said the Aline Siward who had brought two manors to her husband in her own right, but saw no difference between her guest and herself, and innocently ignored the equally proud and honourable standards of those born to craft and commerce instead of land. 'The Corbières are distant kin of Earl Ranulf of Chester himself. And he does seem a most estimable young man.'

'But not of my kind,' said Emma, as shrewd and wary as she sounded regretful. 'I am a stone-mason's daughter, and niece to a merchant. No landed lord is likely to become a suitor for someone like me.'

'But it's not someone *like* you in question,' said Aline reasonably. 'It is *you*!'

Brother Cadfael looked about him, late in the evening after Compline, saw all things in cautious balance, Emma securely settled in the guest-hall, Beringar already home. He went thankfully to bed with his brothers, for once at the proper time, and slept blissfully until the bell rang to wake him for Matins. Down the night stairs and into the church the brothers filed in the midnight silence, to begin the new day's worship. In the faint light of the altar candles they took their places, and the third day of Saint Peter's Fair had begun. The third and last.

Cadfael always rose for Matins and Lauds not sleepy and unwilling, but a degree more awake than at any other time, as though his senses quickened to the sense of separateness of the community gathered here, to a degree impossible by daylight. The dimness of the light, the solidity of the enclosing shadows, the muted voices, the absence of lay worshippers, all contributed to his sense of being enfolded in a sealed haven, where all those who shared in it were his own flesh and blood and spirit, responsible for him as he for them, even some for whom, in the active and arduous day, he could feel no love, and pretended none. The burden of his vows became also his privilege, and the night's first worship was the fuel of the next day's energy.

So the shadows had sharp edges for him, the shapes of pillar and capital and arch clamoured like vibrant notes of music, both vision and hearing observed with heightened sensitivity, details had a quivering insistence. Brother Mark's profile against the candle-light was piercingly clear. A note sung off-key by a sleepy elder stung like a bee. And the single pale speck lying under the trestle that supported Master Thomas's coffin was like a hole in reality, something that could

not be there. Yet it persisted. It was at the beginning of Lauds that it first caught his eye, and after that he could not get free of it. Wherever he looked, however he fastened upon the altar, he could still see it out of the corner of his eye.

When Lauds ended, and the silent procession began to file back towards the night stairs and the dortoir, Cadfael stepped aside, stooped, and picked up the mote that had been troubling him. It was a single petal from a rose, its colour indistinguishable by this light, but pale, deepening round the tip. He knew at once what it was, and with this midnight clarity in him he knew how it had come there.

Fortunate, indeed, that he had seen Emma bring her chosen rose and lay it in the coffin. If he had not, this petal would have told him nothing. Since he had, it told him all. With hieratic care and ceremony, after the manner of the young when moved, she had brought her offering cupped in both hands, and not one leaf, not one grain of yellow pollen from its open heart, had fallen to the floor.

Whoever was hunting so persistently for something believed to be in Master Thomas's possession, after searching his person, his barge and his booth, had not stopped short of the sacrilege of searching his coffin. Between Compline and Matins it had been opened and closed again; and a single petal from the wilting rose within had shaken loose and been wafted unnoticed over the side, to bear witness to the blasphemy.

The Third Day of the Fair

Chapter One

Emma arose with the dawn, stole out of the wide
bed she shared with Constance, and dressed
herself very quietly and cautiously, but even so
the sense of movement, rather than any sound,
disturbed the maid's sleep, and caused her to open
eyes at once alert and intelligent.

Emma laid a finger to her lips, and cast a meaning
glance towards the door beyond which Hugh and
Aline were still sleeping. 'Hush!' she whispered. 'I'm
only going to church for Prime. I don't want to wake
anyone else.'

Constance shrugged against her pillow, raised her
brows a little, and nodded. Today there would be the
Mass for the dead uncle, and then the transference of
his coffin to the barge that would take him home. Not
surprising if the girl was disposed to turn this day into
a penitential exercise, for the repose of her uncle's soul
and the merit of her own. 'You won't go out alone, will
you?'

'I'm going straight to the church,' promised Emma
earnestly.

Constance nodded again, and her eyelids began to
close. She was asleep before Emma had drawn the
door to very softly, and slipped away towards the great
court.

Brother Cadfael rose for Prime like the rest, but left

141

his cell before his companions, and went to take counsel with the only authority in whom he could repose his latest discovery. Such a violation was the province of the abbot, and only he had the right to hear of it first.

With the door of the abbot's austere cell closed upon them, they were notably at ease together, two men who knew their own minds and spoke clearly what they had to say. The rose petal, a little shrunken and weary, but with its yellow and pink still silken-bright, lay in the abbot's palm like a golden tear.

'You are sure this cannot have fallen when our daughter brought it as an offering? It was a gentle gift,' said Radulfus.

'Not one grain of dust fell. She carried it like a vessel of wine, in both hands. I saw every move. I have not yet seen the coffin by daylight, but I doubt not it has been dealt with competently, and looks as it looked when the master-carpenter firmed it down. Nevertheless, it has been opened and closed again.'

'I take your word,' said the abbot simply. 'This is vile.'

'It is,' said Cadfael and waited.

'And you cannot put name to the man who would do this thing?'

'Not yet.'

'Nor say if he has gained by it? As God forbid!'

'No, Father! But God will forbid.'

'Give your might to it,' said Radulfus, and brooded for a while in silence. Then he said: 'We have a duty to the law. Do what is best there, for I hear you have the deputy sheriff's ear. As for the affront to the church, to our house, to our dead son and his heiress, I am left to read between rubrics. There will be a Mass this morning for the dead man. The holy rite will cleanse all foulness from his passing and his coffin. As for the child, let her be at peace, for so she may, her dead is in

142

the hand of God, there has no violence been done to his soul.'

Brother Cadfael said, with hearty gratitude: 'She will rest the better if she knows nothing. She is a good girl, her grief should have every consolation.'

'See to it, brother, as you may. It is almost time for Prime.'

Cadfael was hurrying from the abbot's lodging towards the cloister when he saw Emma turn in there ahead of him, and slowed his steps to be unnoticed himself while he watched what she would do. On this of all days Emma was entitled to every opportunity of prayer and meditation, but she also had a very private secular preoccupation of her own, and which of these needs she was serving by this early-rising zeal there was no telling.

In at the south door went Emma, and in after her, just as discreetly, went brother Cadfael. The monks were already in their stalls, and concentrating all upon the altar. The girl slipped silently round into the nave, as though she would find herself a retired spot there in privacy; but instead of turning aside, she continued her rapid, silent passage towards the west door, the parish door that opened on to the Foregate, outside the convent walls. Except during times of stress, such as the siege of Shrewsbury the previous year, it was never closed.

In at one door and out at another, and she was free, for a little while, to go where she would, and could return by the same way, an innocent coming back from church.

Brother Cadfael's sandals padded soundlessly over the tiled floor after her, keeping well back in case she should look round, though here within he was reasonably sure she would not. The great parish door was unlatched, she had only to draw it open a little way, her slenderness slipped through easily, and since this

was facing due west, no betraying radiance flooded in. Cadfael gave her a moment to turn right or left outside the door, though surely it would be to the right, towards the fairground. What should she have to do in the direction of the river and the town?

She was well in sight when he slid through the doorway and round the corner of the west front, and looked along the Foregate. She did not hurry now, but curbed her pace to that of the early buyers who were sauntering along the highroad, halting at stalls already busy, handling goods, arguing over prices. The last day of the fair was commonly the busiest. There were bargains to be snapped up at the close, and lowered prices. There was bustle everywhere, even at this hour, but the pace of the ambulant shoppers was leisurely. Emma matched hers to it, as though she belonged among them, but for all that, she was making her way somewhere with a purpose. Cadfael followed at a respectful distance.

Only once did she speak to anyone, and then she chose the holder of one of the larger stalls, and it seemed that she was asking him for directions, for he turned and pointed ahead along the street, and towards the abbey wall. She thanked him, and went on in the direction he had indicated, and now she quickened her pace. Small doubt that she had known all along to whom she was bound; apparently she had not known precisely where to find him. Now she knew. By this time all the chief merchants gathered here knew where to find one another.

Emma had come to a halt, almost at the end of the Foregate, where a half-dozen booths were backed into the abbey wall. It seemed that she had arrived at her destination, yet now stood hesitant, gazing a little helplessly, as if what she confronted surprised and baffled her. Cadfael drew nearer. She was frowning doubtfully at the last of the booths, backed into a

corner between buttress and wall. Cadfael recognised it; a lean, suspicious face had peered out from that hatch as the sheriff's officers had hoisted Turstan Fowler on to a board and borne him away to an abbey cell on the eve of the fair. The booth of Euan of Shotwick. Here they came again, those imagined gloves, so feelingly described, so soon stolen!

And Emma was at a loss, for the booth was fast-closed, every panel sealed, and business all around in full swing. She turned to the nearest neighbour, clearly questioning, and the man looked, and shrugged, and shook his head. What did he know? There had been no sign of life there since last night, perhaps the glover had sold out and departed.

Cadfael drew nearer. Beneath the austere white wimple, so sharp a change from the frame of blue-black hair, Emma's young profile looked even more tender and vulnerable. She did not know what to do. She advanced a few steps and raised a hand, as though she would knock at the closed shutter, but then she wavered and drew back. From across the street a brawny butcher left his stall, patted her amiably on the shoulder, and did the knocking for her lustily, then stood to listen. But there was no move from within.

A large hand clapped Cadfael weightily on the back, and the cavernous voice of Rhodri ap Huw boomed in his ear in Welsh: 'What's this, then? Master Euan not open for trade? That I should see the day! I never knew him to miss a sale before, or any other thing to his advantage.'

'The stall's deserted,' said Cadfael. 'The man may have left for home.'

'Not he! He was there past midnight, for I took a turn along here to breathe the cool before going to my inn, and there was a light burning inside there then.' No gleam from within now, though the slanting sunlight might well pale it into invisibility. But no, that

was not so, either. The chinks between shutter and frame were utterly dark.

It was all too like what Roger Dod had found at another booth, only one day past. But there the booth had been barred from within, and the bar hoisted clear with a dagger. Here there was a lock, to be mastered from within or without, and certainly no visible key.

'This I do not like,' said Rhodri ap Huw, and strode forward to try the door, and finding it, as was expected, locked, to peer squint-eyed through the large keyhole. 'No key within,' he said shortly over his shoulder, and peered still. 'Not a movement in there.' He had Cadfael hard on his heels by then, and three or four others closing in. Give me room!'

Rhodri clenched the fingers of both hands in the edge of the door, set a broad foot against the timber wall, and hauled mightily, square shoulders gathered in one great heave. Wood splintered about the lock, small flinders flying like motes of dust, and the door burst open. Rhodri swayed and recovered in recoil, and was first through the opening, but Cadfael was after him fast enough to ensure that the Welshman touched nothing within. They craned into the gloom together, cheek by jowl.

The glover's stall was in chaos, shelves swept clear, goods scattered like grain over the floor. On a straw palliasse along the rear wall his cloak lay sprawled, and on an iron stand beside, a quenched candle sagged in folds of tallow. It took them a few seconds to accustom their eyes to the dimness and see clearly. Tangled in his spilled stock of belts, baldricks, gloves, purses and saddle-bags, Euan of Shotwick lay on his back, knees drawn up, a coarse sacking bag drawn half-over his lean face and greying head. Beneath the hem of the hood his thin-lipped mouth grinned open in a painful rictus, large white teeth staring, and the angle at which his head lay had the horrible suggestion of a broken

wooden puppet.

Cadfael turned and flung up the shutter of the booth, letting in the morning light. He stooped to touch the contorted neck and hollow cheek. 'Cold,' said Rhodri, behind him, not attempting to verify his judgment, which for all that was accurate enough. Euan's flesh was chilling. 'He's dead,' said Rhodri flatly.

'Some hours,' said Cadfael.

In the stress of the moment he had forgotten Emma, but the shriek she gave caused him to swing round in haste and dismay. She had crept in fearfully to peer over the shoulders of the neighbours, and stood staring with eyes wide with horror, both small fists crushed against her mouth. 'Oh, no!' she said in a whisper. 'Not dead! Not he, too ...'

Cadfael took her in his arms, and thrust her bodily before him out of the booth, elbowing the gaping onlookers out of his way. 'Go back! You mustn't stay here. Go back before you're missed, and leave this to me.' He wondered if she even heard his rapid murmur into her ear; she was shaking and white as milk, her blue eyes fixed and huge with shock. He looked about him urgently for someone to whom he could safely confide her, for he doubted if she should be left to return alone, and yet he did not care to leave this scene until Beringar should be here to take charge, or one of the sheriff's sergeants at least. The sudden alarmed shout of recognition that came from the rear of the gathering crowd was a most welcome sound.

'Emma! Emma!' Ivo Corbière came cleaving an unceremonious way through the press, like a sudden vehement wind in a cornfield, bludgeoning the standing stems out of its path. She turned at the call, and a spark of returning life sprang up in her eyes. Thankfully Cadfael thrust her into the young man's arms, which reached eagerly and anxiously to receive

her.

'For God's sake, what has happened to her? What …' His glance flashed from her stunned visage to Cadfael's, and beyond, to the open door with its splintered panel. Over her head his lips framed silently for Cadfael: 'Not again? Another?'

'Take her back,' said Cadfael shortly. 'Take care of her. And tell Hugh Beringar to come. We have sheriff's business here within.'

All the way back along the Foregate, Corbière kept a supporting arm about her, and curbed his long stride to hers, and all the way he poured soothing, caressing words into her ear, while she, until they had almost reached the west door of the church, said nothing at all, simply walked docilely beside him, distantly aware of the lulling sound and the comforting touch. Then suddenly she said: 'He's dead. I saw him, I know.'

'A bare glimpse you had,' said Ivo consolingly. 'It may not be so.'

'No,' said Emma, 'I know the man is dead. How could it happen? Why?'

'There are always such acts, somewhere, robberies, violence and evil. It is sad, but it is not new.' His fingers pressed her hand warmly. 'It is no fault of yours, and alas, there is nothing you or I can do about it. I wish I could make you forget it. In time you will forget.'

'No,' she said. 'I shall never forget this.'

She had meant to return by the church, as she had left, but now it no longer mattered. As far as he or any other was concerned, she had simply set out early to buy some gloves, or at least to view what the glover had to offer. She went in with Ivo by the gatehouse. By the time he had brought her tenderly on his arm to the guest-hall she had regained her composure. There was a little colour in her face again, and her voice was alive, even if its tone indicated that life was painful.

'I'm recovered now, Ivo,' she said. 'You need not trouble for me further. I will tell Hugh Beringar that he is needed.'

'Brother Cadfael entrusted you to me,' said Ivo with gentle and confident authority, 'and you did not reject me. I shall fulfil my errand exactly. As I hope,' he said smiling, 'I may perform any other missions you may care to entrust to me hereafter.'

Hugh Beringar came with four of the sheriff's men, dispersed the crowd that hung expectantly round the booth of Euan of Shotwick, and listened to the accounts rendered by the neighbouring stall-holders, by the butcher from over the road, and by Rhodri ap Huw, for whom Cadfael interpreted sentence by sentence. In no haste to go, for as he said, his best lad was back with the boat from Bridgnorth and competent to take charge of what stock he still had to sell, the Welshman nonetheless showed no unbecoming desire to linger, once his witness was taken. Imperturbable and all-beholding, he ambled away at the first indication that the law had done with him. Others, more persistent, hung about the booth in a silent, watchful circle, but were kept well away from earshot. Beringar drew the door to. The opened hatches gave light enough.

'Can I take the man's account for fair and true?' asked Hugh, casting a glance after Rhodri's retreating back. There was no backward glance from the Welshman, his assurance was absolute.

'To the letter, for all that happened here from the time I came on the scene. He's an excellent observer, there's little he misses of what concerns him, or may concern him, and what does not. He does business, too, his trade here is no pretext. But it may be only half his business that we see.'

There were only the two of them within there now,

two living and the dead man. They stood one either side of him, drawn back to avoid disturbing either his body or the litter of leatherwork scattered about and over him.

'He says there was a light showing through the chinks here past midnight,' said Beringar. 'The light is quenched now, not burned out. And if he locked his door after closing the booth for the night ...'

'As he would,' said Cadfael. 'Rhodri's account of him rings true. A man complete in himself, trusting no one, able to take care of himself, until now. He would have locked his door.'

'Then he also unlocked it, to let in his murderer. The lock never was forced until now, as you saw. Why should a wary man unlock his door to anyone in the small hours?'

'Because he was expecting someone,' said Cadfael, 'though not the someone who came. Because, it may be, he had been expecting someone all these three days, and was relieved when the expected message came at last.'

'So relieved that he ceased to be cautious? Given your Welshman's estimate of him, I should doubt it.'

'So should I,' agreed Cadfael, 'unless there was a private word he was waiting for, and it was known and given. A name, perhaps. For you see, Hugh, I think he was already well aware that the one he had expected to deliver the message was never going to tap at his door by night, or stop in the Foregate to pass the time with him.'

'You mean,' said Hugh, 'Thomas of Bristol, who is dead.'

'Who else? How many strange chances can come together, all against what is likely, or even possible? A merchant is killed, his barge searched, his booth searched, then, dear God, his coffin! I have not yet had time, Hugh, to tell you of that.' He told it now. He had

150

the rose-petal in the breast of his habit, wrapped in a scrap of linen; it still spoke as eloquently as before. 'You may trust my eyes, I know it did not fall earlier, I know it has been in the coffin with him. Now that same man's niece makes occasion to come by stealth to this glover's stall, only to find the glover dead like her uncle. It is a long list of assaults upon all things connected with Thomas of Bristol. Now, since this unknown treasure was not found even in his coffin, for safe-conduct back to Bristol in default of delivery, the next point of search has been here – where Master Thomas should have delivered it.'

'They would need to have foreknowledge of that.'

'Or good reason to guess aright.'

'By your witness,' said Hugh, pondering, 'the coffin was opened and closed between Compline and Matins. Before midnight. When would you say, Cadfael – your experience is longer than mine – when would you say this man died?'

'In the small hours. By the second hour after midnight, I judge, he was dead. After the coffin, it seems, they were forced to the conclusion that somehow, for all they had a watch on Master Thomas from his arrival, and disposed of him before ever the fair started, yet somehow he, or someone else on his behalf, must have slipped through their net, and delivered the precious charge. This poor soul certainly opened his door last night to someone he believed had business with him. The mention of a privileged name … a password … He let in his murderer, but what he had expected was the thing promised.'

'Then even now,' said Hugh sharply, 'with two murders on their souls, they have not what they wanted. He thought they were bringing it. They trusted to find it here. And neither of them had it. Both were deceived.' He brooded with a brown fist clamping his jaw, and his black brows down-drawn in

unaccustomed solemnity. 'And Emma came here ... by stealth.'

'She did. Not every man,' said Cadfael, 'has your view of women, or mine. Most of your kind, most of mine, would never dream of looking in a woman's direction to find anything of importance in hand. Especially a mere child, barely grown. Not until every other road was closed, and they were forced to notice a woman there in the thick of the matter. Who just might be what they sought.'

'And who has now betrayed herself,' said Hugh grimly. 'Well, at least she reached the guest-hall safely, thanks to Corbière. I have left her with Aline, very shaken, for all her strength of will, and she will not stir a step this day unguarded. That I can promise. Between us I think we can take care of Emma. Now let's see if this poor wretch has anything to tell us that we don't yet know.'

He stooped and drew back the coarse sack that covered half the glover's narrow face, from eyebrow on one side to jaw on the other. A broken bruise in the greying hair above the left temple indicated a right-handed blow as soon as the door was opened to his visitor, meant to stun him, probably, until he could be muffled in the sack and gagged like Warin. Here it was a case of gaining entry and confronting a wide-awake man, not a timid sleeper.

'Much the same manner as the other one,' said Cadfael, 'and I doubt if they ever meant to kill. But he was not so easily put out of the reckoning. He put up a fight. And his neck is broken. By the look of it, one made round behind him to secure this blindfold, and in the struggle he gave them, tried all too hard to haul him backwards by it. He was wiry and agile, but his bones were aging, and too brittle to sustain it. I don't think it was intended. We should have found him neatly bound and still alive, like Warin, if he had not

fought them. Once they knew he was dead, they made their search in haste, and left all as it fell.'

Beringar brushed aside the light tangle of girdles and straps and gloves that littered the floor and lay over the body. Euan's right arm was covered from the elbow down by the skirts of his own gown, kicked out of the way of the searchers in their hunt. When the folds were drawn down Hugh let out a sharp whistle of surprise, for in the dead man's hand was a long poniard, the naked blade grooved, and ornamented with gilding near the hilt. At his belt, half-hidden now under his right hip, the scabbard lay empty.

'A man of his hands! And see, he's marked one of them for us!' There was blood on the point of the blade, and drawn up by the grooving for some three fingers' breadth in two thin crimson lines, now drying to black.

'Rhodri ap Huw said of him,' Cadfael remembered, 'that he was a solitary soul who trusted nobody – his own porter and his own watchman. He said he wore a weapon, and knew how to use it.' He went on his knees beside the body, and cleared away the debris that still lay about it, eyeing and handling from head to foot. 'You'll have him away to the castle, I suppose, or the abbey, and look him over more carefully, but I do believe the only blood he's lost is this smear on his brow. This on the dagger is not his.'

'If only we could as easily say whose it is!' said Hugh dryly, sitting on his heels with the nimbleness of the young on the other side of the body. Brother Cadfael eased creaky elderly knees on the hard boards, and briefly envied him. The young man lifted the stiffening arm, and tested the grip of the clenched fingers. 'He holds fast!' It took him some effort to loosen the convulsive grasp enough to slip the hilt of the dagger free. In the slanting light from the open hatch something gleamed briefly, waving at the tip of

the blade, and again vanished, as motes of dust come and go in gold in bright sunlight. There was also what seemed at first to be a thin encrustation of blood fringing the steel on one edge. Cadfael exclaimed, leaning to point. 'A yellow hair – There it shows again!' The flashing gleam curled and twisted as Hugh turned the dagger in his hand.

'Not a hair, a fine, yellowish thread. Thread of flax, not bleached. This grooving has ripped out a shred of cloth, and the blood has stuck it fast. See!'

A mere wisp of brown material it was, a fringe along the groove that had held it. Narrow as a blade of grass, but when Cadfael carefully took hold of a thread at the end and drew it out straight, it stretched to the length of his hand. The colour, though fouled by dried blood, showed plain at one edge, a light russet-brown; and at the end of the sliver floated gaily the long, fine flax thread, scalloped like a curly hair.

'A sliced tear a hand long,' said Cadfael, 'and ending at a hem, for surely this thread sewed the edging, and the dagger ripped out a length of the stitching.' He narrowed his eyes, and considered, imagining Euan facing the door as he opened it, the instant blow that failed to tame him, and then his rapid drawing of his poniard and striking with it. Almost brow to brow and breast to breast, a man good with his right hand, and his attacker's heart an open target.

'He struck for the heart,' said Cadfael with conviction. 'So would I, or so would I have done once. The other man, surely, slipped behind him and spoiled the stroke, but that is where he aimed. Someone, somewhere, has a torn cotte. It might be in the left breast, or it might be in the sleeve. The man's arms would be raised, reaching to grapple him. I should say the left sleeve, ripping from the hem halfway to the elbow. The sewing thread was caught first, and pulled out a length of stitches.'

Hugh considered that respectfully, and found no fault with it. 'Much of a scratch, would you guess? He did not drip blood to the doorway. It could not have been enough to need much stanching.'

'The sleeve would hold it. Likely only a graze, but a long graze. It will be there to be seen.'

'If we knew where to look!' Hugh gave a short bark of laughter at the thought of sending sergeants about this teeming marketplace to ask every man to roll up his left sleeve and show his arm. 'A simple matter! Still, no reason why you and I, and all the men I can spare and trust, should not be keeping our eyes open all the rest of this day for a torn sleeve – or a newly cobbled one.'

He rose, and turned to beckon his nearest man from the open hatch. 'Well, we'll have him away from here, and do what we can. A word with your Rhodri ap Huw wouldn't come amiss, and I fancy you might get more out of him in his own tongue than ever I should at second hand. If he knows this man so well, prick him on to talk, and bring me what you learn.'

'That I'll do,' said Cadfael, clambering stiffly from his knees.

'I must go first to the castle, and report what we've found. One thing I'll make certain of this time,' said Hugh. 'The sheriff was in no mood to listen too carefully last night, but after this he'll have to turn young Corviser loose on his father's warranty, like the rest of them. It would take a more pig-headed man than Prestcote to believe the lad had any part in the first death, seeing the trail of offences that have followed while he was in prison. He shall eat his dinner at home today.'

Rhodri was not merely willing to spend an hour pouring the fruits of his wisdom and experience into Brother Cadfael's ear, he was hovering with that very

155

thing in mind as soon as the corpse of Euan of Shotwick had been carried away, and the booth closed, with one of the sheriff's men on guard. Though ever-present, he had the gift of being unobtrusive until he chose to obtrude, and then could appear from an unexpected direction, and as casually as if only chance had brought him there.

'No doubt you'll have sold all you brought with you,' said Cadfael, encountering him thus between the stalls, clearly untroubled by business.

'Goods of quality are recognised everywhere,' said Rhodri, sharp eyes twinkling merrily. 'My lads are clearing the last few jars of honey, and the wool's long gone. But I've a half-full bottle there, if you care to share a cup at this hour? Mead, not wine, but you'll be happy with that, being a Welshman yourself.'

They sat on heaped trestles already freed from their annual use by the removal of small tradesmen who had sold out their stock, and set the bottle between them.

'And what,' asked Cadfael, with a jerk of his head towards the guarded booth, 'do you make of that affair this morning? After all that's gone before? Have we more birds of prey this way than usual, do you think? It may be they've taken fright and left the shires where there's still fighting, and we get the burden of it.'

Rhodri shook his shaggy head, and flashed his large white teeth out of the thicket in a grin. 'I would say you've had a more than commonly peaceful and well-mannered fair, myself – apart from the misfortunes of two merchants only. Oh, tonight's the last night, and there'll be a few drunken squabbles and a brawl or two, I daresay, but what is there in that? But chance has played no part in what has happened to Thomas of Bristol. Chance never goes hounding one man for three days through hundreds of his fellows, yet never grazes one of the others.'

'It has more than grazed Euan of Shotwick,'

remarked Cadfael dryly.

'Not chance! Consider, brother! Earl Ranulf of Chester's eyes and ears comes to a Shropshire fair and is killed. Thomas of Bristol, from a city that holds by Earl Robert of Gloucester, comes to the same fair, and is killed the very night of his coming. And after his death, everything he brought with him is turned hither and yon, but precious little stolen, from all I hear.' And certainly he had a way of hearing most of what was said within a mile of him, but at least he had made no mention of the violation of Master Thomas's coffin. Either that had not reached his ears, and never would, or else he had been the first to know of it, and would be the last ever to admit it. The parish door was always open, no need to set foot in the great court or pass the gatehouse. 'Something Thomas brought to Shrewsbury is of burning interest to somebody, it seems to me, and the somebody failed to get hold of it from man, barge or stall. And the next thing that happens is that Euan of Shotwick is also killed in the night, and all his belongings ransacked. I would not say but things were stolen there. They may have learned enough for that, and his goods are small and portable, and why despise a little gain on the side? But for all that – No, two men from opposite ends of a divided country, meeting midway, on important private business? It could be so! Gloucester's man and Chester's man.'

'And whose,' wondered Cadfael aloud, 'was the third man?'

'The third?'

'Who took such an interest in the other two that they died of it. Whose man would he be?'

'Why, there are other factions, and every one of them needs its intelligencers. There's the king's party – they might well feel a strong interest if they noted Gloucester's man and Chester's man attending the

same fair midway between. And not only the king –
there are others who count themselves kings on their
own ground, besides Chester, and they also need to
know what such a one as Chester is up to, and will go
far to block it if it threatens their own profit. And then
there's the church, brother, if you'll take it no offence
is meant to the Benedictines. For you'll have heard by
now that the king has dealt very hardly with some of
his bishops this last few weeks, put up all manner of
clerical backs, and turned his own brother and best
ally, Bishop Henry of Winchester, who's papal legate
into the bargain, into a bitter enemy. Bishop Henry
himself might well have a finger in this pie, though I
doubt if he can have had word of things afoot here in
time, being never out of the south. But Lincoln, or
Worcester – all such lords need to know what's
going on, and for men of influence there are always
plenty of bully-boys for hire, who'll do the labouring
work while their masters sit inviolable at home.'

And so, thought Cadfael, could wealthy men sit
inviolable here in their stalls, in full view of hundreds,
while their hired bully-boys do the dirty work. And this
black Welshman is laying it all out for me plain to be
seen, and taking delight in it, too! Cadfael knew when
he was being deliberately teased! what he could not be
quite sure of was whether this was the caprice of a
blameless but mischievous man, or the sport of a guilty
one taking pleasure in his own immunity and
cleverness. The black eyes sparkled and the white teeth
shone. And why grudge him his enjoyment, if
something useful could yet be gleaned from it?
Besides, his mead was excellent.

'There must,' said Cadfael thoughtfully, 'be others
here from Cheshire, even some from close to Ranulf's
court. You yourself, for instance, come from not so far
away, and are knowledgeable about those parts, and
the men and the mood there. If you are right, whoever

has committed these acts knew where to look for the thing they wanted, once they gave up believing that it was still among the effects of Thomas of Bristol. Now how would they be able to choose, say, between Euan of Shotwick and you? As an instance, of course! No offence!'

'None in the world!' said Rhodri heartily. 'Why, bless you! The only reason I know myself is because I *am* myself, and know I'm not in Ranulf of Chester's employ. But *you* can't know that, not certainly, and neither can any other. There's a small point, of course – Thomas of Bristol, I doubt, spoke no Welsh.'

'And you no English,' sighed Cadfael. 'I had forgotten!'

'There was a traveller from down towards Gloucester stayed overnight at Ranulf's court not a month ago,' mused Rhodri, twinkling happily at his own omniscience, 'a jongleur who got unusual favour, for he was called in to play a stave or two to Ranulf and his lady in private, after they left the hall at night. If Earl Ranulf has an ear for music, it's the first I've heard of it. It would certainly need more than a French virelai to fetch him in for his father-in-law's cause. He would want to know what were the prospects of success, and what his reward might be.' He slanted a radiant smile along his shoulder at Cadfael, and poured out the last of the mead. 'Your health, brother! You, at least, are delivered from the greed for gain. I have often wondered, is there a passion large enough to take its place? I am still in the world myself, you understand.'

'I think there might be,' said Cadfael mildly. 'For truth, perhaps? Or justice?'

Chapter Two

The gaoler unlocked the door of Philip's cell somewhat before noon, and stood back to let the provost enter. Father and son eyed each other hard, and though Geoffrey Corviser continued to look grimly severe, and Philip obdurate and defiant, nevertheless the father was mollified and the son reassured. By and large, they understood each other pretty well.

'You are released to my warranty,' said the provost shortly. 'The charge is not withdrawn, not yet, but you're trusted to appear when called, and until then, let's hope I may get some sensible work out of you.'

'I may come home with you?' Philip sounded dazed; he knew nothing of what had been going on outside, and was unprepared for this abrupt release. Hurriedly he brushed himself down, all too aware that he presented no very savoury spectacle to walk through the town at the provost's side. 'What made them change their mind? There's no one been taken for the murder?' That would clear him utterly in Emma's eyes, no doubts left.

'Which murder?' said his father grimly. 'Never mind now, you shall hear, once we have you out of here.'

'Ay, stir yourself, lad,' advised the goodhumoured warder, jingling his keys, 'before they change their minds again. The rate things are happening at this year's fair, you might find the door slammed again

before you can get through it.'

Philip followed his father wonderingly out of the castle. The noon light in the outer ward fell warm and dazzling upon him, the sky was a brilliant, deep blue, like Emma's eyes when she widened them in anxiety or alarm. It was impossible not to feel elated, whatever reproaches might still await him at home; and hope and the resilience of youth blossomed in him as his father recounted brusquely all that had happened while his son fretted in prison without news.

'Then there have been two attacks upon Mistress Vernold's boat and booth, her goods taken, her men assaulted?' He had quite forgotten his own bedraggled appearance, he was striding towards home with his head up and his visage roused and belligerent, looking, indeed, very much as he had looked when he led his ill-fated expedition across the bridge on the eve of the fair. 'And no one seized for it? Nothing done? Why, she herself may be in danger!' Indignation quickened his steps. 'For God's sake, what's the sheriff about?'

'He has enough to do breaking up unseemly riots by you and your like,' said his father smartly, but could not raise so much as a blush from his incensed offspring. 'But since you want to know, Mistress Vernold is in the guest-hall of the abbey, safe enough, in the care of Hugh Beringar and his lady. You'd do better to be thinking about your own troubles, my lad, and mind your own step, for you're not out of the wood yet.'

'What did I do that was so wrong? I went only one pace beyond what you did yourself the day before.' He did not even sound aggrieved about being judged hard, he made that brief defence only absently, his mind all on the girl. 'Even in the guest-hall she may not be out of reach, if this is all some determined plot against her uncle and all his family.' In the death of one more tradesman at the fair he showed less interest,

161

shocking though it was, since it seemed to have little or nothing to do with the vindictive catalogue of offences against Master Thomas and all his possessions. 'She spoke so fairly,' he said. 'She would not have me accused of worse than I did.'

'True enough! She was a fine, honest witness, no denying it. But no business of yours now, she's well cared for. It's your mother you need to be thinking of, she's been in a fine taking over you all this while, and now they're looking in other directions for the one who did the killing – with one eye still on you, though, mind! – she'll likely take some sweetening. One way or another, you'll get a warm welcome.'

Philip was far beyond minding that, though as soon as he entered the house behind the shoemaker's shop he did indeed get a warm welcome, not one way or another, but both ways at once. Mistress Corviser, who was large, handsome and voluble, looked round from her fireside hob, uttered a muted shriek, dropped her ladle, and came billowing like a ship in full sail to embrace him, shake him, wrinkle her nose at the prison smell of him, abuse him for the damage to his best cotte and hose, box his ears for laughing at her tirade, exclaim lamentably over the dried scar at his temple, and demand that he sit down at once and let her crop the hair that adhered to the matted blood, and clean up the wound. By far the easiest thing to do was to submit to all, and let her talk herself out.

'The trouble and shame you've put us to, the heartaches you've cost me, wretch, you don't deserve that I should feed you, or wash and mend for you. The provost's son in prison, think of our mortification! Are you not ashamed of yourself?' She was sponging away the encrusted blood, and relieved to find so insignificant a scar remaining; but when he said blithely: 'No, mother!' she pulled his hair smartly.

'Then you should be, you good-for-nothing! There,

162

that's not so bad. Now I hope you're going to settle down to work, and make up for all the trouble you've made for us, instead of traipsing about the town egging on other people's sons to mischief with your wild ideas ...'

'They were the same ideas father and all the guild merchant had, mother, you should have scolded them. And you ask those who're wearing my shoes whether there's much amiss with my work.' He was a very good workman, in fact, as she would have asserted valiantly if anyone else had cast aspersions on his diligence and ability. He hugged her impulsively, and kissed her cheek, and she put him off impatiently, with what was more a slap than a caress. 'Get along with you, and don't come moguing me until you're cleared of the worse charge, and have paid your fine for the riot. Now come and eat your dinner!'

It was an excellent dinner, such as she produced on festivals and saints' days. After it, instead of shedding the clothes he had worn day and night in his cell, he shaved carefully, made a bundle of his second-best suit, and left the house with it under his arm.

'*Now* where are you going?' she demanded inevitably.

'To the river, to swim and get clean again.' They had a garden upstream, below the town hall, as many of the burgesses had, for growing their own fruit and vegetables, and there was a small hut there, and a sward where he could dry in the sun. He had learned to swim there, shortly after he learned to walk. He did not tell her where he was going afterwards. It was a pity he would have to present himself in his second-best coat, but in this hot summer weather perhaps he need not put it on at all; in shirt and hose most men look the same, provided the shirt is good linen and well laundered.

The water was not even cold in the sandy shallow by

the garden, but after his meal he did not stay in long, or swim out into deep water. But it was good to feel like himself again, cleansed even of the memory of his failure and downfall. There was a still place under the bank where the water hung almost motionless, and showed him a fair image of his face, and the thick bush of red-brown hair which he combed and straightened with his fingers. He dressed as carefully as he had shaved, and set off back to the bridge, and over it to the abbey. The town's grievance, which he had had on his mind the last time he came this way, was quite forgotten; he had other important business now on the abbey side of Severn.

'There's one here,' said Constance, coming in from the great court with a small, private smile on her lips. 'Who asks to speak with Mistress Vernold. And not a bad figure of a young fellow, either, though still a thought coltish about the legs. He asked very civilly.'

Emma had looked up quickly at the mention of a young man; now that she had gone some way towards accepting what had happened, and coming to terms with a disaster which, after all, she had not caused, she had been remembering words Ivo had used, almost disregarded then in her shocked daze, but significant and warming now.

'Messire Corbière?'

'No, not this time. This one I don't know, but he says his name is Philip Corviser.'

'I know him,' said Aline, and smiled over her sewing. 'The provost's son, Emma, the boy you spoke for in the sheriff's court. Hugh said he would see him set free today. If there's one soul can say he has done no evil to you or any these last two days, he's the man. Will you see him? It would be a kindness.'

Emma had almost forgotten him, even his name, but she recalled the plea he had made for her belief in him.

164

So much had happened between. She remembered him now, unkempt, bruised and soiled, pallid-sick after his drunkenness, but still with a despairing dignity. 'Yes, I remember him. Of course I'll see him.'

Philip followed Constance into the room. Fresh from the river, with damp hair curling thickly about his head, shaven and glowing and in fierce earnest, but without the aggression of the manner she had first seen in him, this was a very different person from the humiliated prisoner of the court. The last look he had given her, chin on shoulder, as he was dragged out ... yes, she saw the resemblance there. He made his reverence to Aline, and then to Emma.

'Madam, I am released on my father's bail. I came to say my thanks to Mistress Emma for speaking so fairly for me, when I had no right to expect goodwill from her.'

'I'm glad to see you free, Philip,' said Aline serenely, 'and looking none the worse. You will like to speak with Emma alone, I daresay, and company other than mine may be good for her, for here we talk nothing but babies.' She rose, folding her sewing carefully to keep the needle in view as she carried it. 'Constantine and I will sit on the bench by the hall door, in the sun. The light is better there, and I am no such expert needlewoman as Emma. You can be undisturbed here.'

Out she went, and they saw a ray of sun from the open outer door sparkle in her piled gold hair, before Constance followed, and closed the door between. The two of them were left, gazing gravely at each other.

'The first thing I wanted to do with freedom,' said Philip, 'was to see you again, and thank you for what you did for me. As I do, with all my heart. There were some who bore witness there who had known me most of my life, and surely had no grudge against me, and yet testified that I had been the first to strike, and done all manner of things I knew I had not done. But you,

165

who had suffered through my act, though God knows I never willed it, you spoke absolute truth for me. It took a generous heart and a fair mind to do so much for an unknown whom you had no cause to love.' He had not chosen that word, it had come naturally in the commonplace phrase, but when he heard it, it raised a blush like fire in his own face, faintly reflected the next moment in hers.

'All I did was to tell the truth of what I had seen,' she said. 'So should we all have done, it's no virtue, but an obligation. It was shame that they did not. People do not think what it is they are saying, or trouble to be clear about what they have seen. But that's all by now. I'm very glad they've let you go. I was glad when Hugh Beringar said they must, taking into account what has been happening, for which you certainly can bear no blame. But perhaps you have not heard ...'

'Yes, I have heard. My father has told me.' Philip sat down beside her in the place Aline had vacated, and leaned towards her earnestly. 'There is some very evil purpose against you and yours, surely, how else to account for so many outrages? Emma, I am afraid for you ... I fear danger threatening even you. I'm grieved for your loss, and all the distress you've suffered. I wish there might be some way in which I could serve you.'

'Oh, but you need not be troubled for me,' she said. 'You see I am in the best and kindest hands possible, and tomorrow the fair will all be over, and Hugh Beringar and Aline will help me to find a safe way to go home.'

'Tomorrow?' he said, dismayed.

'It may not be tomorrow. Roger Dod will take the barge down-river tomorrow, but it may be that I must stay a day or two more. We have to find a party going south by Gloucester, for safe-conduct, and with some other women for company. It may take a day or two.'

Even a day or two would be gold; but after that she would be gone, and he might never see her again. And still, confronted by this cause for unhappiness on his own part, he could only think of her. He could not rid himself of the feeling that she was threatened.

'In only two days, see how many ill things have happened, and always close to you, and what may not still happen in a day or two more? I wish you were safe home this moment,' he said passionately, 'though God knows I'd rather lose my right hand than the sight of you.' He was not even aware that that same right hand had taken possession of her left one, and was clasping it hard. 'At least find me some way of serving you before you go. If nothing more, tell me you know that I never did harm to your uncle ...'

'Oh, yes,' she said warmly, 'that I can, most willingly. I never did truly believe it. You are no such person, to strike a man dead by stealth. I never thought it. But still we don't know who did it! Oh, don't doubt me, I'm sure of *you*. But I wish it could be shown clear to the world, for your sake.'

It was said very prettily and sincerely, and he took it to his heart gratefully, but it was said out of generous fellow-feeling, and nothing deeper, and he was gallingly sure of it while he hugged at least the kindness to him.

'For mine, too,' she said honestly, 'and for the sake of justice. It is not right that a mean murderer should escape his due, and it does aggrieve me that my uncle's death should go unpaid for.'

Find me some way of serving you, he had said; and perhaps she had. There was nothing he would not have undertaken for her; he would have lain over the threshold of any room in which she was, like a dog on guard, if she had needed it, but she did not, she was cared for by the sheriff's own deputy and his lady, and they would watch over her until they saw her safely on

her way home. But when she spoke of the unknown who had slipped a dagger in her uncle's back, her great eyes flared with the angry blue of sapphires, and her face grew marble-clear and taut. Her complaint was his commission. He would achieve something for her yet.

'Emma,' he began in a whisper, and drew breath to commit himself deep as the sea.

The door opened, though neither of them had heard the knock; Constance put her head into the room.

'Messire Corbière waits to see you, when you are free,' she said, and withdrew, but left the door ajar. Evidently Messire Corbière ought not to be kept waiting long.

Philip was on his feet. Emma's eyes had kindled at the name like distant stars, forgetting him. 'You may remember him,' she said, still sparing a morsel of her attention for Philip, 'the young gentleman who came to help us on the jetty, along with Brother Cadfael. He has been very kind to me.'

Philip did remember, though his bludgeoned senses at the time had seen everything distorted; a slender, elegant, assured lordling who leaped a rolling cask to catch her in his arm at the water's edge, and further, to be just to him, had appeared in the sheriff's court and borne out Emma's honest story – even if he had also produced his falconer to testify to the silly threats Philip had been indulging in, drunk as he was, later that evening. Testimony Philip did not dispute, since he knew he had been incapable of clear thought or positive recollection. He recalled his disgusting self, and smarted at the thought. And the young lord with the bright gold crest and athlete's prowess had showed so admirable by contrast.

'I'll take my leave,' said Philip, and allowed her hand to slip out of his, though with reluctance and pain. 'For the journey, and always, I wish you well.'

'So do I you,' she said, and with unconscious cruelty added: 'Will you ask Messire Corbière to come in?'

Never in his life until then had Philip been required to draw himself to his full stature, body and mind. His departure was made with a dignity he had not dreamed he could achieve, and meeting Corbière face to face in the hall, he did indeed bid him within, at Mistress Emma's invitation, very civilly and amiably, while he burned with jealousy inwardly. Ivo thanked him pleasantly, and if he looked him over, did so with interest and respect, and with no apparent recollection of ever having seen him in less acceptable circumstances.

No one would have guessed, thought Philip, marching out into the sunshine of the great court, that a working shoemaker and a landed lord rubbed shoulders there. Well, he may have several manors in Cheshire and one in Shropshire, and be distant kin of Earl Ranulf, and welcome at his court; but I have something I can try to do for her, and I have a craft as honourable as his noble blood, and if I succeed, whether she comes my way or no, she'll never forget me.

Brother Cadfael came in at the gatehouse after some hours of fruitless prowling about the fair and the riverside. Among hundreds of men busy about their own concerns, the quest of a gashed sleeve, or one recently and hastily mended, is much the same as hunting one straw in a completed stack. His trouble was that he knew no other way to set about it. Moreover, the hot and settled weather continued unbroken, and most of those about the streets and the stalls were in their shirt-sleeves. There was a point there, he reflected. The glover's dagger had drawn blood, therefore it had reached the skin, but never a thread of white or unbleached linen had it brought

away with the sliver of brown cloth. If the intruder had worn a shirt, he had worn it with sleeves rolled up, and it had emerged unscathed, and could now cover his graze, and if the wound had needed one, his bandage. Cadfael returned to tend the few matters needing him in his workshop, and be ready for Vespers in good time, more because he was at a loss how to proceed than for any other reason. An interlude of quiet and thought might set his wits working again.

In the great court his path towards the garden happened to cross Philip's from the guest-hall to the gatehouse. Deep in his own purposes, the young man almost passed by unnoticing, but then he checked sharply, and turned to look back.

'Brother Cadfael!' Cadfael swung to face him, startled out of just as deep a preoccupation. 'It is you!' said Philip. 'It was you who spoke for me, after Emma, in the sheriff's court. And I knew you then for the one who came to help me to my feet and out of trouble, when the sergeants broke up the fight on the jetty. I never had the chance to thank you, brother, but I do thank you now.'

'I fear the getting you out of trouble didn't last the night,' said Cadfael ruefully, looking this lanky youngster over with a sharp eye, and approving what he saw. Whether it was time spent in self-examination in the gaol, or time spent more salutarily still in thinking of Emma, Philip had done a great deal of growing up in a very short time. 'I'm glad to see you about again among us, and none the worse.'

'I'm not clear of the load yet,' said Philip. 'The charge still stands, even the charge of murder has not been withdrawn.'

'Then it stands upon one leg only,' said Cadfael heartily, 'and may fall at any moment. Have you not heard there's been another death?'

'So they told me, and other violence, also. But surely

this last bears no connection with the rest? Until this, all was malice against Master Thomas. This man was a stranger, and from Chester.' He laid a hand eagerly on Cadfael's sleeve. 'Brother, spare me some minutes. I was not very clear in my wits that night, now I need to know – all that I did, all that was done to me. I want to trace every minute of an evening I can barely piece together for myself.'

'And no wonder, after that knock on the head. Come and sit in the garden, it's quiet there.' He took the young man by the arm, and turned him towards the archway through the pleached hedge, and sat him down on the very seat, had Philip known it, where Emma and Ivo had sat together the previous day. 'Now, what is it you have in mind? I don't wonder your memory's hazy. That's a good solid skull you have on you, and a blessedly thick thatch of hair, or you'd have been carried away on a board.'

Philip scowled doubtfully into distance between the roses, hesitated how much to say, how much to keep painfully to himself, caught Brother Cadfael's comfortably patient eye, and blurted: 'I was coming now from Emma. I know she is in better care than I could provide her, but I have found one thing, at least, that might still be done for her. She wants and needs to see the man who killed her uncle brought to justice. And I mean to find him.'

'So does the sheriff, so do all his men,' said Cadfael, 'but they've had little success as yet.' But he did not say it in reproof or discouragement, but very thoughtfully. 'So, for that matter, do I, but I've done no better. One more mind probing the matter could just as well be the mind that uncovers the truth. Why not? But how will you set about it?'

'Why, if I can prove – *prove*! – that I did not do it, I may also rub up against something that will lead me to the man who did. At least I can make a start by trying

to follow what happened to me that night. Not only for my own defence,' he said earnestly, 'but because it seems to me that I gave cover to the deed by what I had begun, and whoever did it may have had me and my quarrel in mind, and been glad of the opening I made for him, knowing that when murder came of the night, the first name that would spring to mind would be mine. So whoever he may be, he must have marked my comings and goings, or I could be no use to him. If I had been with ten friends throughout, I should have been out of the reckoning, and the sheriff would have begun at once to look elsewhere. But I was drunk, and sick, and took myself off alone to the river for a long time, so much I do know. Long enough for it to have been true. And the murderer knew it.'

'That is sound thinking,' agreed Cadfael approvingly. 'What, then, do you mean to do?'

'Begin from the riverside, where I got my clout on the head, and follow my own scent until I get clear what's very unclear now. I do remember what happened there, as far as you hauling me out of the way of the sheriff's men, and then being hustled away between two others, but my legs were grass and my wits were muddied, and I can't for my life recall who they were. It's a place to start, if you knew them.'

'One of them was Edric Flesher's journeyman,' said Cadfael. 'The other I've seen, though I don't know his name, a big, sturdy young fellow twice your width, with tow-coloured hair …'

'John Norreys!' Philip snapped his fingers. 'I seem to recall him later in the night. It's enough, I'll begin with them, and find out where they left me, and how – or where I shook them off, for so I might have done, I was no fit company for Christians.' He rose, draping his coat over one shoulder. 'That whole evening I'll unravel, if I can.'

'Good lad!' said Cadfael heartily. 'I wish you success

with all my heart. And if you're going to be threading your way through a few of the ale-houses of the Foregate, as you seem to have done that night, keep your eyes open on my behalf, will you? If you can find your murderer, you may very well also be finding mine.' Carefully and emphatically he told him what to look for. 'An arm raising a flagon, or spread over a table, may show you what I'm seeking. The left sleeve sliced open for a hand's-length from the cuff of a russet-brown coat, that was sewn with a lighter linen thread. It would be on the underside of the arm. Or where arms are bared, look for the long scratch the knife made when it slit the sleeve, or for the binding that might cover it if it still bleeds. But if you find him, don't challenge him or say word to him, only bring me, if you can, his name and where to find him again.'

'This was the glover's slayer?' asked Philip, marking the details with grave nods of his brown head. 'You think they may be one and the same?'

'If not the same, well known to each other, and both in the same conspiracy. Find one, and we shall be very close to the other.'

'I'll keep a good watch, at any rate,' said Philip, and strode away purposefully towards the gatehouse to begin his quest.

Chapter Three

Afterwards Brother Cadfael pondered many times over what followed, and wondered if prayer can even have a retrospective effect upon events, as well as influencing the future. What had happened had already happened, yet would he have found the same situation if he had not gone straight into the church, when Philip left him, with the passionate urge to commit to prayer the direction of his own efforts, which seemed to him so barren? It was a most delicate and complex theological problem, never as far as he knew, raised before, or if raised, no theologian had ventured to write on the subject, probably for fear of being accused of heresy.

Howbeit, the urgent need came over him, since he had lost some offices during the day, to recommit his own baffled endeavours to eyes that saw everything, and a power that could open all doors. He chose the transept chapel from which Master Thomas's coffin had been carried that morning, resealed into sanctity by the Mass sung for him. He had time, now, to kneel and wait, having busied himself thus far in anxious efforts like a man struggling up a mountain, when he knew there was a force that could make the mountain bow. He said a prayer for patience and humility, and then laid that by, and prayed for Emma, for the soul of Master Thomas, for the child that should be born to Aline and Hugh, for young Philip and the parents who

had recovered him, for all who suffered injustice and wrong, and sometimes forgot they had a resource beyond the sheriff.

Then it was high time for him to rise from his knees, and go and see to his primary duty here, whatever more violent matters clamoured for his attention. He had supervised the herbarium and the manufactory derived from it, for sixteen years, and his remedies were relied upon far beyond the abbey walls; and though Brother Mark was the most devoted and uncomplaining of helpers, it was unkind to leave him too long alone with such a responsibility. Cadfael hastened towards his workshop with a lightened heart, having shifted his worries to broader shoulders, just as Brother Mark would be happy to do on his patron's arrival.

The heavy fragrance of the herb-garden lay over all the surrounding land, after so many hours of sunshine and heat, like a particular benediction meant for the senses, not the soul. Under the eaves of the workshop the dangling bunches of dried leafage rustled and chirped like nests of singing birds in waves of warmed air, where there was hardly any wind. The very timbers of the hut, dressed with oil against cracking, breathed out scented warmth.

'I finished making the balm for ulcers,' said Brother Mark, making dutiful report, and happily aware of work well done. 'And I have harvested all the poppy-heads that were ripe, but I have not yet broken out the seed, I thought they should dry in the sun a day or two yet.'

Cadfael pressed one of the great heads between his fingers, and praised the judgment. 'And the angelica water for the infirmary?'

'Brother Edmund sent for it half an hour ago. I had it ready. And I had a patient,' said Brother Mark, busy stacking away on a shelf the small clay dishes he used

175

for sorting seeds, 'earlier on, soon after dinner. A groom with a gashed arm. He said he did it on a nail in the stables, reaching down harness, though it looked like a knife-slash to me. It was none too clean, I cleansed it for him, and dressed it with some of your goose-grass unguent. They were gambling with dice up there in the loft last night, I daresay it came to a fight, and somebody drew on him. He'd hardly admit to that.' Brother Mark dusted his hands, and turned with a smile to report for the sum of his stewardship. 'And that's all. A quiet afternoon, you need not have worried.' At sight of Cadfael's face his brows went up comically, and he asked in surprise: 'Why are you staring like that? Nothing there, surely, to open your eyes so wide.'

My mouth, too, thought Cadfael, and shut it while he reflected on the strangeness of human effort, and the sudden rewards that fell undeserved. Not undeserved, perhaps, in this case, since this had fallen to Brother Mark, who modestly made no demands at all.

'Which arm was gashed?' he asked, further baffling Brother Mark, who naturally could not imagine why that should matter.

'The left. From here, the outer edge of the wrist, down the underside of the forearm. Almost to the elbow. Why?'

'Had he his coat on?'

'Not when I saw him,' said Mark, smiling at the absurdity of this catechism. 'But he had it over his sound arm. Is that important?'

'More than you know! But you shall know, later, I am not playing with you. Of what colour was it? And did you see the sleeve that should cover that arm?'

'I did. I offered to stitch it for him – I had little to do just then. But he said he'd already cobbled it up, and so he had, very roughly, and with black thread. I could

176

have done better for him, the original was unbleached linen thread. The colour? Reddish dun, much like most of the grooms and men-at-arms wear, but a good cloth.'

'Did you know the man? Not one of our own abbey servants?'

'No, a guest's man,' said Brother Mark, patient in his bewilderment. 'Not a word to his lord he said! It was one of Ivo Corbière's grooms, the older one, the surly fellow with the beard.'

Gilbert Prestcote himself, unescorted and on foot, had taken an afternoon turn about the fairground to view the public peace with his own eyes, and was in the great court on his way back to the town, conferring with Hugh Beringar, when Cadfael came in haste from the garden with his news. When the blunt recital was ended, they looked at him and at each other with blank and wary faces.

'Corbière's within at this moment,' said Hugh, 'and I gather from Aline has been, more than an hour. Emma has him dazed, I doubt if he's had any other thought, these last two days. His men have been running loose much as they pleased, provided the work was done. It could be the man.'

'His lord has the right to be told,' said Prestcote. 'Households grow lax when they see the country torn, and their betters flouting law. There's nothing been said or done to alarm this fellow, I take it? He has no reason to make any move? And surely he values the shelter of a name like Corbière.'

'No word has been said to any but you,' said Cadfael. 'And the man may be telling the truth.'

'The tatter of cloth,' said Hugh, 'I have here on me. It should be possible to match or discard.'

'Ask Corbière to come,' said the sheriff.

Hugh took the errand to himself, since Ivo was a

177

guest in his rooms. While they waited in braced silence, two of the abbey's men-at-arms came in at the gatehouse with unstrung long-bows, and Turstan Fowler between them with his arbalest, the three of them hot, happy and on excellent terms. On the last day of the fair there were normally matches of many kinds, wrestling, shooting at the butts along the river meadows, long-bow against cross-bow, though the long-bow here was usually the short bow of Wales, drawn to the breast, not the ear. The six-foot weapon was known, but a rarity. There were races, too, and riding at the quintain on the castle tiltyard. Trade and play made good companions, and especially good profits for the ale-houses, where the winners very soon parted with all they had won, and the losers made up their losses.

These three were wreathed together in argumentative amity, passing jokes along the line; each seemed to be vaunting his own weapon. They had strolled no more than halfway across the court when Hugh emerged from the guest-hall with Ivo beside him. Ivo saw his archer crossing towards the stable-yard, and made him an imperious signal to stay.

There was no fault to be found with Turstan's service since his disastrous fall from grace on the first evening; motioned to hold aloof but remain at call, he obeyed without question, and went on amusing himself with his rivals. He must have done well at the butts for they seemed to be discussing his arbalest, and he braced a foot in the metal stirrup and drew the string to the alert for them, demonstrating that he lost little in speed against their instant arms. No doubt the dispute between speed and range would go on as long as both arms survived. Cadfael had handled both in his time, as well as the eastern bow, the sword, and the lance of the mounted man. Even at this grave moment he spared a long glance for the amicable wrangle going on

a score of paces away.

Then Ivo was there among them, and shaken out of his easy confidence and grace. His face was tense, his dark eyes large and wondering under the proudly raised auburn brows and golden cap of curls. 'You wanted me, sir? Hugh has not been specific, but I took it this was urgent matter.'

'It is a matter of a man of yours,' said the sheriff.

'My men?' He shook a doubtful head, and gnawed his lip. 'I know of nothing … Not since Turstan drank himself stiff and stupid, and he's been a penitent and close to home ever since, and he did no harm then to any but himself, the dolt. But they all have leave to go forth, once their work's done. The fair is every man's treat. What's amiss concerning my men?'

It was left to the sheriff to tell him. Ivo paled visibly as he listened, his ruddy sunburn sallowing. 'Then my man is suspect of the killing I brushed arms with – Good God, this very morning! That you may know, his name is Ewald, he comes from a Cheshire manor, and his ancestry is northern, but he never showed ill traits before, though he is a morose man, and makes few friends. I take this hard. I brought him here.'

'You may resolve it,' said Prestcote.

'So I may. His mouth tightened. 'And will! About this hour I appointed to ride, my horse has had little exercise here, and he'll be bearing me hence tomorrow. Ewald is the groom who takes care of him. He should be saddling him up in the stables about this time. Shall I send for him? He'll be expecting my summons. No!' he interrupted his own offer, his brows contracting. 'Not send for him, go for him myself. If I sent Turstan, there, you might suspect that a servant would stand by a servant, and give him due warning. Do you think he has not been watching us, this short while? And do you think this colloquy has the look of simple talk among us?'

Assuredly it had not. Turstan, dangling his braced bow, had lost interest in enlightening his rivals, and they, sensing that there was something afoot that did not concern them, were drawing off and moving away, though with discreet backward glances until they vanished into the grange court.

'I'll go myself,' said Ivo, and strode away towards the stable-yard at a great pace. Turstan, hesitant, let him pass, since he got no word out of him in passing, but then turned and hurried on his heels, anxiously questioning. For a little way he followed, and they saw Ivo turn his head and snap some hasty orders at his man. Chastened, Turstan drew back and returned towards the gatehouse, and stood at a loss.

Some minutes passed before they heard the sharp sound of hooves on the cobbles of the stable-yard, brittle and lively. Then the tall, dusky bay, glowing like the darkest of copper and restive for want of work, danced out of the yard with the stocky, bearded groom holding his bridle, and Ivo stalking a yard or so ahead.

'Here is my man Ewald,' he said shortly, and stood back, as Cadfael noted, between them and the open gateway. Turstan Fowler drew nearer by discreet inches, and silently, sharp eyes flicking from one face to another in quest of understanding. Ewald stood holding the bridle, uneasy eyes narrowed upon Prestcote's unrevealing countenance. When the horse, eager for action, stirred and tossed his head, the groom reached his left hand across to take the bridle, and slid the right one up to the glossy neck, caressing by rote, but without for an instant shifting his gaze.

'My lord says your honour has something to ask me,' he said in a slow and grudging voice.

Under his left forearm the cobbled mend in his sleeve showed plainly, the cloth puckered between large stitches, and the end of linen thread shivered in sun and breeze like a gnat dancing.

'Take off your coat,' ordered the sheriff. And as the man gaped in real or pretended bewilderment: 'No words! Do it!'

Slowly Ewald slipped out of his coat, somewhat awkwardly because he was at pains to retain his hold on the bridle. The horse had been promised air and exercise, and was straining towards the gate, the way to what he desired. He had already shifted the whole group, except Cadfael, who stood mute and apart, a little nearer the gate.

'Turn back your sleeve. The left.'

He gave one wild glance round, then lowered his head like a bull, set his jaw, and did it, his right arm through the bridle as he turned up the coarse homespun to the elbow. Brother Mark had bound up the gash in a strip of clean linen over his dressing. The very cleanness of it glared.

'You have hurt yourself, Ewald?' said Prestcote, quietly grim.

He has his chance now, thought Cadfael, if he has quick enough wit, to change his story and say outright that he took a knife-wound in a common brawl, and told Brother Mark the lie about a nail simply to cover up the folly. But no, the man did not stop to think; he had his story, and trusted it might still cover him. Yet if Mark, on handling the wound, could tell a cut from a tear, so at the merest glance could Gilbert Prescote.

'I did it on a nail in the stables, my lord, reaching down harness.'

'And tore your sleeve through at the same time? It was a jagged nail, Ewald. That's stout cloth you wear.' He turned abruptly to Hugh Beringar. 'You have the slip of cloth?'

Hugh drew out from his pouch a folded piece of vellum, and opened it upon the insignificant strip of fabric, that looked like nothing so much as a blade of dried grass fretted into fibres and rotting at the edge.

Only the wavy tendril of linen thread showed what it really was, but that was enough. Ewald drew away a pace, so sharply that the horse backed off some yards towards the gateway, and the groom turned and took both hands to hold and soothe the beast. Ivo had to spring hurriedly backwards to avoid the dancing hooves.

'Hand here your coat,' ordered Prestcote, when the bay was appeased again, and willing to stand, though reluctantly.

The groom looked from the tiny thing he had recognised to the sheriff's composed but unrelenting face, hesitated only a moment, and then did as he was bid, to violent effect. He swung back his arm and flung the heavy cotte into their faces, and with a leap was over the bay's back and into the saddle. Both heels drove into the glossy sides, and a great shout above the pricked ears sent the horse surging like a flung lance for the gateway.

There was no one between but Ivo. The groom drove the bay straight at him, headlong. The young man leaped aside, but made a tigerish spring to grasp at the bridle as the horse hurtled by, and actually got a hold on it and was dragged for a moment, until the groom kicked out at him viciously, breaking the tenuous hold and hurling Ivo out of the way, to fall heavily and roll under the feet of the sheriff and Hugh as they launched themselves after the fugitive. Out at the gateway and round to the right into the Foregate went Ewald, at a frantic gallop, and there was no one mounted and ready to pursue, and for once the sheriff was without escort or archers.

But Ivo Corbière was not. Turstan Fowler had rushed to help him to his feet, but Ivo waved him past, out into the Foregate, and heaving himself breathlessly from the ground, with grazed and furious face ran limping after. The little group of them stood in the

middle of the highroad, helplessly watching the bay and his rider recede into distance, and unable to follow. He had killed, and he would get clear away, and once some miles from Shrewsbury, he could disappear into forest and lie safe as a fox in its lair.

In a voice half-choked with rage, Ivo cried: 'Fetch him down!'

Turstan's arbalest was still braced and ready, and Turstan was used to jumping to his command. The quarrel was out of his belt, fitted and loosed, in an instant, the thrum and vibration of its flight made heads turn and duck and women shriek along the Foregate.

Ewald, stooped low over the horse's neck, suddenly jerked violently and reared up with head flung high. His hands slackened from the reins and his arms swung lax on either side. He seemed to hang for a moment suspended in air, and then swung heavily sidewise, and heeled slowly out of the saddle. The bay, startled and shocked, ran on wildly, scattering the frightened vendors and buyers on both sides, but his flight was uncertain now, and confused by this sudden lightness. He would not go far. Someone would halt and soothe him, and lead him back.

As for the groom Ewald, he was dead before ever the first of the appalled stallholders reached him, dead, probably, before ever he struck the ground.

Chapter Four

he was my villein,' asserted Ivo strenuously, in the room in the gatehouse where they had brought and laid the body, 'and I enjoy the power of the high justice over my own, and this one had forfeited life. I need make no defence, for myself or my archer, who did nothing more than obey my order. We have all seen, now, that this fellow's wound is no tear from a nail, but the stroke of a dagger, and the fret you took from the glover's blade matches this sleeve past question. Is there doubt in any mind that this was a murderer?'

There was none. Cadfael was there with them in the room, at Hugh's instance, and he had no doubts at all. This was the man Euan of Shotwick had marked, before he himself died. Moreover, some of Euan of Shotwick's goods and money had been found among the sparse belongings Ewald had left behind him; his saddle-roll held a pouch of fine leather full of coins, and two pairs of gloves made for the hands of girls, presents, perhaps, for wife or sister. This was certainly a murderer. Turstan, who had shot him down, obviously did not consider himself anything of the kind, any more than one of Prestcote's archers would have done, had he been given the order to shoot. Turstan had taken the whole affair stolidly, as none of his business apart from his duty to his lord, and gone away to his evening meal with an equable appetite.

'I brought him here,' said Ivo bitterly, wiping smears of blood from his grazed cheek. 'It is my honour he has offended, as well as the law of the land. I had a right to avenge myself.'

'No need to labour it,' said Prestcote shortly. 'The shire has been saved a trial and a hanging, which is to the good, and I don't know but the wretch himself might prefer this way out. It was a doughty shot, and that's a valuable man of yours. I never thought it could be done so accurately at that distance.'

Ivo shrugged. 'I knew Turstan's quality, or I would not have said what I did, to risk either my horse or any of the hundreds about their harmless business in the Foregate. I don't know that I expected a death …'

'There's only one cause for regret,' said the sheriff. 'If he had accomplices, he can never now be made to name them. And you say, Beringar, that there were probably two?'

'You're satisfied, I hope,' said Ivo, 'that neither Turstan nor my young groom Arald had any part with him in these thefts?'

Both had been questioned, he had insisted on that. Turstan had been a model of virtue since his one lapse, and the youngster was a fresh-faced country youth, and both had made friends among the other servants and were well liked. Ewald had been morose and taciturn, and kept himself apart, and the revelation of his villainy did not greatly surprise his fellows.

'There's still the matter of the other offences. What do you think? Was it this man in all of them?'

'I cannot get it out of my mind,' said Hugh slowly, 'that Master Thomas's death was the work of one man only. And without reason or proof, by mere pricking of thumbs, I do not believe it was this man. For the rest – I don't know! Two, the merchant's watchman said, but I am not sure he may not be increasing the odds to excuse his own want of valour – or his very good sense,

185

however you look at it. Only one, surely, would enter the barge in full daylight, no doubt briskly, as if he had an errand there, something to fetch or something to bestow. Where there were two, this must surely be one of them. Who the other was, we are still in the dark.'

After Compline Cadfael went to report to Abbot Radulfus all that had happened. The sheriff had already paid the necessary courtesy visit to inform the abbot, but for all that Radulfus would expect his own accredited observer to bring another viewpoint, one more concerned with the repute and the standards of a Benedictine house. In an order which held moderation in all things to be the ground of blessing, immoderate things were happening.

Radulfus listened in disciplined silence to all, and there was no telling from his face whether he deplored or approved such summary justice.

'Violence can never be anything but ugly,' he said thoughtfully, 'but we live in a world as ugly and violent as it is beautiful and good. Two things above all concern me, and one of them may seem to you, brother, a trivial matter. This death, the shedding of this blood, took place outside our walls. For that I am grateful. You have lived both within and without, what must be accepted and borne is the same to you, within or without. But many here lack your knowledge, and for them, and for the peace we strive to preserve here as refuge for others beside ourselves, the sanctity of this place is better unspotted. And the second thing will matter as deeply to you as to me: Was this man guilty? Is it certain he himself had killed?'

'It is certain,' said Brother Cadfael, choosing his words with care, 'that he had been concerned in murder, most likely with at least one other man.'

'Then harsh though it may be, this was justice.' He

186

caught the heaviness of Cadfael's silence, and looked up sharply. 'You are not satisfied?'

'That the man took part in murder, yes, I am satisfied. The proofs are clear. But what is justice? If there were two, and one bears all, and the other goes free, is that justice? I am certain in my soul that there is more, not yet known.'

'And tomorrow all these people will depart about their own affairs, to their own homes and shops, wherever they may be. The guilty and the innocent alike. That cannot be the will of God,' said the abbot, and brooded a while in silence. 'Nevertheless, it may be God's will that it should be taken out of our hands. Continue your vigil, brother, through the morrow. After that others, elsewhere, must take up the burden.

Brother Mark sat on the edge of his cot, in his cell in the dortoire, with his elbows on his knees and his head in his hands, and grieved. From a child he had lived a hard life, privation, brutality and pain were all known to him as close companions until he came into this retreat, at first unwilling. But death was too monstrous and too dark for him, coming thus instant in terror, and without the possibility of grace. To live misused, ill-fed, without respite from labour, was still life, with a sky above it, and trees and flowers and birds around it, colour and season and beauty. Life, even so lived, was a friend. Death was a stranger.

'Child, it is with us always,' said Cadfael, patient beside him. 'Last summer ninety-five men died here in the town, none of whom had done murder. For choosing the wrong side, they died. It falls upon blameless women in war, even in peace at the hands of evil men. It falls upon children who never did harm to any, upon old men, who in their lives have done good to many, and yet are brutally and senselessly slain.

187

Never let it shake your faith that there is a balance hereafter. What you see is only a broken piece from a perfect whole.'

'I know,' said Brother Mark between his fingers, loyal but uncomforted. 'But to be cut off without trial ...'

'So were the ninety-four last year,' said Cadfael gently, 'and the ninety-fifth was murdered. Such justice as we see is also but a broken shred. But it is our duty to preserve what we may, and fit together such fragments as we find, and take the rest on trust.'

'And unshriven!' cried Brother Mark.

'So went his victim also. And he had neither robbed nor killed, or if he had, only God knows of it. There has many a man gone through that gate without a safe-conduct, who will reach heaven ahead of some who were escorted through with absolution and ceremony, and had their affairs in order. Kings and princes of the church may find shepherds and erfs preferred before them, and some who claim they have done great good may have to give place to poor wretches who have done wrong and acknowledge it, and have tried to make amends.'

Brother Mark sat listening, and at least began to hear. Humbly he recognised and admitted the real heart of his grievance. 'I had his arm between my hands, I saw him wince when I cleansed his wound, and I felt his pain. It was only a small pain, but I felt it. I was glad to help him, it was pleasure to anoint the cut with balm, and wrap it clean, and know he was eased. And now he's dead, with a cross-bow bolt through him ...' Briefly and angrily, Brother Mark brushed away tears, and uncovered his accusing face. 'What is the use of mending a man, if he's to be broken within a few hours, past mending?'

'We were speaking of souls,' said Cadfael mildly, 'not mere bodies. and who knows but your touch with

ointment and linen may have mended to better effect
the one that lasts the longer? There's no arrow cleaves
the soul. But there may be balm for it.

Chapter Five

head-down on his own traces, Philip had run his friend John Norreys to earth at last at the butts by the riverside, where the budding archers of the town practised, and together they hunted out Edric Flesher's young journeyman from the yard behind his master's shop. Philip's odyssey on the eve of the fair had begun with these two, who had had him bundled into their arms by Brother Cadfael when the sheriff's men descended on the Gaye.

By their own account, they had hauled him away through the orchards and the narrow lanes behind the Foregate, avoiding the highroads, and sat him down in the first booth that sold drink, to recover his addled wits. And very ungrateful they had found him, as soon as the shock of his blow on the head began to pass, and his legs were less shaky under him.

Furious with himself, he had turned his ill-temper on them, snarled at them, said John tolerantly, that he was capable of looking after himself, and they had better go and warn some of the other stalwarts who had rushed on along the Foregate overturning stalls and scattering goods, before the officers reached them. Which they had taken good-humouredly enough, knowing his head was aching villainously by that time, and had followed him for a while at a discreet distance as he blundered away through the fair-ground, until he turned on them again and

ordered them away. They had stood to watch him, and then shrugged and left him to his own devices, since he would have none of them.

'You had your legs again,' said John reasonably, 'and since you wouldn't let us do anything for you, we thought best to let you go your own way. Let alone, you wouldn't go far, but if we followed, you might do who knows what, out of contrariness.'

'There was another fellow who looked after you a thought anxiously,' said the butcher's man, thinking back, 'when we left that booth with you. Came out after us, and set off the same way you took. He thought you were already helpless drunk, I fancy, and might need helping home.'

'That was kind in him,' said Philip, stiffening indignantly, and meaning that it was damned officious of whoever it was. 'That would be what hour? Not yet eight?'

'Barely. I did hear the bell for Compline shortly after, over the wall. Curious how it carries over all the bustle between.' In the upper air, so it would; people in the Foregate regulated their day by the office bells.

'Who was this who followed me? Did you know him?'

They looked at each other and hoisted indifferent shoulders; among the thousands at a great fair the local people are lost. 'Never seen him before. Not a Shrewsbury man. He may not have been following, to call it that, at all, just heading the same way.'

They told him exactly where he had left them, and the direction he had taken. Philip made his way purposefully to the spot indicated, but in that busy concourse, spreading along the Foregate and filling every open space beyond, he was still without a map. All he knew was that before nine, according to the witness in the sheriff's court, he had been very drunk and still drinking in Wat's tavern, and blurting out hatred and grievance and the intent of vengeance

against Master Thomas of Bristol. The interval it was hard to fill. Perhaps he had made his way there at once, and been well advanced in drink before the stranger noted his threats.

Philip gritted his teeth and set off along the Foregate, so intent on his own quest that he had no ears for anything else, and missed the news that was being busily conveyed back and forth through the fair, with imaginative variations and considerable embellishments before it reached the far corner of the horse-fair. It was news more than two hours old by then, but Philip had heard no word of it, his mind was on his own problem. All round him stalls were being stripped down to trestle and board, and rented booths being locked up, and the keys delivered to abbey stewards. Business was almost put away, but the evening was not yet outworn, there would be pleasure after business.

Walter Renold's inn lay at the far corner of the horse-fair, not on the London highroad, but on the quieter road that bore away north-eastwards. It was handy for the country people who brought goods to market, and at this hour it was full. It went against the grain with Philip even to order a pot of ale for himself while he was on this desperate quest, but ale-houses live by sales, and at least he was so formidably sober now that he could afford the indulgence. The pot-boy who brought him his drink was hardly more than a child, and he did not remember the tow hair and pock-marked face. He waited to speak with Wat himself, when there was a brief interlude of calm.

'I heard they'd let you go free,' said Wat, spreading brawny arms along the table opposite him. 'I'm glad of it. I never thought you'd do harm, and so I told them where they asked. When was it they loosed you?'

'A while before noon.' Hugh Beringar had said he should eat his dinner at home, and so he had, though

192

at a later hour than usual.

'So nobody could point a finger at you over the latest ill-doings. Such a fair as we've had! Good weather and good sales, and good attendance all round, even good behaviour,' said Wat weightily, considering the whole range of his experience of fairs. 'And yet two merchants murdered, the second of them a northern man found only this morning broken-necked in his stall. You'll have heard about that? When did we ever have such happenings! It's not the lads of Shrewsbury, I said when they asked me, that get up to such villainies, you look among the incomers from other parts. We're decent folk hereabouts!'

'Yes, I know of that,' said Philip. 'But it's not that death they pointed at me, it's the first, the Bristol merchant …' North and south had met here, he reflected, fatally for both. Now why should that be? Both the victims strangers from far distances, where some born locally were as well worth plundering.

'This one they could hardly charge to your account,' said Wat, grinning broadly, 'even if you'd been at large so early. It's all past and gone. You hadn't heard? There was a grand to-do along the Foregate, a few hours ago. The murderer's found out red-handed, and made a break for his freedom on his lord's horse, and kicked his lord into the dust on the way. And he's shot down dead as a storm-struck tree, at his lord's orders. A master's shot, they say. The glover's soon avenged. And you'd not heard of it?'

'Not a word! The last I heard they were looking for a man who might have a slit sleeve to show, and a gash in his arm. When was this, then?' It seemed that Brother Cadfael must have found his man, unaided, after all.

'Not an hour before Vespers it must have been. All I heard was the shouting at the abbey end of the Foregate. But they tell me the sheriff himself was there.'

About five in the afternoon, perhaps less than an hour after Philip had left Brother Cadfael and gone back into the town to look for John Norreys. A short hunt that had been, no need any longer for him to cast a narrowed eye at men's sleeves wherever he went. 'And it's certain they got the right man?'

'Certain! The merchant had marked him, and they say there were goods and money from the glover's stall found in his pack. Some groom called Ewald, I heard ...'

A mere sneak-thief, then, who had gone too far. Nothing there to bear on Philip's own quest. He was free to concentrate his mind once again, and even more intently, upon his own pilgrimage. It had begun as a penitential exercise, but was gradually abandoning that aspect. Certainly he had made a fool of himself, but the original impulse on which he had acted, and roused others to act, had not been so foolish, after all, and was nothing to be ashamed of. Only when it collapsed about him in ruins had he thrown good sense to the winds, and indulged his misery like a sulking child.

'Now if only I could find out as certainly who it was did for Master Thomas! It was that night there was grave matter urged against me, and I will own I laid myself open. It's all very well being let out on my father's bail, but no one has yet said I'm clear of the charge. The rest I'll pay my score for, but I want to prove I never did the merchant any violence. I know I was here that night – the eve of the fair, you'll remember? From what hour? I've no recollection of times, myself. According to his men, master Thomas was alive until a third of the hour past nine.'

'Oh, you were here, no question!' Wat could not help grinning at the memory. 'There was noise enough, we were busy, but you made yourself heard! No offence, lad, who hasn't made a fool of himself in his cups from

time to time? It can't have been more than a quarter after eight when you came in, and I doubt you'd had much, up to then.'

Only a quarter after the hour of Compline – then he must have come straight here after shaking off his friends. Not straight, perhaps that was an inappropriate word, but weavingly and unsteadily, though at that rate not calling anywhere else on the way. It was a natural thing to do, to hurry clean through the thick of the fair, and put as much ground as possible between himself and his solicitous companions before calling a halt.

'I tell you what, boy,' said the expert kindly, 'if you'd taken it slowly you'd have been sober enough. But you had to rush the matter. I doubt I've ever seen a fellow put so much down in the time, no wonder your belly turned against it.'

It was not cheering listening, but Philip swallowed it doggedly. Evidently he had been as foolish as he had been dreading, and the archer's account of his behaviour had not been at all exaggerated.

'And was I yelling vengeance against the man who struck me? That's what they said of me.'

'Well, now, I wouldn't go so far as that, and yet it's not too far off the mark, either. Let's say you were not greatly loving him, and no wonder, we could all see the dunt he'd given you. Arrogant and greedy you called him, and a few other things I don't recall, and mark your words, you kept telling us, pride like his was due for a disastrous fall, and soon. That must be what they had in mind who witnessed against you. I never heard word of any going to this hearing from my tavern, not until afterwards. Who were they that testified, then?'

'It was one man,' said Philip. 'Not that I can blame him, it seems he told no lies – indeed, I never thought he had, I know I was the world's fool that night.'

'Why, bless you, lad, with a cracked head a man's

liable to act like one cracked, he has the right. But who's this one man? What with all the incomers at the fair, I had more strangers than known customers of these evenings.'

'It was a man attending one of the abbey guests,' said Philip. 'Turstan Fowler, they said his name was. He said he was here drinking, and went from ale to wine, and then to strong liquor – it seems he ended up as drunk as I was myself, they took him up helpless later, and slung him into a cell at the abbey overnight. A well-set-up fellow, but slouching and unkempt when I saw him in the court. About thirty-five years old, at a guess, sunburned, a bush of brown hair ...'

Wat shook his head, pondering the description. 'I don't know him, not by that, though I've got a rare memory for faces. An ale-house keeper has to have. Ah, well, if he's a stranger he'd no call to give false witness, I suppose he was but honest, and put the worst meaning on your bletherings for want of knowing you.'

'What time was it when I left here?' Philip winced ever at the recollection of the departure, sudden and desperate, with churning stomach and swimming head, and both hands clamped hard over his grimly locked jaw. Barely time to weave a frantic way across the road and into the edge of the copse beyond, where he had heaved his heart out, and then blundered some distance further in cover towards the orchards of the Gaye, and collapsed shivering and retching into the grass, to pass into a sodden sleep. He had not dragged himself out of it until the small hours.

'Why, reckoning from Compline, I'd say an hour had passed, it would be about nine of the clock.'

Thomas of Bristol had set out from his booth to return to his barge only a quarter of an hour or so later. And someone, someone unknown, had intercepted him on the way, dagger in hand. No wonder the

law had looked so narrowly at Philip Corviser, who had reason to resent and hate, and had blundered out of sight and sound of other men around that time, after venting his grievance aloud for all to hear.

Wat rose to go and cope with the custom that was overwhelming his two potboys, and Philip sat brooding with his chin on his fist. Most of the flares must be out by now along the Foregate, most of the stalls packed up and ready for departure. Another balmy summer night, heaven dropping fat blessings on the abbey receipts and the profits of trade, after a lost summer of warfare and a winter of uncertainty. And the town walls still unrepaired, and the streets still broken!

The door stood propped wide on the warm, luminous twilight, and the traffic in and out was brisk. Youngsters came with jugs and pitchers to fetch for their elders, maids tripped in for a measure of wine for their masters, labourers and abbey servants wandered in to slake their thirst between spells of work. Saint Peter's Fair was drawing to its contented and successful close.

Through the open door came a fresh-faced youngster in a fine leather jerkin, and on his heels a sturdy, brown-faced man at least fifteen years older, in the same good livery. It took Philip a long moment of staring to recognise Turstan Fowler, sober, well-behaved, in good odour with his lord and all the world. Still longer to cause him to reflect afresh how he himself must have looked, drunk, if the difference could stretch so far. He watched the little potboy serve them. Wat was busy with others, and the room was full. The end of the fair was always a busy time. Another day, and these same hours would hang heavy and dark.

Philip never quite knew why he turned his head away, and hoisted a wide shoulder between himself and Ivo Corbière's men. He had nothing against either

of them, but he did not want to be recognised and condoled with, or congratulated on his release, or in any way, sympathetic or not, have public attention called to him. He kept his shoulder hunched between, and was glad to have the room so full of people, and most of them strangers.

'Fairs are good business,' remarked Wat, returning to his place and plumping down on the bench with a sigh of pleasure, 'but I wish we could spread them round the rest of the year. My feet are growing no younger, and I've hardly been off them an hour in all, the last three days. What was it we were saying?'

'I was trying to describe for you the fellow who reported me as threatening revenge,' said Philip. 'Cast a look over yonder now, and you'll see the very man. The two in leather who came in together – the elder of the two.'

Wat let his sharp eyes rove, and surveyed Turstand Fowler with apparent disinterest, but very shrewdly. 'Slouching and hangdog, was he? Smart as a new coat now.' His gaze returned to Philip's face. 'That's the man? I remember *him* well enough. I seldom forget a man's face, but his name and condition I've no way of knowing.'

'He can't have looked quite so trim that evening,' said Philip, 'seeing he owned to being well soused. He was lost to the world two hours later, by his own tale.'

'And he said he got it all here?' Wat's eyes had narrowed thoughtfully.

'So he said. "Where I got my skinful" is what he said.'

'Well, let me tell you something interesting, friend ...' Wat leaned confidentially across the table. 'Now I see him, I know how I saw him the last time, for if you'll credit me, he looked much as he looks now. And what's more, now I know of the connection he had with you and your affairs, I can recall small things that happened that night, things I never gave a

198

thought to before, and neither would you have done. He was in here twice that evening, or rather, he was in the doorway once, before he came over the threshold later. In that doorway he stood, and looked round him, a matter of ten minutes or so after you came in. I made nothing of it that he gave you a measuring sort of look, for well he might, you were in full cry then. But look at you he did, and weighed you up, and went away again. And the next we saw of him, it might be half an hour later, he came in and bought a measure of ale, and a big flask of strong geneva liquor, and sat supping his ale quietly, and eyeing you from time to time – as again well he might, it was about then you were greenish and going suspicious quiet. But do you know when he drank up and left, Philip, lad? The minute after you made for the door in a hurry. And his flask under his arm, unopened. Drunk? *Him*? He was stone cold sober when he went out of here.'

'But he took the juniper liquor with him,' pointed out Philip, reasonably. 'He was drunk enough two hours later, there were several of them to swear to that. They had to carry him back to the abbey on a trestle-board.'

'And how much of the juniper spirit did they find remaining? Did they ever mention that? Did they find the flask at all?'

'I never heard mention of it,' owned Philip, startled and doubtful. 'Brother Cadfael was there, I could ask him. But why?'

Wat laid a kindly if patronising hand on his shoulder. 'Lad, it's easy to see you never went beyond wine or ale, and if you'll heed me you'll leave the strong stuff to strong stomachs. I said a large flask, and large I meant. There was a quart of geneva spirits in that bottle! If any man drank that dry in two hours, it wouldn't be dead drunk they'd be carrying him away, it would be plain dead. Or if he did live to tell of it, it

wouldn't be the next day, nor for several after. Sober as the sheriff himself was that fellow when he went out of here on your heels, and why he should want to lie about it is more than I can say, but lie about it he did, it seems. Now you tell me why a man should go to some pains to convict himself of a debauch he never even had, and get himself slung into a cell for recompense. Unless,' added Wat, considering the problem with lively interst, 'it was to get himself out of something worse.'

The elder potboy, a freckled lad born and bred in the Foregate, came by with a cluster of empties in either hand, and paused to nudge Wat in the ribs with an elbow, and lean to his ear.

'Do you know who you have there, master?' A jerk of his head indicated the two in leather jerkins. 'The young one's fellow-groom to the one that got a bolt through him along the Foregate a while ago. And the other – Will Wharton just told me, and he was close by and saw it all! – that's the fellow who loosed the bolt! His comrade in the same price, mark! Should he be here and in such spirits the same night? That's a stronger stomach than mine. "Fetch him down!" says the master, and down the fellow fetches him, sharp and cool. You'd have thought his hand would have shook too much to get near the target, but no! – thump between the shoulders and through to the breast, so Will says. And that's the very man that did it, supping ale like any Christian.'

They were both of them staring at him open-mouthed, and turned away only to stare again, briefly and intently, at Turstan Fowler sitting at ease with his tankard, sturdy legs splayed under the table. It had never even occurred to Philip to ask in whose service the dead malefactor was employed, and perhaps Wat would not have known the name if he had asked. He would have mentioned it else

'That's the man? You're sure?' pressed Philip.

'Will Wharton is sure, and he helped to pick up the poor devil who was killed.'

'Turstan Fowler? The falconer to Ivo Corbière? And Corbière ordered him to shoot?'

'The name I don't know, for neither did Will. Some young lord at the abbey guest-hall. Very handsome sprig, yellow-haired, Will says. Though it's no great blame to him for wanting a murderer and thief stopped in his tracks, granted, and any road, the man had just stolen his horse, and kicked him off into the dust when he tried to halt him. And I suppose when a lord orders, his man had better jump to obey. Still, it's a grim thing to work side by side with a man maybe months and years, and then to be told, strike him dead! And to do it!' And the potboy rolled up his eyes and loosed a long, soft whistle, and passed on with his handful of tankards, leaving them so sunk in reconsideration that neither of them had anything to say.

But there could not be anything in it of significance for him, surely? Philip looked back briefly as he left the inn, and Turstan Fowler and the young groom were sitting tranquilly with their ale, talking cheerfully with half a dozen other sober drinkers around them. They had not noticed him, or if they had, had not recognised him, and neither of them seemed to have anything of grave moment on his mind. Strange, though, how this same man seemed to be entangled in every untoward episode, never at the centre of things yet always somewhere in view.

As for the matter of the flask of juniper spirits, what did it really signify? The man had been picked up too drunk to talk, no one had looked round for his bottle, it might well have been left lying, still more than half-full, if the stuff was a potent as Wat said, and some

201

scavenger by night might have picked it up and rejoiced in his luck. There were a dozen ways of accounting for the circumstances. And yet it was strange. Why should he have said he was drunk before he left Wat's inn, if he had really left it cold sober? More to the point, why should he have left so promptly on Philip's heels? Yet Wat was a good observer.

The tiny discrepancies stuck like barbs in Philip's mind. It was far too late to trouble anyone else tonight, Compline was long over, the monks of Shrewsbury, their guests, their servants, would all be in their beds or preparing to go there, except for the few lay stewards who had almost completed their labours, and would be glad enough to make a modestly festive night of it. Moreover, his parents would be vexed that he had abandoned them all the day and he could expect irate demands for explanations at home. He had better make his way back.

All the same, he crossed the road and made for the copse, as on the night he was repeating, and found some faint signs of his wallow still visible, dried into the trampled grass. Then back towards the river, avoiding the streets, keeping to the cover of woodland, and there was the sheltered hollow where he had slept off the worst of his orgy, before gathering himself up stiffly and hobbling back to the town. There was enough lambent starlight to see his way, and show him the scuffled and flattened grasses.

But no, this was not the place! Here there was a faint, trodden path, and he had certainly moved much deeper into the bushes and trees, down-river, hiding even from the night. This glade looked very like the other, but it was not the same. Yet someone or something, large as a man, had lain here, and not peacefully. Surely more than one pair of feet had ploughed the turf. A pair of opportunist lovers, enjoying one of the traditional pleasures of the fair?

Or another kind of struggle? No, hardly a struggle, though something had been dragged downhill towards the river, which was just perceptible as a gleam between the trees. There was a patch of bare soil, dry and pale as clay, between the spreading roots of the birch tree against which he leaned, and ribbons of dropped bark littered it. The largest of them showed curiously dark instead of silvery, like the rest. He stooped and picked it up, and his fingertips recoiled from the black, encrusted stain. In the grass, if he searched by daylight, there might well be other such blots.

In looking for the place of his own humiliation, he had found something very different, the place where Master Thomas had been killed. And below, from that spur of grass standing well above the undermined bank, his body had been thrown into the river.

After the Fair

Chapter One

Brother Cadfael came out from Prime, next morning, to find Philip hovering anxiously in the great court, fidgeting from one foot to the other as if the ground under him burned, and so intent and grim of face that there was no doubting the urgency of what he had to impart. At sight of Cadfael he came bounding alongside to lay a hand on his sleeve.

'Will you come with me to Hugh Beringar? You know him, he'll listen if you vouch for me. I didn't know if he'd be stirring this early, so I waited for you. I think I've found the place where Master Thomas was killed.'

It was certainly not what he had been looking for, and came as a total irrelevance for a moment to Brother Cadfael, who checked and blinked at an announcement so unexpected. 'You've done *what?*'

'It's true, I swear it! It was so late last night, I couldn't pester anyone with it then, and I've not been there by daylight – but someone bled there – someone was dragged down to the water –'

'Come!' said Cadfael, recovering. 'We'll go together.' And he set out at a brisk trot for the guest-hall, Philip's long strides keeping easy pace with him. 'If you're right ... He'll want you to show the place. Can you find it again with certainty?'

'I can, you'll see why.'

Hugh came out to them yawning, in shirt and hose, but wide awake and shaven all the same. 'Speak low!' he said, finger on lip, and softly closed the door of his rooms behind him. 'The women are still asleep. Now, what is it? I know better than to turn away anyone who comes with Brother Cadfael's warranty.'

Philip told only what was needful. For his own personal need there would be time later. What mattered now was the glade in the edge of the woods, beyond the orchards of the Gaye.

'I was following my own scent, last night, and I made too short a cast at the way I took down to the river. I came on a place in the trees there – I can find it again – where some heavy thing had lain, and been dragged down to the water. The grass is flattened where he lay, and combed downhill, where he was dragged, and for all the three days between, it still shows the traces. I think there are also spots of blood.'

'The merchant of Bristol?' asked Hugh, after an instant of startled silence.

'I think so. Daylight may show for certain.'

Hugh turned to drain his morning ale in purposeful haste, and demolish the end of oatcake he had been eating. 'You slept at home? In the town?' He was brushing his black crest hastily as he talked, tying the laces of his shirt and reaching for his cotte. 'And came to me rather than to the sheriff! Well, no harm, we're nearer than he, it will save time.' Sword and sword-belt he left lying, and thrust his feet into his shoes. 'Cadfael, you'll be missing breakfast, take these cakes with you, and drink something now, while you may. And you, friend, have you eaten?'

'No escort?' said Cadfael.

'To what end? Your eyes and mine are all we require here, and the fewer great boots stamping about the sward, the better. Come, before Aline wakes, she has a bird's hearing, and I'd rather have her rest. Now,

Philip, lead! You're on your home turf, take us the quickest way.'

Aline and Emma were at breakfast, resigned to Hugh's sudden and silent departures, when Ivo came asking admittance. Punctilious as always, he asked for Hugh.

'But as that husband of mine has already gone forth somewhere on official business,' said Aline, amused, 'and as it's certainly you he really wants to see, shall we let him in? I felt sure he would not go away without paying his respects to you yet again. He has probably been exercising his wits to find a way of ensuring it shan't be the last time, either. He was hardly at his best last night, and no wonder, after so many shocks, and grazed and bruised from his fall.'

Emma said nothing, but her colour rose agreeably. She had risen from her bed with a sense of entering a life entirely new, and more her own to determine than ever it had been before. By this hour Master Thomas's barge must be well down the Severn on its way home. She was relieved of the necessity of avoiding Roger Dod's grievous attentions, and eased of the sense of guilt she felt in doing him what was probably the great wrong of fearing and distrusting his intentions towards her. Her belongings were neatly packed for travelling, in a pair of saddle-bags bought at the fair, for whatever was to become of her now, she would be leaving the abbey today. If no immediate escort offered for the south, she would go home with Aline, to await whatever arrangements Hugh could make for her, and in default of any other trustworthy provision, he himself had promised her his safe-conduct home to Bristol.

The bustle of departure filled the stable-yard and the great court, and half the rooms in the guest-hall had already been vacated. No doubt Turstan Fowler and the young groom were also assembling their lord's

purchases and effects, and saddling up the bay horse, returned to the abbey by an enterprising errand-boy who had been lavishly rewarded, and their own shaggy ponies. Two of them! The third would be on a leading rein.

Emma felt cold when she remembered what had befallen the rider of the third pony, and the things he had done. So sudden a death filled her with horror. But the man had done murder, and had not scrupled to ride down his own lord when he was unmasked. It was reasonable to blame Ivo for what had happened, even if his order had not been given in an understandable rage at the misuse of his patronage and the assault upon his own person. Indeed, Emma had been touched, the previous evening, when the very vehemence with which Ivo had defended his action had so clearly betrayed his own doubts and regrets. It had ended in her offering reassurance and comfort. It was a terrible thing in itself, she thought, to have the power of life and death over your fellowmen, whatever crimes they might have committed.

If Ivo had lacked something of his normal balance and confidence last night, he had certainly regained them this morning. His grooming was always immaculate, and his dress, however simple, sat upon his admirable body with a borrowed elegance. It had been hateful to him to be spilled into the dust, and rise limping and defaced before a dozen or more witnesses. This morning he had made sure of his appearance, and wore even the healing grazes on his left cheek like ornaments; but as soon as he entered, Emma saw that he was still limping after his fall.

'I'm sorry to have missed your husband,' he said as he came into the room where they were sitting, 'but they tell me he's already gone forth. I had a scheme to put to him for approval. Dare I put it to you, instead?'

'I'm already curious,' said Aline, smiling.

'Emma has a problem, and I have a solution. I've been thinking about it ever since you told me, Emma, two days ago, that you would not be returning to Bristol with the barge, but must find a safe escort south by road. I have no right at all to advance any claim, but if Beringar will consent to trust you to me … You need to get home, I'm sure, as quickly as you can.'

'I must,' said Emma, eyeing him with wondering expectation. 'There are so many things I must see to there.'

Ivo addressed himself very earnestly to Aline. 'I have a sister at Stanton Cobbold who is determined to take the veil, and the convent of her choice has consented to take her. And by luck it happens that she wished to join a Benedictine house, and the place is the prior at Minchinbarrow, which is some few miles beyond Bristol. She is waiting for me to take her there, and to tell the truth, I've been delaying to give her time to change her mind, but the girl's set on her own way. I'm satisfied she means it. Now if you'll confide Emma to my care, as I swear you may with every confidence, for it will be my pleasure to serve her, then why should not she and Isabel travel down very comfortably together? I have men enough to provide a safe guard, and naturally I should myself be their escort. That's the plan I wanted to put to your husband, and I hope he would have felt able to fall in with it and give his approval. It's great pity he is not here –'

'It sounds admirable,' said Aline, wide-eyed with pleasure, 'and I'm sure Hugh would feel completely happy in trusting Emma to your care. Had we not better ask Emma herself what she has to say?'

Emma's flushed face and dazzled smile were speaking for her. 'I think it would be the best possible answer, for me,' she said slowly, 'and I'm most grateful for so kind a thought. But I must really go as soon as possible, and your sister – you said, you wanted her to

have time to be sure ...'

Ivo laughed, a little ruefully. 'I've already reached the point of giving up the hope of persuading her to stay in the world. Never fear that you may be forcing Isabel's hand, ever since she was accepted she has been trying to force mine. And if it's what she wants, whom am I to prevent? She has everything ready, it will give her only pleasure if I come home to say that we can start tomorrow. If you're willing to trust yourself to me alone for the few miles to Stanton Cobbold, and sleep under our roof tonight, we can be on our way in the morning. We can provide you horse and saddle, if you care to ride, or a litter for the pair of you, as you please.'

'Oh, I can ride,' she said, glowing. 'It would be a delight.'

'We would try and make it so. *If*,' said Ivo, turning his grazed smile almost diffidently upon Aline, 'if I may have your approval, and my lord Beringar's. I would not presume without that. But since this is a journey I must make, sooner or later, and Isabel insists the sooner the better, why not take advantage of it to serve Emma's need, too?'

'It would certainly solve everything very happily,' agreed Aline. And there could be no doubt, thought Emma, bolstering her own dear wish with the persuasion of virtue, that Aline would be relieved and happy if Hugh could be spared a journey, and she several days deprived of his company. 'Emma knows,' said Aline, 'that she may choose as she thinks best, for both you and we, it seems, are equally at her service. As for approval, why, of course I approve, and so, I'm sure, would Hugh.'

'I wish he would put in an appearance,' said Ivo, 'I should be the happier with his blessing. But if we are to go, I think we should set out at once. I know I said all's ready with Isabel, but for all that we may need to make

the most of this day.'

Emma wavered between her desire and her regret at leaving without making her due and grateful farewell to Hugh. But it was gain for him, great gain, to be rid of the responsibility he had assumed, and so securely as this promised. 'Aline, you have been the soul of kindness to me, and I leave you with regret, but it is better to spare an extra journey, in such times, and then, Hugh has been kept so busy on my account already, and you've seen so little of him these days ... I should like to go with Ivo, if you'll give me your blessing. Yet I hate to go without thanking him properly ...'

'Don't fret about Hugh, he will surely think you wise to take advantage of so kind and fortunate an offer. I will give him all the pretty messages you're thinking of. Once I lose sight of him, now, I never know when he'll return, and I'm afraid Ivo is right, you may yet need every moment of the day, or certainly Isabel may. It's a great step she's taking.'

'So I've told her,' he said, 'but my sister has the boldness of mind to take great steps. You won't mind, Emma, riding pillion behind me, the few miles we have to go today? At home we'll find you saddle and horse and all.'

'Really,' said Aline, eyeing the pair of them with a small and private smile, 'I begin to be envious!'

He sent the young groom to fetch out her saddle-bags. Their light weight was added to the bales of Corbière's purchases on the spare pony, her cloak, which she certainly would not need on so fine a day, folded and stowed away with the bags. It was like setting out into a new world, sunlit and inviting, but frighteningly wide. True, she had solemn duties waiting for her in Bristol, not least the confession of a failure, but for all that, she felt as if she had almost shed the past, and could be

glad of the riddance, and was stepping into this unknown world unburdened and unguarded, truly her own mistress.

Aline kissed her affectionately, and wished them both a happy journey. Emma cast frequent glances towards the gatehouse until the last moment, in case Hugh should appear, but he did not; she had still to leave her messages to Aline for delivery. Ivo mounted first, since the bay, as he said, was in a skittish mood and inclined to play tricks, and then turned to give her a steady, sustaining hand as Turstan Fowler hoisted her easily to the pillion.

'Even with two of us up,' said Ivo over his shoulder, smiling, 'this creature can be mettlesome when he's fresh out. For safety hold me fast about the waist, and close your hands on my belt – so, that's well!' He saluted Aline very gracefully and courteously. 'I'll see she reaches Bristol safely, I promise!'

He rode out at the gatehouse in shirt-sleeves, just as he had ridden in, his men, now two only, at his heels, and the pack-pony trotting contentedly under his light load. Emma's arms easily spanned Ivo's slenderness, and the feel of his spare, strong body was warm and muscular and vital through the fine linen. As they threaded the Foregate, now emptying fast, he laid his own left hand over her clasped ones, pressing them firmly against his flat middle, and though she knew he was simply assuring himself that her hold was secure, she could not help feeling that it was also a caress.

She had laughed and shaken her head over Aline's romantic fantasies, refusing to believe in any union between landed nobility and trade, except for mutual profit. Now she was not so sure that wisdom was all with the sceptics.

The hollow where the big, heavy body had lain still showed at least the approximate bulk of Master

214

Thomas's person, and round about it the grass was trodden, as though someone, or perhaps more than one, had circled all round him as he lay dead. And so they surely had, for here he must have been stripped and searched, the first of those fruitless searches Brother Cadfael had deduced from the events following. Out of the hollow, down to the raised bank of the river, went the track by which he had been dragged, the grass, growing longer as it emerged from shade, all brushed in one direction.

Nor was there any doubt about the traces of blood, meagre though they were. The sliver of birch bark under the tree showed a thin crust, dried black. Careful search found one or two more spots, and a thin smear drawn downhill, where it seemed the dead man had been turned on his back to be hauled the more easily down to the water.

'It's deep here,' said Hugh, standing on the green hillock above the river, 'and undercuts the bank, it would take him well out into the current. I fancy the clothes went after him at once, we may find the rest yet. One man could have done it. Had they been two, they would have carried him.'

'Would you say,' wondered Cadfael, 'that this is a reasonable way he might take to get back to his barge? He'd know his boat lay somewhat down-river from the bridge, I suppose he might try a chance cut through from the Foregate, and overcast by a little way. You see the end of the jetty, where the barge tied up, is only a small way upstream from us. Would you say he was alone, and unsuspecting, when he was struck down?'

Hugh surveyed the ground narrowly. It was not the scene of a struggle, there was the flattened area of the body's fall, and the trampling of feet all round its stillness. The brushings of the grass this way and that were ordered, not the marks of a fight.

'Yes. There was no resistance. Someone crept

behind, and pierced him without word or scruple. He went down and lay. He was on his way back, preferring the byways, and came out a little downstream of where he aimed. Someone had been watching and following him.'

'The same night,' said Philip flatly, 'someone had been watching and following *me*.'

He had their attention at once, both of them eyeing him with sharp interest. 'The same someone?' suggested Cadfael mildly.

'I haven't told you my own part,' said Philip. 'It went out of my head when I stumbled on this place, and guessed at what it meant. What I set out to do was to find out just what I did that night, and prove I never did murder. For I'd come to think that whoever intended this killing had his eye on me from the start. I came from that riot on the jetty, with my head bleeding and my mood for murder, I was a gift, if I could but be out of sight and mind when murder was done.' He told them everything he had discovered, word for word. By the end of it they were both regarding him with intent and frowning concentration.

'The man Fowler?' said Hugh. 'You're sure of this?'

'Walter Renold is sure, and I think him a good witness. The man was there to be seen, I pointed him out, and Wat told me what he'd seen of him that night. Fowler looked in, saw and heard the condition I was in, and went away again for it might be as much as half an hour, says Wat. Then he came back, took one measure of ale to drink, and brought a big flask of geneva spirit.'

'And left with it unopened,' Brother Cadfael recalled, 'as soon as you took yourself off with your misery into the bushes. No need to blush for it now, we've all done as foolishly once or twice in our lives, many of us have bettered it. And the next that's known of him,' he said, meeting Hugh's eyes across the glade,

216

'is two hours later, when we discover him lying sodden-drunk under a store of trestles by the Foregate.'

'And Wat of the tavern swears he was sober as a bishop when he quit the inn.'

'And I would swear by Wat's judgment,' said Philip stoutly. 'If any man drank that flagon dry in two hours, he says, it would be the death of him, or go very near. And Fowler was testifying in court next day, and little the worse for wear.'

'Good God!' said Hugh, shaking his head. 'I stooped over him, I pulled back the cloak from his shoulders. The fellow reeked. His breath would have felled an ox. Am I losing my wits?'

'Or was it rather the reek you loosed by moving the cloak? I begin to have curious thoughts,' said Cadfael, 'for I fancy that juniper liquor was bought for his outside, not his inside.'

'A costly freak,' mused Hugh, 'the price such liquors are. Cheap enough, though, if it bought him immunity from all suspicion of a thing that could have cost him a deal higher. What was the first thing I said? – more fool I! By the look of him, I said, he must have been here some hours already. And where did he go from there? Safely into an abbey punishment cell, and lay there overnight. How could he be guilty of anything but being a drunken sot? Children and drunken men are the world's only innocents! If murder was done that night, who was to look at a man who had put himself out of the reckoning from the time Master Thomas was last seen alive to the time when his body was brought back to Shrewsbury?'

Cadfael's mind had probed even beyond that point, though nothing beyond was yet clear. 'I have a fancy, Hugh, to look again at the place where we picked up that sodden carcase, if it can be found. Surely an honest drunk should have had his bottle lying beside

him for all to see. But I remember none. If we missed it, and some stray scavenger found it by night, still half-full or more, well and good. But if by any chance it was hidden – so that no questions need ever be asked about how much had been drunk, and what manner of head could have borne it – would that be the act of a simple sot? He could not walk through the fairground stinking as he did, whether from outside or in. His baptism was there, where we found him tucked away. So should his bottle have been.'

'And if he was neither simple nor a sot that night, Cadfael, how do you read his comings and goings? He looked in at the tavern, took note of this lad's state, listened to his complaints, and went away – where?'

'As far as Master Thomas's booth, perhaps, to make sure the merchant was there, busy about his wares, and likely to be busy for a while longer? And so back to the tavern to keep watch on Philip, so handy a scapegoat, and so clearly on the way to ending the evening blind and deaf. And afterwards, when he had followed him far enough into the copse to know he was lost to the world, back to dog Master Thomas's footsteps as he made his way back to the barge. Made his way, that is, as far as this place.'

'It is all conjecture,' said Hugh reasonably.

'It is. But read it so, and it makes sense.'

'Then back with his flask of spirits ready, to slip unseen into a place withdrawn and private, and become the wretched object we found. How long would it take, would you say, to kill his man, search and strip him down to the river?'

'Counting the time spent following him unseen, and returning unnoticed to the fairground after all was done, more than an hour of those two hours lost between drunk and sober. No,' said Cadfael sombrely, 'I do not think he spent any of that time drinking.'

'Was it he, also, who boarded the barge? But no, that

he could not, he was at the sheriff's court. Concerning the merchant of Shotwick, we already know his slayer.'

'We know one of them,' said Cadfael. 'Can any of these matters be separated from the rest? I think not. This pursuit is all one.'

'You do grasp,' said Hugh, after a long moment of furious thought, 'what it is we are saying? Here are these two men, one proven a murderer, the other suspect. And yesterday the one of them fetched down the other to his death. Coldly, expertly ... Before we say more,' said Hugh abruptly, casting a final glance about the glade, 'let's do as you suggested, look again at the place where we found him lying.'

Chapter Two

Philip, who was learning how to listen and be silent, followed at their heels all the way back through the orchards and gardens of the Gaye. Neither of them found fault with his persistence. He had earned his place, and had no intention of being put off. All the larger boats were already gone from the jetty. Soon the labourers would begin dismantling the boards and piers until the following year, and stowing them away in the abbey storehouses. Along the Foregate stalls were being taken down and stacked for removal, while two of the abbey carts worked their way along from the horse-fair towards the gatehouse.

'More than halfway along, I remember,' said Hugh, 'and well back from the roadway. There were few lights, most of the stalls here were for the country people who come in by the day. Somewhere in this stretch.'

There had been trestles stacked that night, and canvas awnings leaning against them ready for use. This morning there were also piles of trestles and boards, ready now to be put away for the next fair. They surveyed all the likely area, but to lay a finger on the exact place was impossible. One of the collecting carts had reached this stretch, and two lay servants were hoisting the heaped planks aboard, and stacking the trestles one within another in high piles. Cadfael watched as the ground was gradually cleared.

'You've found some unexpected discards,' he commented, for a corner of the cart carried a small pile of odd objects, a large shoe, a short cotte, bedraggled but by no means old or ragged, a child's wooden doll with one arm missing, a green capuchon, a drinking-horn.

'There'll be many more such, brother,' said the carter, grinning, 'before the whole ground's cleared. Some will be claimed. I fancy some child will want to know where she lost her doll. And the cotte is good stuff, some young gentleman took a drop too much, and forgot to collect that when he moved. The shoe's as good as new, too, and a giant's size, somebody may sneak in, shamefaced, to ask after that. I hope he had not far to go home with only one. But it wasn't a rowdy night – not like many a night I've seen.' He slid powerful arms under a stack of trestles, and hoisted them bodily. 'You'd hardly credit where we found that flagon there.'

His nod indicated the front of the car, to which Cadfael had hitherto devoted no attention. Slung by a thin leather thong from the shaft hung a flattened glass bottle large enough to hold a quart. 'Stuck on top of the canvas over one of the country stalls. An old woman who sells cheeses had the stall, I know her, she comes every year, and seeing she's not so nimble nowadays, we put up the stall for her the night before the fair opened. The bottle all but brained Daniel here, when we took it down, this morning! Fancy tossing a bottle like that away as if it had no value! He could have got a free drink at Wat's if he'd taken it back, whoever he was.'

His armful of trestles thumped into the cart, and he turned to heave a stack of boards after it.

'It came from Wat's tavern then, did it?' asked Cadfael, very thoughtfully gazing.

'It has his mark on the thong. We all know where

221

they belong, these better vessels. But they're not often left for us.'

'And where was the stall where this one was left?' asked Hugh over Cadfael's shoulder.

'Not ten yards back from where you're standing.' They could not resist looking back to measure, and it would do. It would do very well. 'The odd thing is, the old woman swore, when she came to put out her wares, that there was a stink of spirits about the place. Said she could smell it in her skirts at night, as if she'd been wading in it. But after the first day she forgot about it. She's half-Welsh, and has a touch of the strange about her, I daresay she imagined it.'

Cadfael would have said, rather, that she had a keen nose, and some knowledge of the distilling of spirits, and had accurately assessed the cause of her uneasiness. Somewhere in the grass close to her stall, he was now certain, a good part of that quart of liquor had been poured out generously over clothing and ground, no wonder the turf retained it. A taste of it, perhaps, to scent the breath and steady the mind, might have gone down a throat; but no more, for the mind had been steady indeed, when stranger stooped over its fleshly habitation, and sniffed at its flagrant drunkenness. Strangers, all but one! Cadfael began to see what could hardly be called light, for he was looking into a profound darkness.

'It so happens,' he said, 'that we have some business with Walter Renold. Will you let us take your bottle back to him? You shall have the credit for it with him.'

'Take it, brother,' agreed the carter cheerfully, unleashing the bottle from the shaft. 'Tell him Rychart Nyall sent it. Wat knows me.'

'Nothing in it, I suppose, when you found it?' hazarded Cadfael, hefting the fated thing in one hand.

'Never a drop, brother! Fair-goers may abandon the bottle, but they make sure of what's inside before they

fall senseless!'

The boards were stowed, the stripped ground lay trampled and naked, the cart moved on. It would take no more than a handful of days and the next summer showers, and all the green, fine hair would grow again, and the bald clay coil into ringlets.

'It's mine, surely,' said Wat, receiving the bottle into a large hand. 'The only one of its kind I'm short. Who buys this measure of spirits, even at a fair? Who has the money to afford it? And who chooses it afore decent ale and wine? Not many! I've known men desperate to sink their souls fast, at whatever cost, but seldom at a fair. They turn genial at fairs, even the sad fellows get the wind of it, and mellow. I marvelled at that one, even when he asked for it and paid the price, but he was plainly some lord's servant, he had his orders. He had money, and I sell liquor. But yes, if it's of worth to you, that same fellow Philip here knows of, that's the measure he bought.'

A retired corner of Wat's large taproom was as good a place as any to sit down and think before action, and try to make sense of what they had gathered.

'Wat has just put words to it,' said Cadfael. 'We should have been quicker to see. He was plainly some lord's servant, he had his orders, he had money. One man from a lord's household suborned to murder by an unknown, one such setting out on his own account to enrich himself by murder and theft, that I could believe in. But two? From the same household? No, I think not! They never strayed from their own manor. They served but one lord.'

'Their own? *Corbière?*' whispered Philip, the breath knocked out of him by the enormity of the implications. 'But he ... The way I heard it, the groom tried to ride him down. Struck him into the dust when

he tried to stop him. How can you account for that? There's no sense in it.'

'Wait! Take it from the beginning. Say that on the night Master Thomas died, Fowler was sent out to deal with him, to get possessions of whatever it is someone so much desires. His lord has spied out the land, told him of a handy scapegoat who may yet be useful, given him money for the drink that will put him out of the reckoning when the deed is done. The man would demand immunity, he must be *seen* to be out of the reckoning. His lord keeps in close touch, joins us when we go forth to look for the missing merchant. Recollect, Hugh, it was *Corbière*, not we, who discovered his truant man. *We* had passed him by, and that would not have done. He must be found, must be seen to be so drunk as to have been helpless and harmless some hours, and must then be manifestly under lock and key many hours more. Ten murders could have been committed that night, and no one would ever have looked at Turstan Fowler.'

'All for nothing,' pointed out Hugh. 'Sooner or later he had to tell his master that murder had been done in vain. Master Thomas did not carry his treasure on him.'

'I doubt if he found that out until morning, when he had his man let out of prison. Therefore he brought Fowler to lay evidence that made sure the finger was pointed at Philip here, and while we were all blamelessly busy at the sheriff's hearing, sent his second man to search the barge. And again, vainly. Am I making sense of it thus far?'

'Sound enough,' said Hugh sombrely. 'The worst is yet to come. Which man, do you suppose, did the work that day?'

'I doubt if they ever involved the young one. Two were enough to do the business. The groom Ewald, I think. Those two were the hands that did all. But they

were not the mind.'

'That same night, then, they broke into the booth, and made their search there, and still without success. The next night came the attack that killed Euan of Shotwick.' Hugh said no word of the violation of Master Thomas's coffin. 'And, as I remember you argued, once more in vain. So far, possible enough. But come to yesterday's thorny business. For God's sake, how can sense be made of that affair? I was there watching the man, I saw him change colour, I swear it! Shock and anger and affronted honour, he showed them all. He would not send for the groom, for fear a fellow-servant might warn him, he would fetch him himself. He placed himself between his man and the gate, he risked maiming or worse, trying to halt his flight ...'

'All that,' agreed Cadfael heavily, 'and yet there is sense in it all, though a more abominable sense even than you or I dreamed of. Ewald was in the stables, there was no escape for him unless he could break out of our walls. Corbière came at the sheriff's bidding, and was told all. His man was detected past denying, and driven into a corner, he would pour out everything he knew, lay the load on his lord. Consider the order in which everything happened from that moment. Fowler had been at the butts, and had his arbalest with him. Corbière set off to summon Ewald from the stables, Turstan made to follow him, yes, and some words were exchanged that sent him back. But what words? They were too distant to be heard. Nor could we guess what was said in the stable-yard. We waited – you'll agree? – several minutes before they came. Long enough for Corbière to tell the groom how things stood, bid him keep his head, promise him escape. Bring the horse, *I* will ensure that only I stand between you and the gate, pick your moment, mount and away. Lie up in hiding – doubtless at his manor –

and you shan't be the loser. But make it clear that I have no part in this – attack me, make it good for your part, I will make it good for mine. And so he did – the finest player of a part that ever I saw. He set himself between Ewald and the gate, and between them they used the lively horse to edge us all that way. He made a gallant grab at the rein, and took a heavy fall, and the groom was clear.'

They were both gazing at him in mute fascination, wide-eyed.

'Except that his lord had one more trick to play,' said Cadfael. 'He had never intended to let him go. Escape was too great a risk, he might yet be taken, and open his mouth. "Fetch him down!" said Corbière, and Turstan Fowler did it. Without compunction, like master, like man. A dangerous mouth – dangerous to both of them – closed at no cost.'

There was a long moment of appalled silence. Even Beringar, whose breadth of mind could conceive, though with detestation, prodigies of evil and treachery, was shocked out of words. Philip stared aghast, huge of eye, and came slowly to his feet. His experience was narrow, local and decent, it was hard to grasp that men could be monsters.

'You mean it! You believe it! But this man – he visits her, he pays court to her! And you say there was something he wanted from her uncle, and has missed getting – not on his body, not in his barge, not in his booth – Where is there left, but with Emma? And we delay here!'

'Emma is with my wife,' said Hugh reasonably, 'in the abbey guest-hall, what harm can come to her there?'

'What harm?' cried Philip passionately. 'When you tell me we are dealing not with men, but with devils?' And he whirled on the heel of a trodden shoe and ran, out of the tavern and arrow-straight along the road

226

towards the Foregate, long legs flashing.

Cadfael and Hugh were left regarding each other mutely across the table, but for no more than a moment. 'By God,' said Hugh then, 'we learn of the innocents! Come on, we'd best make haste after. The lad's shaken me!'

Philip came to the guest-hall out of breath. With chest heaving from his running he asked for Aline, and she came out, smiling but alone.

'Why, Philip, what's the matter?' Then she thought she knew, and was sorry for a lovesick boy who came too late even to take a dignified farewell, and receive what comfort a few kind words, costing nothing, could provide him. 'Oh, Philip, I am sorry you've missed her, but they could not linger, it was necessary to leave in good time. She would have wished me to say her goodbye to you, and wish you ... The words faded on her lips. 'Philip, what is it? What ails you?'

'Gone?' he said, hard and shrill. 'She's gone? *They*, you said! Who? *Who* is gone with her?'

'Why, she left with Messire Corbière, he has offered to escort her to Bristol with his sister, who goes to a convent there. It seemed a lucky chance ... *Philip!* What have I said? What is wrong?' He had let out a great groan of fury and anguish, and even reached a hand to grip her wrist.

'Where? Where is he taking her? *Now, today!*'

'To his manor of Stanton Cobbold for tonight – his sister is there ...'

But he was gone, the instant she had named the place, running like a purposeful demon, and not towards the gatehouse, but across the court to the stable-yard. There was no time to ask leave of any man, or respect any man's property, Whatever the consequences. Philip took the best-looking horse he saw ready to hand, which by luck – Philip's luck, not the

owner's! – stood saddled and waiting for departure, on a tether in the yard. Before Aline, bewildered and frightened, reached the doorway of the hall, Philip was already out of the gate, and a furious groom was haring across the court in voluble and hopeless pursuit.

Since the nearest way to the road leading south towards Stretton and Stanton Cobbold was to turn left at the gate, and left again by the narrow track on the near side of the bridge, Brother Cadfael and Hugh Beringar, hastening along the Foregate, saw nothing of the turmoil that attended Philip's departure. They came to the gatehouse and the great court without any intimation that things could have gone amiss. There were still guests departing, the normal bustle of the day after the fair, but nothing to give them pause. Hugh made straight for the guest-hall, and Cadfael, following hard on his heels, was suddenly arrested by a large hand on his shoulder, and a familiar, hearty voice hailing him in amiable Welsh.

'The very man I was looking for! I come to make my farewells, brother, and thank you for your companionship. A good fair! I'm off to my boat now, and away home with a handsome profit.'

Rhodri ap Huw beamed merrily from within the covert of his black beard and thorn-bush of black hair.

'Far from a good fair to two, at least, who came looking for a profit,' said Cadfael ruefully.

'Ah, but in cash, or some other currency? Though it all comes down to cash in the end, cash or power. What else do men labour for?'

'For a cause, perhaps, now and then one. You said yourself, I remember, no place like one of the great fairs for meeting someone you'd liefer not be seen meeting. Nowhere so solitary as the middle of a market place!' And he added mildly: 'I daresay Owain

Gwynedd himself may have had his intelligencers here. Though they'd need to have good English,' he said guilelessly, 'to gather much profit from it.'

'They would so. No use employing me. I daresay you're right, though. Owain needs to have forward information, as much as any man, if he's to keep his princedom safe, and add a few more miles to it here and there. Now I wonder which of all these traders I've rubbed shoulders with will be making his report in Owain's ear!'

'And what advice he'll be giving him,' said Cadfael.

Rhodri stroked his splendid beard, and his dark eyes twinkled. 'I think he might take him word that the message Earl Ranulf expected from the south – who knows, maybe even from overseas – will never be delivered, and if he wants to get the best out of the hour, he should be aiming to enlarge his rule away from Chester's borders, for the earl will be taking no risks, but looking well to his own. Owain would do better to make his bid in Maelienydd and Elfael, and let Ranulf alone.'

'Now I come to think,' mused Cadfael, 'it would be excellent cover for Owain's intelligencers to ask the help of an interpreter in these parts, and be seen to need him. Tongues wag more freely before the deaf man.'

'A good thought,' approved Rhodri. 'Someone should suggest it to Owain.' Though there was every indication that the prince of Gwynedd needed no other man's wits to fortify his own, but had been lavishly endowed by God in the first place. Cadfael wondered how many other tongues this simple merchant knew. French, almost certainly enough for his purposes. Flemish, possibly a little, he had undoubtedly travelled in Flanders. It would be no surprise if he knew some Latin, too.

'You'll be coming to Saint Peter's Fair next year?'

'I may, brother, I may, who knows! Will you come forth again and speak for me, if I do?'

'Gladly. I'm a Gwynedd man myself. Take my greetings back with you to the mountains. And good speed on the way!'

'God keep you!' said Rhodri, still beaming, and clapped him buoyantly on the shoulder, and set off towards the riverside.

Hugh had no sooner set foot in the hall when Aline flew into his arms, with a cry of relief and desperation mingled, and began to pour into his ears all her bewilderment and anxiety.

'Oh, Hugh, I think I must have done something terrible! Either that, or Philip Corviser has gone mad. He was here asking after Emma, and when I told him she was gone he rushed away like a madman, and there's a merchant from Worcester in the stables accusing him of stealing his horse and making off with it, and what it all means I daren't guess, but I'm afraid ...'

Hugh held her tenderly, dismayed and solicitous. 'Emma's gone? But she was coming home with us. What happened to change it?'

'You know he's been paying attentions to her ... He came this morning asking for you – he said he has a sister who is entering the nunnery at Minchinbarrow, and since he must escort her there, and it's barely five miles from Bristol, he could as well take Emma home in his sister's company. He said they'd sleep overnight at his manor, and set off tomorrow. Emma said yes, and I thought no wrong, why should I? But the very name has sent Philip off like a man demented ...'

'Corbière?' demanded Hugh, holding her off by the shoulders to peer anxiously into her face.

'Yes! Yes, Ivo, of course – but what's so wrong in that? He takes her to his sister at Stanton Cobbold – I

thought it ideal, so did she, and you were not here to say yes or no. Besides, she is her own mistress ...'

True, the girl had a will of her own, and liked the man who had made the offer, and was flattered at being singled out for his favours. Even for the sake of her own independence she would have chosen to go, and Hugh, had he been present, would not then have known or suspected enough to prevent. He tightened his arms comfortingly round his trembling wife, his cheek pressed against her hair. 'My love, my heart, you could not have done anything but what you did, and I should have done the same. But I must go after. No questions now, you shall know everything later. We'll bring her back – there'll be no harm done ...'

'It's true, then!' whispered Aline, her breath fluttering against his throat. 'There's reason to fear harm? I've let her go into danger?'

'You could not stop her. She chose to go. Think no more of your part, you played none – how could you know? Where's Constance? Love, I hate to leave you like this ...'

He was thinking, of course, like all men, she thought, that any grievous upset to his wife in this condition was a potential upset to his son. That roused her. She was not the girl to keep a man dancing anxious attention on her, even if she had a wife's claim on him, when he was needed more urgently elsewhere. She drew herself resolutely out of his arms.

'Of course you must leave me. I've taken no harm, and shall take none. Go, quickly! They have a good three hours start of you, and besides, if you delay, Philip may run his head into trouble alone. Send quickly for what men you can muster, and I'll go see what I can do to placate the merchant whose horse has been borrowed ...' He was loath, all the same, to let go of her. She took his head between her hands, kissed him hard, and turned him about just as Cadfael came

231

in at the hall door.

'She's gone with Corbière,' said Hugh, conveying news in the fewest words possible. 'Bound for his one Shropshire manor. The boy's off after them, and so must I. I'll send word to Prestcote to have a guard follow as fast as may be. You'll be here to take care of Aline …'

Aline doubted that, seeing the spark flare up in Brother Cadfael's bright and militant eye. Hastily she said: 'I need no one to nurse me. Only go – both of you!'

'I have licence,' said Cadfael, clutching at virtue to cover his ardour. 'Abbot Radulfus gave me the charge of seeing that his guest came to no harm under his roof, and I'll stretch that to extend beyond his roof, and make it good, too. You have a horse to spare, Hugh, besides that raw-boned dapple of yours. Come on! It's a year since you and I rode together.'

Chapter Three

The manor of Stanton Cobbold lay a good
seventeen miles from Shrewsbury, in the south
of the shire, and cheek by jowl with the large
property of the bishops of Hereford in those parts,
which covered some nine or ten manors. The road lay
through the more open and sunlit stretches of the
Long Forest, and at its southernmost fringe plunged in
among the hump-backed hills at the western side of a
long, bare ridge that ran for some miles. Here and
there a wooded valley backed into its bare flank, and
into one of these Corbière turned, along a firm
cart-track. It was the height of the early afternoon
then, the sun at its highest, but even so the crowding
trees cast sudden chill and shadow. The bay horse had
worked off his high spirits, and went placidly under his
double burden. Once in the forest they had halted
briefly, and Ivo had produced wine and oat-cakes as
refreshment on the journey, and paid Emma every
possible delicate attention. The day was fair, the
countryside strange to her and beautiful, and she was
embarked on an agreeable adventure. She approached
Stanton Cobbold with only the happiest anticipation,
flattered by Ivo's deference, and eager to meet his
sister.

A rivulet ran alongside the track, coming down from
the ridge. The path narrowed, and the trees closed in.

'We are all but home,' said Ivo over his shoulder; and

in a few minutes more the rising ground opened before them into a narrow, level plot enclosed before with a wooden stockade. Within, the manor house backed solidly into the hillside, trees at the back, trees shutting it in darkly at either end. A boy came running to open the gate for them, and they rode into the enclosure. Barns and byres lined the stockade within. The manor itself showed a long undercroft of stone, buttressed, and pierced with two doors wide enough for carts, and a living floor above, also of stone for most of its length, where the great hall and the kitchens and pantries lay, but at the right, stone gave place to timber, and stone mullions to wooden window-frames and stout shutters; and this wooden living apartment was taller than the stone portion, and seemed to have an additional floor above the solar. A tall stone stair led up to the hall door.

'Modest enough,' said Ivo, turning his head to smile at her, 'but it has room and a welcome for you.'

He was well served. Grooms came running before the horse had halted, a maid appeared in the hall doorway, and began to flutter down to meet them.

Ivo kicked his feet free of the stirrups, swung a leg nimbly over the horse's bowing head, and leaped down, waving Turstan Fowler aside, to stretch up his arms to Emma and lift her down herself. Her slight weight gave him no trouble, he held her aloft for a long moment to prove it, laughing, before he set her down.

'Come, I'll take you up to the solar.' He put off the maid with a flick of his hand, and she stood aside and followed them demurely up the steps, but let them go on without her when they reached the hall. The thick stone walls struck inward with a palpable chill. The hall was large and lofty, the high ceiling smoke-stained, but now, in the summer, the huge fireplace was empty and cold. The mullioned windows let in air far more genial

than that within, and a comforting light, but they were narrow, and could do little to temper the oppression of the room. 'Not my most amiable home,' said Ivo with a grimace, 'but in these Welsh borders we built for defence, not for comfort. Come up to the solar. The timber end was built on later, but even there this is a chill, dark house. Even on summer evenings we need some firing.'

A short staircase at the end of the hall led up to a broad gallery and a pair of doors. 'The chapel,' he said, indicating that on the left. 'There are two small bedchambers above, dark, since they look into the hillside and the trees at close quarters. And in here, if you'll forgive me while I attend to your baggage and mine, and see the horses stabled, I'll rejoin you shortly.'

The solar into which he led her contained a massive table, a carved bench, cushioned chairs, tapestries draping the walls, and rugs on the floor, and was a place of some comfort and elegance, if also somewhat dim and cold, chiefly by reason of the looming hillside and the shrouding trees, and the narrow windows that let in so little of the day, and so filtered through heavy branches. Here there was no fireplace, the only chimney serving the hall and the kitchens; but the centre of the floor was set with large paving stones to make a hearth proof against cinders, and on this square a brazier burned, even on this summer day. Charcoal and wood glowed, discreetly massed, to give a central spark of comfort without smoke. Summer sunlight failed to warm through the arm's-length thickness of the stone walls below, and here the sun, though confronted only with friendly timber, hardly ever reached.

Emma went forward into the room and stood looking about her curiously. She heard Ivo close the door between them, but it was only a very small sound

in a large silence.

She had expected his sister to appear immediately on his return, and felt a pang of disappointment, though she knew it was unreasonable. He had sent no word ahead, how could the girl have known? She might, with good reason, be out walking on the open hill in the full summer warmth, or she might have duties elsewhere. When she did come, it would be to the pleasure of having her brother home, and with a visitor of her own sex and approximate age, into the bargain, and to hear that she was to have her will without further delay. Yet her absence was a disappointment, and his failure to remark on it or apologise for it was a check to her eagerness.

She began to explore the room, interested in everything. Her own city home was cushioned and comfortable by comparison, though no less dark and shut in, if not among trees, among the buildings the trees provided. She was aware that she had been born to comparative wealth, but wealth concentrated into one commodious and well-furbished dwelling, whereas this border manor represented only perhaps a tenth of what Ivo possessed, without regard to the land attached to all those manors. He had said himself that this was not the most genial of his homes, yet it held sway over she could not guess how many miles of land, and how many free tenants and unfree villeins. It was another world. She had looked at it from a distance, and been dazzled, but never to blindness.

She felt a conviction suddenly that it was not for her, though whether she was glad or sorry remained a mystery.

All the same, there was knowledge and taste here beyond her experience. The brazier was a beautiful thing, a credit to the smith who made it; on three braced legs like saplings, the fire-basket a trellis of vine-leaves. If it had a fault, it was that it was raised

rather too high, she thought, to be completely stable. The cushions of the chairs were of fine embroidery of hunting scenes, though dulled by use and friction and the touch of slightly greasy fingers. On a shelf built under the table there were books, a psalter, a vellum folder of music, and a faded treatise with strange diagrams. The carving of chairs and table and bench-ends was like live plants growing. The tapestries that covered all the walls between windows and door were surely old, rich, wonderfully worked, and once had had glorious colours that showed still, here and there, in the protected folds; but they were smoke-blackened almost beyond recognition, rotted here and there into tinder. She parted a fold, and the hound, plunging with snarling jaws and stretched paws between her fingers, disintegrated into powdery dust, and floated on the air in slow dissolution. She let fall the threads she held, and retreated in dismay. The very dust on her palms felt like ash.

She waited, but nobody came. Probably the time she waited was not as long as she supposed, by no means as long as it felt to her, but it seemed an age, a year of her life.

In the end, she thought she might not be offending by wandering along the gallery into the chapel. She might at least hear if there was any activity below. Ivo had bought Flemish tapestries for his new Cheshire manor, he might well be unbaling them and delighting in their fresh colours. She could forgive a degree of neglect in such circumstances.

She set her hand to the latch of the door, and trustingly lifted it. The door did not give. She tried it again, more strongly, but the barrier remained immovable. No doubt of it, the door was locked.

What she felt first was sheer incredulity, even amusement, as if some foolish accident had dropped a latch and shut her in by mistake. Then came the

instinctive wish of every creature locked in, to get out; and only after that the flare of alarm and the startled and furious reappraisal, in search of understanding. No mistake, no! Ivo's own hand had turned the key on her.

She was not the girl to fall into a frenzy and batter on the door. What good would that do? She stood quite still with the latch in her hand, while her wits ran after truth as fiercely as the hound in the tapestry after the hart. She was here in an upstairs room, with no other door, and windows not only narrow for even her slender body to pass through, but high above ground, by reason of the slope. There was no way out until someone unlocked the door.

She had come with him guilelessly, in good faith, and he turned into her gaoler. What did he want of her? She knew she had beauty, but suddenly was certain he would not go to such trouble on that account. Not her person, then, and there was only one thing in her possession for which someone had been willing to go to extremes. Deaths had followed it wherever it passed. One of those deaths a servant of his had helped to bring about, and he had dealt out summary justice. A sordid attack for gain, a theft that accidentally ended in murder, and the stolen property found to prove it! She had accepted that as everyone had accepted it. To doubt it was to see beyond into a pit too black to be credited, but she was peering into that darkness now. It was Ivo, and no other, who had caged her.

If she could not pass through the windows, the letter she carried could, though that would be to risk others finding it. Its weight was light, it would not carry far. All the same, she crossed to the windows and peered out through the slits at the slope of grass and the fringe of trees below; and there, sprawled at ease against the bole of a beech with his arbalest beside him, was

Turstan Fowler, looking up idly at these very windows. When he caught sight of her face between the timbers of the frame, he grinned broadly. No help there.

She withdrew from the window, trembling. Quickly she drew up, from its resting-place between her breasts, the small, tightly-rolled vellum bag she had carried ever since Master Thomas had hung it about her neck, before they reached Shrewsbury. It measured almost the length of her hand, but was thin as two fingers of that same hand, and the thread on which it hung was of silk, cobweb-fine. It did not need a very large hiding-place. She coiled the silk thread about it, and rolled it carefully into the great swathe of blue-black tresses coiled within her coif of silken net, until its shape was utterly shrouded and lost. When she had adjusted the net to hold it secure, and every strand of hair lay to all appearances undisturbed, she stood with hands clasped tightly to steady them, and drew in long breaths until the racing of her heart was calmed. Then she put the brazier between herself and the door, and looking up across the room, felt the heart she had just steeled to composure leap frantically in her breast.

Once again she had failed to hear the key turn in the lock. He kept his defences well oiled and silent. He was there in the doorway, smiling with easy confidence, closing the door behind him without taking his eyes from her. She knew by the motion of his arm and shoulder that he had transferred the key to the inner side, and again turned it. Even in his own manor, with his household about him, he took no risks. Even with no more formidable opponent than Emma Vernold! It was, in its way, a compliment, but one she could have done without.

Since he could not know whether she had or had not tried the door, she chose to behave as if nothing had happened to disturb her. She acknowledged his

entrance with an expectant smile, and opened her lips to force out some harmless enquiry, but he was before her.

'Where is it? Give it to me freely, and come to no harm. I would advise it.'

He was in no hurry, and he was still smiling. She saw now that his smile was a deliberate gloss, as cold, smooth and decorative as a coat of gilt. She gazed at him wide-eyed, the blank, bewildered stare of one suddenly addressed in an unknown tongue. 'I don't understand you! What is it I'm to give you?'

'Dear girl, you know only too well. I want the letter your uncle was carrying to Earl Ranulf of Chester, the same he should have delivered at the fair, by prior agreement, to Euan of Shotwick, my noble kinsman's eyes and ears.' He was willing to go softly with her, since time was now no object, he even found the prospect amusing, and was prepared to admire her playing of the game, provided he got his own way in the end. 'Never tell me, sweet, that you have not even heard of any such letter. I doubt if you make as good a liar as I do.'

'Truly,' she said, shaking her head helplessly, 'I understand you not at all. There is nothing else I could say to you, for I know nothing of a letter. If my uncle carried one, as you claim, he never confided in me. Do you suppose a man of business takes his womenfolk into his confidence over important matters? You're mistaken in him if you believe that.'

Corbière came forward an idle pace or two into the room, and she saw that no trace of his limp remained. The brazier had burned into a steady, scarlet glow, the light from it reflected like the burnish of sunset along the waving gold of his hair. 'So I thought,' he agreed, and laughed at the memory. 'It took me a long time, too long, to arrive at you, my lady. *I* would not have trusted a woman, no … But Master Thomas, it seems,

240

had other ideas. And I grant you, he had an unusual young woman to deal with. For what it's worth, I admire you. But I shall not let that stand in my way, believe me. What you hold is too precious to leave me any scruples, even if I were given to such weaknesses.'

'But I don't hold it! I can't give you what I have not in my possession. How can I convince you?' she demanded, with the first spurt of impatience and indignation, though she knew in advance that she was wasting all pretences. He knew.

He shook his head at her, smiling. 'It is not in your baggage. We've taken apart even the seams of your saddle-bags. Therefore it is here, on your person. There is no other possibility. It was not on your uncle, it was neither in his barge nor in his booth. Who was left but you? You, and Euan of Shotwick, if I had somehow let a messenger slip through my guard. You, I knew, would keep, and come tamed to my hand – but for a sudden qualm I had, that you might have sent it back in Thomas's coffin for safe-keeping, but that was to overrate you, my dear, clever as you are. And Euan never received it. Who was then left, but you? Not his crew – all of them far too simple, even if he had not had orders to keep strict secrecy, as I know he had. I doubt if he told even you what was in the letter.'

It was true, she had no idea of its contents. She had simply been given it to wear and guard, as the obvious innocent who would never come under suspicion of being anyone's courier, but its importance had been impressed upon her most powerfully. Lives, her uncle had said, hung upon its safe delivery, or, failing that, its safe return to the sender. Or, in the last resort, its total destruction.

'I am tired of telling you,' she said forcefully, 'that you are wrong in supposing that I know anything about it, or believe it ever existed but in your imagination. You brought me here, my lord, on the

241

pretext of providing me the companionship of your sister, and conducting us both to Bristol. Do you intend to do as you promised?'

He threw his head back and laughed aloud, the red glow dancing on his fine cheekbones. 'You would not have come with me if there had not been a woman in the story. If you behave sensibly now you may yet meet, some day, the only sister I have. She's married to one of Ranulf's knights, and keeps me informed of what goes on in Ranulf's court. But devil a nun she'd ever have made, even if she were not already a wife. But send you safe home to Bristol – yes, that I'll do, when you've given me what I want from you. And what I will have!' he added with a snap, and his shapely, smiling lips thinned and tightened into a sword-blade.

There was a moment, then, when she almost considered obeying him, and giving up what she had kept so obstinately through so many shocks. Fear was a reality by this time, but so was anger, all the more fierce because she was so resolutely suppressing it. He came a step towards her, his smile as narrow as a cat's bearing down on a bird, and she moved just as steadily to keep the brazier between them; that also amused him, but he had ample patience.

'I don't understand,' she said, frowning as if she had begun to feel genuine curiosity, 'why you should set such store on a letter. If I had it, do you think I should refuse it to you, when I'm in your power? But why does it matter to you so much? What can there be in a mere letter?'

'Fool girl, there can be life and death in a letter,' he said condescending to her simplicity, 'wealth, power, even land to be won or lost. Do you know what that single packet could be worth? To King Stephen, his kingdom entire! To me, maybe an earldom. And to a number of others, their necks! For I think you must know, for all your innocence, that Robert of Gloucester

has his plans made to bring the Empress Maud to England, and make a fight of it for her claim to the throne, and has been touting through his agents here to get Earl Ranulf's support for her cause when they do land. My noble kinsman has a hard heart, and has demanded proof of the strength of that cause before he lifts a hand or stirs a foot to commit himself. Names, numbers, every detail, if I know my Ranulf, they've been forced to set down in writing for him. All the tale of the king's enemies, the names of all those who pay him lip service now but are preparing to betray him. There could be as many as fifty names on the list, and it will serve, believe me, for Ranulf's ruin no less, since if his name is not there, he had reached the point of considering adding it. What will not King Stephen give, to have that delivered into his hand? All committed to writing, it may be even the date they plan to sail, and the port where they hope to land. All his enemies cut off before they can forgather, a prison prepared for Maud before ever she gets foot ashore. That, my child, is what I propose to offer to the king, and never doubt but I shall get my price for it.'

She stood staring at him with drawn brows and shocked eyes across the brazier, and felt her blood chill in her veins and all her body grow cold. And he was not even a partisan! He had killed, or procured others to kill for him, three times already, not for a cause, but coldly and methodically for his own gain and advancement. He cared nothing at all for which of them wore the crown, Stephen or Maud. If he could have got his hands rather on information of value to Maud, and felt that she was likely to prevail and reward him well, he would have betrayed Stephen and all his supporters just as blithely.

For the first time she was terrified, the weight of all those imperilled lives lay upon her heart like a great stone. She had no doubt that this estimate of what

would be in the letter must be very close to the truth, close enough to destroy a great many men who adhered to the same side her uncle had served with devotion. He had been a passionate partisan, and it had cost him his life. Now, unless she could bring about a miracle, the message he had carried would cost many more lives, bloodshed, bereavement, ruin. And all for the enrichment and advancement of Ivo Corbière! She had followed and supported Master Thomas as a matter of family loyalty. Now that meant nothing any longer, and all she felt was a desperate desire to avoid more killing, not to betray any man on either side of the quarrel to his enemies on the other. To help every fugitive, to hide every hunted man, to keep the wives unwidowed and the children still fathered, was better by far than to fight and kill either for Stephen or for Maud.

And she would not let him have them! Whatever the cost, he should not tread his way unscathed to his earldom over other men's faces.

'I have nothing against you,' Corbière was saying, confident and at ease. 'Give me the letter, and you shall reach Bristol in safety, and not be the loser. But don't think I'll scruple to pay you in full, either, if you thwart me.'

She stood fixed and still, her hands cupping her face, as though pressing hard to contain fear. The tips of her fingers worked unseen under the edge of her tissue net into the coils of her hair, feeling for the little cylinder of vellum, but face to face with her he saw no movement at all.

'Come, you are not so attractive to me that you need fear rape,' he said, disdainfully smiling, 'provided you are sensible, but for all that, it would be no hardship to me to strip you with my own hands, if you are obstinate. It might even give me pleasure, if the act proves stimulating. Give, or have it taken from you by

force. You should know by now that I let no man stand in my way, much less a little shopkeeper's girl of no account.'

Of no account! No, she had never been of any account to him, never for a moment, only of use in his ruthless pursuit of his own ambitous interests. Still she stood as if frozen, except that when he advanced upon her at leisure, his smile now wolfish and hungry, she circled inch by inch to keep the brazier between them. Its heart was a red glow. She stood close, as if only that core of warmth gave her some comfort and protection; and suddenly she tore down the coil of her hair and clawed out the letter, tearing off her silken net with it in her haste. She dared not simply cast it into the fire, it might roll clear or be too easily retrieved. She made a desperate lunge, and thrusting it deep into the heart of the glow, held it there for an agonised moment, snatching back burned fingers with a faint cry that sounded half of pain and half of triumph.

He uttered a bellow of rage, and lunged as quickly to snatch it out again, but the net had flared at a touch, tiny worms of fire climbed to lick his hand, and all he touched of the precious letter, before he recoiled, was the wax of the seal, which had melted at once, and clung searingly to his fingers as he wrung them and whined with pain. She heard herself laughing, and could not believe she was the source of the sound. She heard him frantically cursing her, but he was too intent on recovering his prize to turn upon her then. He tore off his cotte, wrapped a corner of the skirt about his hand, and leaned to grasp again at the glowing cylinder thrust upright in the fire-basket. And he would get it, defaced and incomplete, perhaps, but enough for his purpose. The outer covering was not yet burned through everywhere. He should not have it, she would not bear it! She stooped as he snatched at it, clutched with her good hand at the leg of the

brazier, and overturned it over his ankles and feet.

He screamed aloud and leaped back. Glowing coals flew, cascading over the floor, starting a brown furrow, a flurry of smoke and a stink of burning wood across the nearest rug, and reached the tinder-dry skirts of the tapestries on the wall between the two windows. There was a strange sound like a great indrawn breath, and an instant serpent of flame climbed the wall, and after it a tree of fire grew, thickened, put out lightning branches on all sides, enveloped all the space between the windows, and coursed both ways like hounds at fault, to reach the dusty hangings on the neighbouring walls. A brittle shell of fire encased the room before Emma could even stir from her horrified stillness. She saw the huntsmen and huntresses in the tapestries blaze for an instant into quivering life, the hounds leap, the forest trees shimmer in fierce light, before they disintegrated into glittering dust. Smoke rose from a dozen burning fragments over half the floor, and vision dimmed rapidly.

Somewhere in that abrupt hell beyond the hearth, Ivo Corbière, shirt and hair aflame, a length of blazing tapestry fallen upon him, rolled and shrieked in agony, the sounds he made tearing her senses. Behind her one wall of the room was still clean, but the circling flames were licking round both ways towards it.

There was a rug untouched at her back, she dragged it up and tried to reach the burning man with it, but smoke thickened quickly, stinging and blinding her eyes, and flashing tongues of fire jetted out of the smoke and drove her back. She flung the rug, in case he could still clutch at it and roll himself in its smothering folds, but she knew then that it was too late for anyone to help him. The room was already thick with smoke, she clutched her wide sleeve over mouth and nostrils, and drew back from the awful screaming that shrilled in her ears. And he had the key of the

room on him! No hope of reaching him now, no hope of recovering the key. The room was ablaze, timber at window and wall and floor began to cry out in loud cracks and splitting groans, spurting strange jets of flame.

Emma drew back, shielding her face, and hammered at the door, shrieking for help against the furious sounds of the fire. She thought she heard cries somewhere below, but distantly. She knotted her hands in the tapestries on either side the door, where the flames had not yet reached, tore the rotting fabric down, rolled it up tightly to resist sparks, and hurled it into the furnace on the other side of the room. Let the door at least remain passable. All the hangings that were not yet burning she dragged down. Her seared hand she had forgotten, she used it as freely as the other. All those other lives, surely, were safe enough, no one was ever going to read the letter that had failed to reach Ranulf of Chester. Even that fearful life shut in this room with her must be all but over, the sounds were almost lost in the voice of the fire. A busy, preoccupied voice, not unlike the obsessed hum of the fairground. She had a life to lose, too. She was young, angry, resolute, she would not lose it tamely. She hammered at the door, and called again. No one came. She heard no voices, no hasty footsteps on the stairs to the gallery, nothing but the singing of the fire, mounting steadily from a hum to a roar, like a rioting crowd, but better harmonised, the triumphant utterance of a single will.

Emma stooped to the keyhole, and called through it as long as breath and strength lasted. She could neither see nor think by then, all about her was gathering blackness, and a throttling hand upon her throat. From stooping she sank to her knees, and from her knees sagged forward along the base of the door, and lay there with mouth and nose pressed against the gap

that let in a thread of clean air. After a while she was not aware of anything, even of breathing.

Chapter Four

Philip lost himself briefly in the tangle of small valley tracks that threaded the hills, after leaving the Long Forest, and was forced to hunt out a local man from the first assart he came to, to put him on the road for Stanton Cobbold. The region he knew vaguely, but not the manor. The cottar gave him precise instructions, and turning to follow his own pointing, saw the first thin column of smoke going up into a still sky, and rapidly thickening and darkening as he stared at it.

'That could be the very place, or near it. The woods are dry enough for trouble. God send they can keep it from the house, if some fool's set a spark going ...'

'How far is it?' demanded Philip, wildly staring.

'A mile and over. You'd best ...' But Philip was gone, heels driving into his stolen horse's sides, off at a headlong gallop. He kept his eyes upon that growing, billowing column of smoke more often than upon the road, and took risks on those little-used and eccentric paths, that might have fetched him down a dozen times if luck had not favoured him. With every minute, the spectacle grew more alarming, the red of flames belching upward spasmodically against the black of smoke. Long before he reached the manor, and came bursting out of the trees towards the stockade, he could hear the bursting of beams, splitting apart in the heart with louder reports than any axe-blow. It was the house, not the forest.

The gate stood open, and within, frantic servants ran confusedly, dragging out from hall and kitchen whatever belongings they could, salvaging from the stables and byres, dangerously near to the wooden part of the house, terrified and shrieking horses, and bellowing cattle. Philip stared aghast at the tower of smoke and flames that engulfed one end of the house. The long stone building of hall and undercroft would stand, though as a gutted shell, but the timbered part was already a furnace. Confused men and screaming maids ran about distractedly and paid him no heed. The disaster had overtaken them so suddenly that they were half out of their wits.

Philip kicked his feet out of the stirrups which were short for him, but which he had never paused to lengthen, and vaulted from the horse, leaving it to wander at will. One of the cowmen blundered across his path, and Philip seized him by the arm and wrenched him round to face him.

'Where's your lord? Where's the girl he brought here today?' The man was dazed and slow to answer; he shook him furiously. 'The girl – what has he done with her?'

Gaping helplessly, the man pointed into the pillar of smoke. 'They're in the solar – my lord as well … It's there the fire began.'

Philip dropped him without a word, and began to run towards the stair to the hall door. The man howled after him: 'Fool, it's the hob of hell in there, nothing could live in it! And the door's locked – he had the key with him … You'll go to your death!'

Nothing of this made any impression upon Philip, until mention of the locked door checked him sharply. If there was no other way in, by a locked door he would have to enter. He cast about him at all the piles of hangings and furnishings and utensils they had dragged out into the courtyard, for something he

250

could use to break through such a barrier. The kitchen had been emptied, there were meat-choppers and knives, but, better still, there was a pile of arms from the hall. One of Corbière's ancestors, it seemed, had favoured the battle-axe. And these craven creatures of the household had made no attempt to use so handy a weapon! Their lord could roast before they would risk a burned hand for him.

Philip went up the stone steps three at a time, and into the black and stifling cavern of the hall. The heat, after all, was not so intense here, the stone walls were thick, and the floor, too, was laid with stones over the great beams of the undercroft. The worst enemy was the smoke that bit acrid and poisonous into his throat at the first breath. He spared the few moments it took to tear off his shirt and bind it round his face to cover nose and mouth, and then began to grope his way at reckless speed along the wall towards the other end of the hall, whence the heat and the fumes came. He did not think at all, he did what he had to do. Emma was somewhere in that inferno, and nothing mattered but to get her out of it.

He found the foot of the staircase to the gallery by stumbling blindly over the first step, and went up the flight stooped low, because it seemed that the bulk of the smoke was rolling along the roof. The shape of the solar door he found by the framework of smoke pouring in a thin, steady stream all round it. The wood itself was not yet burning. He hammered and strained at the door, and called, but there was no sound from within but the crackling of the fire. No way but to go through.

He swung the axe like a berserker Norseman, aiming at the lock. The door was stout, the wood old and seasoned, but less formidable axes had felled the trees that made it. His eyes smarted, streaming tears that helped by damping the cloth that covered his

251

mouth. The blows started the beams of the door, but the lock held. Philip went on swinging. He had started a deep crack just above the lock, so deep that he had trouble withdrawing the axe. Time after time he struck at the same place, aware of splinters flying, and suddenly the lock burst clear with a harsh, metallic cry, and the edge of the door gave, only to stick again when he had thrust it open no more than a hand's breadth. The upper part, when he groped round it, offered no resistance. He felt along the floor within, and closed his hand upon a coil of silky hair. She was there, lying along the doorway, and though the heat that gushed out at him was terrifying, yet only the smoke, not the flames, had reached her.

The opening of the door had provided a way through for the wind that fed the flames, such a brightness burned up beyond the black that he knew he had only minutes before the blaze swept over them both. Frantically he leaned to get a grasp of her arm and drag her aside, so that he could open the door for the briefest possible moment, just wide enough to lift her through, and again draw it to against the demon within.

There was a great explosion of scarlet and flame, that sent a tongue out through the opening to singe his hair, and then he had her, the soft, limp weight hoisted on his shoulder, the door dragged to again behind them, and he was half-falling, half-running down the staircase with her in his arms, and the devil of fire had done no worse than snap at their heels. He did not even realise, until he took off his shoes much later, that the very treads of the stairs had been burning under his feet.

He reached the hall doorway with head lolling and chest labouring for breath, and had to sit down with his burden on the stone steps, for fear of falling with her. Greedily he dragged the clean outside air into him,

and pulled down the smoke-fouled shirt from about his face. Vision and hearing were blurred and distant, he did not even know that Hugh Beringar and his guard had come galloping into the courtyard, until Brother Cadfael scurried up the steps to take Emma gently from him.

'Good lad! I have her. Come away down after us – lean on me as we go, so! Let's find you a safe corner, and we'll see what we can do for you both.'

Philip, suddenly shivering, and so feeble he dared not trust his legs to stand, asked in urgent, aching terror: 'Is she …?'

'She's breathing,' said Brother Cadfael reassuringly. 'Come and help me care for her, and with God's blessing, she'll do.'

Emma opened her eyes upon a clean, pale sky and two absorbed and anxious faces. Brother Cadfael's she knew at once, for it bore its usual shrewdly amiable aspect, though how he had come to be there, or where, indeed, she was, she could not yet divine. The other face was so close to her own that she saw it out of focus, and it was wild and strange enough, grimed from brow to chin, the blackness seamed with dried rivulets of sweat, the brown hair along one temple curled and brown from burning! but it had two fine, clear brown eyes as honest as the daylight above, and fixed upon her with such devotion that the face, marred as it was, and never remarkable for beauty, seemed to her the most pleasing and comforting she had ever seen. The face on which her eyes had last looked, before it became a frightful lantern of flame, had been the face of ambition, greed and murder, in a plausible shell of beauty. This face was the other side of the human coin.

Only when she stirred slightly, and he moved his position to accommodate her more comfortably, did she realise that she was lying in his arms. Feeling and

253

awareness came back gradually, even pain took its time. Her head was cradled in the hollow of his shoulder, her cheek rested against the breast of his cotte. A craftsman's working clothes, homespun. Of course, he was a shoemaker. A shopkeeper's boy, of no account! There was much to be said for it. The stink of smoke and burning still hung about them both, in spite of Cadfael's attentions with a pannikin of water from the well. The shopkeeper's boy of no account had come into the manor after her, and brought her out alive. She had mattered as much as that to him. A little shopkeeper's girl …

'Her eyes are open,' said Philip in an eager whisper. 'She's smiling.'

Cadfael stooped to her. 'How is it with you now, daughter?'

'I am alive,' she said, almost inaudibly, but with great joy.

'So you are, God be thanked, and Philip here next after God. But lie still, we'll find you a cloak to wrap you in, for you'll be feeling the cold that comes after danger. There'll be pain, too, my poor child.' She already knew about the pain. 'You've a badly burned hand, and I've no salves here, I can do no more than cover it from the air, until we get back to town. Leave your hand lie quiet, if you can, the stiller the better. How did it come that you escaped clean, but for the one hand so badly burned?'

'I put it into the brazier,' said Emma, remembering. She saw with what startled eyes Philip received this, and realised what she had said; and suddenly the most important thing of all seemed to her that Philip should not know everything, that his candid clarity should not be made to explore the use of lies, deceptions and subterfuges, no matter how right the cause they served. Some day she might tell someone, but it would not be Philip. 'I was afraid of him,' she said, carefully

254

amending, 'and I tipped over the brazier. I never meant to start such a fire ...'

Somewhere curiously distant from the corner of peace where she lay, Hugh Beringar and the sergeant and officers who had followed him from Shrewsbury were mustering the distracted servants in salvage, and damping down all the outhouses that were still in danger from flying sparks and debris, so that the beasts could be housed, and a roof, at least, provided for the men and maids. The fire had burned so fiercely that it was already dying down, but not for some days would the heat have subsided enough for them to sift through the embers for Ivo Corbière's body.

'Lift me,' entreated Emma. 'Let me see!'

Philip raised her to sit beside him in the clean, green grass. They were in a corner of the court, their backs against the stockade. Round the perimeter the barns and byres steamed in the early evening sun from the buckets of water which had been thrown over them. Close to the solar end, men were still at work carrying buckets in a chain from the well. There would be roofs enough left to shelter horses, cattle and people, until better could be done for them. They had the equipment of the kitchen, the stores in the undercroft might be damaged, but would not all be spoiled. In this summer weather they would do well enough, and someone must make shift to have the manor restored before the winter. All that terror, in the end, had taken but one life.

'He is dead,' she said, staring at the ruin from which she, though not he, had emerged alive.

'No other possibility,' said Cadfael simply.

He surmised, but she knew. 'And the other one?'

'Turstan Fowler? He's prisoner. The sergeant has him in charge. It was he, I believe,' said Cadfael gently, 'who killed your uncle.'

She had expected that at the approach of Beringar

and the law he would have helped himself to a horse and taken to his heels, but after all, he had known of no reason why he should. No one had been accusing him when he left Shrewsbury. Everyone at the abbey ought to have taken it for granted that Emma had been duly conducted home to Bristol. Why should they question it? Why *had* they questioned it? She had much to learn, as well as much to tell. There would be time, later. Now there was no time for anything but living, and exulting in living, and being glad and grateful, and perhaps, gradually and with unpractised pleasure, loving.

'What will become of him?' she asked.

'He'll surely tell all he knows, and lay the worst blame where it belongs, on his lord.' Cadfael doubted, all the same, whether Turstan could hope to evade the gallows, and doubted whether he should, but he did not say so to her. She was deeply preoccupied at this moment with life and death, and willed mercy even to the lowest and worst in the largeness of the mercy shown to her. And that was good, God forbid he should say any word to deface it.

'Are you cold?' asked Philip tenderly, feeling her shiver in his arm.

'No,' she said at once, and turned her head a little in the hollow of his shoulder, resting her forehead against his grimy cheek. He felt the soft curving of her lips in the hollow of his throat as she smiled, and was filled with so secure a sense of possession that no one would ever be able to take her away from him.

Hugh Beringar came to them across the trampled grass of the court, even his neatness smoked and odorous.

'What can be done's done,' he said, wiping his face. 'We had better get her back to Shrewsbury, there's no provision here. I'm leaving my sergeant and most of the men here for the time being, but the place for you,'

he said, smiling somewhat wearily at Emma, 'is in a comfortable bed, with your hurt properly dressed, and no need for you to think or stir until you're restored. Bristol will have to wait for you. We'll take you to Aline at the abbey, you'll be easy there.'

'No,' said Philip, with large assurance. 'I am taking Emma to my mother in Shrewsbury.'

'Very well, so you shall,' agreed Hugh, 'it's hardly a step further. But give Cadfael time at the abbey to hunt out the salves and potions he wants from his workshop, and let Aline see for herself that we've not let Emma come to any great harm. And don't forget, friend, you owe Aline something for entertaining the fellow you robbed of his horse, and guarding your back for you until you can restore him.'

Beneath his coating of soot Philip could still blush. 'True enough, I'm likely to end in gaol again for theft, but not until I've seen Emma safe lodged in my mother's care.'

Hugh laughed, and clapped him amiably on the shoulder. 'Nor then nor ever, while I'm in office – not unless you choose to kick the law in the teeth on some other occasion. We'll satisfy the merchant, Aline will have sweetened him into complacency, you'll find. And his horse has been rubbed down and watered and rested, while you've been otherwise occupied, and we'll take him back with us unloaded, none the worse for his adventures. There are horses enough here, I'll find you the pick of them, a steady ride fit to bear two.' He had had one eye on Emma while he had been mustering water-carriers and husbanding household effects, he knew better than to try to wrest her out of Philip's arms, or send for a horse-litter to carry her back. There were two here so joined together that only a fool would attempt to part them even for a few hours; and Hugh was no fool.

They wrapped her gently in a brychan borrowed

from the salvaged bedding, rather for comfortable padding than for warmth, for the evening was still serene and mild, though she might yet suffer the cold that comes after effort is all over. She accepted everything with serenity, like one in a dream, though the pain of her hand must, they reasoned, be acute. She seemed to feel nothing but a supreme inner peace that made everything else of no account. They mounted Philip on a great, broad-backed, steady-paced gelding, and then lifted Emma up to him in her swathing blanket, and she settled into the cradle of his lap and arms and braced shoulder as though God had made her to fit there.

'And perhaps so he did,' said Brother Cadfael, riding behind with Hugh Beringar close beside him.

'So he did what?' wondered Hugh, starting out of very different considerations, for two officers brought a bound Turstand Fowler behind them.

'Direct all,' said Cadfael. 'It is, after all, a way he has.'

Halfway back towards Shrewsbury she fell asleep in his arms, nestled on his breast. For the fall of her black, smoke-scented hair he could see only the lower part of her face, but the mouth was soft and moist and smiling, and all her weight melted and moulded into the cradle of his loving body as into a marriage-bed. In her dream she had gone somewhere beyond the pain of her burned hand. It was as if she had thrust her hand into the future, and found it worth the price. The left hand, the unmarked one, lay clasped warmly round him, inside his coat, holding him close to her in her dream.

Chapter Five

The summer darkness of fine nights, which is never quite dark, showed a horse-fair deserted, no trace of the past three days but the trampled patches and the marks of trestles in the grass. All over for another year. The abbey stewards had gathered in the profits of rent and toll and tax, delivered their accounts, and gone to their beds. So had the monks of the abbey, the lay servants, the novices and the pupils. A sleepy porter opened the gate for them; and mysteriously, at the sounds of their arrival, though circumspect and subdued, the great court awoke to life. Aline came running from the guest-hall with the aggrieved merchant, now remarkably complacent, at her back, Brother Mark from the dortoir, and Abbot Radulfus's own clerk from the abbot's lodging, with a bidding to Brother Cadfael to attend there as soon as he arrived, however late the hour.

'I sent him word what was toward,' said Hugh, 'as we left. It was right he should know. He'll be anxious to hear how it ended.'

While Aline took Emma and Philip, half awake and dazedly docile, to rest and refresh themselves in the guest-hall, and Brother Mark ran to the herbarium to collect the paste of mulberry leaves and the unguent of Our Lady's mantle, known specifics for burns, and the men-at-arms went on to the castle with their prisoner,

Brother Cadfael duly attended Radulfus in his study. Whether at midday or midnight, the abbot was equally wide-awake. By the single candle burning he surveyed Cadfael and asked simply: 'Well?'

'It is well, Father. We are returned with Mistress Vernold safe and little the worse, and the murderer of her uncle is in the sheriff's hands. One murderer – the man Turstan Fowler.'

'There is another?' asked Radulfus.

'There *was* another. He is dead. Not by any man's hand, Father, none of us has killed or done violence. He is dead by fire.'

'Tell me,' said the abbot.

Cadfael told him the whole story, so far as he knew it, and briefly. How much more Emma knew was a matter for conjecture.

'And what,' the abbot wished to show, 'can this communication have been, to cause any man to commit such crimes in pursuit of it?'

'That we do not know, and no man now will know, for it is burned with him. But where there are two warring factions in a land,' said Cadfael, 'men without scruples can turn controversy to gain, sell men for profit, take revenge on their rivals, hope to be awarded the lands of those they betray. Whatever evil was intended, now will never come to fruit.'

'A better ending than I began to fear,' said Radulfus, and drew a thankful sigh. 'Then all danger is now over, and the guests of our house are come to no harm.' He pondered for a moment. 'This young man who did so well for us and for the girl – you say he is son to the provost?'

'He is, Father. I am going with them now, with your permission, to see them safely home and dress their burns. They are not too grave, but they should be cleansed and tended at once.'

'Go with God's blessing!' said the abbot. 'It is

convenient, for I have a message to the provost, which you may deliver for me, if you will. Ask Master Corviser, with my compliments, if he will be kind enough to attend here tomorrow morning, about the end of chapter. I have some business to transact with him.'

Mistress Corviser had undoubtedly been fulminating for hours about her errant son, a good-for-nothing who was no sooner bailed out of prisoner than he was off in mischief somewhere else until midnight and past. Probably she had said at least a dozen times that she washed her hands of him, that he was past praying for, and she no longer cared, let him go to the devil his own way. But for all that, her husband could not get her to go to bed, and at every least sound that might be a footstep at the door or in the street, steady or staggering, she flew to look out, with her mouth full of abuse but her heart full of hope.

And then, when he did come, it was with a great-eyed girl in his arm, a thick handful of his curls singed off at one temple, the smell of smoke in his coat, his shirt in tatters, a monk of Saint Peter's at his heels, and a look of roused authority and maturity about him that quite overcame his draggled and soiled state. And instead of either scolding or embracing him, she took both him and the girl by the hand and drew them inside together, and went about seating, feeding, tending them, with only few words, and those practical and concerned. Tomorrow Philip might be brought to tell the whole story. Tonight it was Cadfael who told the merest skeleton of it, as he cleansed and dressed Emma's hand, and the superficial burns on Philip's brow and arm. Better not make too much of what the boy had done. Emma would take care of that, later; his mother would value it most of all from her.

Emma herself said almost nothing, islanded in her

exhaustion and bliss, but her eyes seldom left Philip, and when they did, it was to take in with deep content the solid, dark furnishings and warm panelling of this burgess house, so familiar to her that being accepted here was like coming home. Her rapt, secret smile was eloquent; mothers are quick to notice such looks. Emma had already conquered, even before she was led gently away to the bed prepared for her, and settled there by Mistress Corviser with all the clucking solicitude of a hen with one chick, with a posset laced with Brother Cadfael's poppy syrup to make sure that she slept, and forgot her pain.

'As pretty a thing as ever I saw,' said Mistress Corviser, coming back softly into the room, and closing the door between. She cast a fond look at her son, and found him asleep in his chair. 'And to think that's what he was about, while I was thinking all manner of bad things about him, who should have known him better!'

'He knows himself a deal better than he did a few days ago,' said Cadfael, repacking his scrip. 'I'll leave you these pastes and ointments, you know how to use them. But I'll come and take a look at her later tomorrow. Now I'll take my leave, I confess I'm more than ready for my own bed. I doubt if I shall hear the bell for Prime tomorrow.'

In the yard Geoffrey Corviser was himself stabling the horse from Stanton Cobbold with his own. Cadfael gave him the abbot's message. The provost raised sceptical eyebrows. 'Now what can the lord abbot want with me? The last time I came cap in hand to chapter, I got a dusty answer.'

'All the same,' advised Cadfael, scrubbing thoughtfully at his blunt brown nose, 'in your shoes I think I'd be curious enough to come and see. Who knows but the dust may have settled elsewhere by this time!'

*

It was no wonder if Brother Cadfael, though he did manage to rise for Prime, took advantage of his carefully chosen place behind a pillar to doze his way through chapter. He was so sound asleep, indeed, that for once he was in danger of snoring, and at the first melodious horn-call Brother Mark took fright, and nudged him awake.

The provost had obeyed the abbot's invitation to the latter, and arrived only at the very end of chapter. The steward of the grange court had just announced that he was in attendance when Cadfael opened his eyes.

'What can the provost be here for?' whispered Mark.

'He was asked to come. Do I know why? Hush!'

Geoffrey Corviser came in in his best, and made his reverence respectfully but coolly. He had no solid cohort at his back this time, and to tell the truth, though he may have felt some curiosity, he was attaching very little importance to this encounter. His mind was on other things. True, the problems of the town remained, and at any other time would have taken foremost place in his concern, but today he was proof against public cares by reason of private elation in a son vindicated and praised, a son to be proud of.

'You sent for me, Father Abbot. I am here.'

'I thank you for your courtesy in attending,' said the abbot mildly. 'Some days ago, master Provost, before the fair, you came with a request to me which I could not meet.'

The provost said not a word; there was none due, and he felt no need to speak at a loss.

'The fair is now over,' said the abbot equably. 'All the rents, tolls and taxes have been collected, and all have been delivered into the abbey treasury, as is due by charter. Do you endorse that?'

'It is the law,' said Corviser, 'to the letter.'

'Good! We are agreed. Right has therefore been done, and the privilege of this house is maintained.

263

That I could not infringe by any prior concession. Abbots who follow me would have blamed me, and with good reason. Their rights are sacrosanct. But now they have been met in full. And as abbot of this house, it is for me to determine what use shall be made of the monies in our hold. What I could not grant away in imperilment of charter,' said Radulfus with deliberation, 'I can give freely as a gift from this house. Of the fruits of this year's fair, I give a tenth to the town of Shrewsbury, for the repair of the walls and repaving of the streets.'

The provost, enlarged in his family content, flushed into startled and delighted acknowledgement, a generous man accepting generosity. 'My lord, I take your tenth with pleasure and gratitude, and I will see that it is used worthily. And I make public here and now that no part of the abbey's right is thereby changed. Saint Peter's Fair is your fair. Whether and when your neighbour town should also benefit, when it is in dire need, that rests with your judgment.'

'Our steward will convey you the money,' said Radulfus, and rose to conclude a satisfactory encounter. 'This chapter is concluded,' he said.

Chapter Six

August continued blessedly fine, and all hands turned gladly to making sure of the harvest. Hugh Beringar and Aline set off with their hopes and purchases for Maesbury, as did the merchant of Worcester for his home town, a day late, but well compensated with a fee for the hire of his horse in an emergency, on the sheriff's business, and a fine story which he would retail on suitable occasions for the rest of his life. The provost and council of Shrewsbury drafted a dignified acknowledgement to the abbey for its gift, warm enough to give proper expression to their appreciation of the gesture, canny enough not to compromise any of their own just claims for the future. The sheriff put on record the closure of a criminal affair, as related to him by the young woman who had been lured away on false pretences, with the apparent design of stealing from her a letter left in her possession, but of the contents of which she was ignorant. There was some suspicion of a conspiracy involved, but as Mistress Vernold had never seen nor been told the significance of what she held, and as in any case it was now irrevocably lost by fire, no further action was necessary or possible. The malefactor was dead, his servant, self-confessed a murderer at his master's orders, awaited trial, and would plead that he had been forced to obey, being villein-born and at his lord's mercy. The dead man's overlord had been

informed. Someone else, at the discretion of the earl of Chester, would take seisin of the manor of Stanton Cobbold.

Everyone drew breath, dusted his hands, and went back to work.

Brother Cadfael went up into the town on the second day, to tend Emma's hand. The provost and his son were at work together, in strong content with each other and the world. Mistress Corviser returned to her kitchen, and left leech and patient together.

'I have wanted to talk to you,' said Emma, looking up earnestly into his face as he renewed the dressing. 'There must be one person who hears the truth from me, and I would rather it should be you.'

'I don't believe,' said Cadfael equably, 'that you told the sheriff a single thing that was false.'

'No, but I did not tell him all the truth. I said that I had no knowledge of what was in the letter, or even for whom it was intended, or by whom it was sent. That was true, I had no such knowledge of my own, though I did know who brought it to my uncle, and that it was to be handed to the glover for delivery. But when Ivo demanded the letter of me, and I span out the time asking what could be so important about a letter, he told me what he believed to be in it. King Stephen's kingdom stood at stake, he said, and the gain to the man who provided him the means to wipe out his enemies would stretch as wide as an earldom. He said the empress's friends were pressing the earl of Chester to join them, and he would not move unless he had word of all the other powers her cause could muster, and this was the promised despatch, to convince him his interest lay with them. As many as fifty names there might be, he said, of those secretly bound to the empress, perhaps even the date when Robert of Gloucester hopes to bring her to England, even the port where they plan to land. All these sold in advance

to the king's vengeance, life and limb and lands, he said, and the earl of Chester with them, who had gone so far as to permit this approach! All these offered up bound and condemned, and *he* would get his own price for them. This is what he told me. This is what I do not know of my own knowledge, and yet in my heart and soul I do know it, for I am sure what he said was true.' She moistened her lips, and said carefully: 'I do not know King Stephen well enough to know what he would do, but I remember what he did here, last summer. I saw all those men, as honest in their allegiance as those who hold with the king, thrown into prison, their lives forfeit, their families stripped of land and living, some forced into exile ... I saw deaths and revenges and still more bitterness if the tide should turn again. So I did what I did.'

'I know what you did,' said Brother Cadfael gently. He was bandaging the healing proof of it.

'But still, you see,' she persisted gravely, 'I am not sure if I did right, and for right reasons. King Stephen at least keeps a kind of peace where his writ runs. My uncle was absolute for the empress, but if she comes, if all these who hold with her rise and join her, there will be no peace anywhere. Whichever way I look I see deaths. But all I could think of, then, was preventing *him* from gaining by his treachery and murders. And there was only one way, by destroying the letter. Since then I have wondered ... But I think now that I must stand by what I did. If there must be fighting, if there must be deaths, let it happen as God wills, not as ambitious and evil men contrive. Those lives we cannot save, at least let us not help to destroy. Do you think I was right? I have wanted someone's word, I should like it to be yours.'

'Since you ask what I think,' said Cadfael, 'I think, my child, that if you carry scars on the fingers of this hand lifelong, you should wear them like jewels.'

'Her lips parted in a startled smile. She shook her head over the persistent tremor of doubt. 'But you must never tell Philip,' she said with sudden urgency, holding him by the sleeve with her good hand. As I never shall. Let him believe me as innocent as he is himself …' She frowned over the word, which did not seem to her quite what she had wanted, but she could not find one fitter for her purpose. If it was not innocence she meant – for of what was she guilty? – was it simplicity, clarity, purity? None of them would do. Perhaps Brother Cadfael would understand, none the less. 'I felt somehow mired,' she said. '*He* should never set foot in intrigue, it is not for him.'

Brother Cadfael gave her his promise, and walked back through the town in a muse, reflecting on the complexity of women. She was perfectly right. Philip, for all his two years advantage, his intelligence, and his new and masterful maturity, would always be the younger, and the simpler, and – yes, she had the just word, after all! – the more innocent. In Cadfael's experience, it made for very good marriage prospects, where the woman was fully aware of her responsibilities.

On the thirtieth of September, just two months after Saint Peter's Fair, the Empress Maud and her half-brother Robert of Gloucester landed near Arundel and entered into the castle there. But Earl Ranulf of Chester sat cannily in his own palatine, minded his own business, and stirred neither hand nor foot in her cause.

CADFAEL COUNTRY

SHROPSHIRE AND THE WELSH BORDERS

Rob Talbot & Robin Whiteman

Introduction by *ELLIS PETERS*

'. . . no ground in the kingdom has been more tramped over by armies, coveted by chieftains, ravaged by battles, sung by poets and celebrated in epics of legend and tragedy' *Ellis Peters*

This beautifully illustrated book is a celebration of Ellis Peters's Shropshire and the world of the medieval sleuth she has created in Brother Cadfael. Robin Whiteman's meticulous and authoritative text, complemented by Rob Talbot's timeless photographs, creates an impression of the Shropshire landscape as it would once have appeared to Brother Cadfael as he travelled its desolate moorlands, dense forests and hidden valleys.

From Salop (Shrewsbury) and the Stiperstones to the remote hills of Clun Forest, from Offas's Dyke to the Devil's Chair, CADFAEL COUNTRY – based on the bestselling *Chronicles of Brother Cadfael* – is an enthralling pilgrimage through this wild and fascinating border country. Informative and comprehensive, it is a must for all fans of Ellis Peters and for those who love the region.

THE CADFAEL
COMPANION

Robin Whiteman
Introduction by Ellis Peters

Since the publication of A MORBID TASTE FOR BONES in 1977, millions of readers throughout the world have been captivated and enthralled by the exploits and adventures of Brother Cadfael – the twelfth-century Welsh monk and herbalist of Shrewsbury Abbey who uses his skills, knowledge and considerable powers of deduction to solve murder mysteries.

The first book was set in the spring of 1137; the second in the summer of 1138. Thereafter, the Chronicles have progressed steadily until they now number eighteen. Set in England and Wales during the turbulent reign of King Stephen, the novels are a rich blend of historical fact and derived fiction: people and places, real and imagined, are woven with such skill and confidence into the fabric of the whole that without access to the author's mind or knowledge of her references it becomes almost impossible to disentangle. But Cadfael fans, like the good monk himself, are endlessly curious . . .

While writing and researching CADFAEL COUNTRY, Robin Whiteman discovered a wealth of fascinating material relating to Cadfael and his colourful world. Indexing the mysteries produced a list of over one thousand characters and locations, factual and fictional – some appearing in only one story, others recurring again and again. An encyclopaedic guide to these, and to Cadfael's plants and herbs, plus a glossary of mediaeval terms, form THE CADFAEL COMPANION.

SAINT PETER'S FAIR